"When is everybody going to realize that I am no longer a little girl?"

"Trust me, Princess," Nick murmured, his voice suddenly husky. "I noticed the moment I saw you tonight."

Her eyes wide, Lindsay looked at him, only to find him looking back at her with an expression that made her mouth go dry. Before she could think of anything to say in response, Nick headed for the door. He glanced back over his shoulder. "Lindsay?"

"Yes?" she asked, in little more than a whisper.

He smiled. "You'll be hearing from me. Lock the door behind me."

"I always lock—"

But he was already gone.

You'll be hearing from me, he'd said. Lindsay knew that he hadn't been talking about resuming the platonic relationship they'd had fourteen years earlier....

Dear Reader,

Welcome to Silhouette **Special Edition**, where each month, we publish six novels with *you* in mind—stories of love and life, tales that you can identify with.

Last year, I requested your opinions on our books. Thank you for the many thoughtful comments. I'd like to share with you quotes from those letters. This seems very appropriate now, while we are in the midst of the THAT SPECIAL WOMAN! promotion. Each one of our readers is a *special* woman, as heroic as the heroines in our books.

We have some wonderful books in store for you this June. *A Winter's Rose* by Erica Spindler is our THAT SPECIAL WOMAN! title and it introduces Erica's wonderful new series, BLOSSOMS OF THE SOUTH. Not to be missed this month is *Heart of the Wolf*, by Lindsay McKenna. This exciting tale begins MORGAN'S MERCENARIES.

Wrapping up this month are books from other favorite authors: Gina Ferris (*Fair and Wise* is the third tale in FAMILY FOUND!), Tracy Sinclair, Laurey Bright and Trisha Alexander.

I hope you enjoy this book, and all of the stories to come!

Sincerely,

Tara Gavin
Senior Editor
Silhouette Books

Quote of the Month: "Why do I read romances? I maintain a positive outlook to life—do not allow negative thoughts to enter my life—but when my willpower wears, a good romance novel gets me back on track fast! The romance novel is adding much to the New Age mentality— keep a positive mind, create a positive world!"

—E.J.W. Fahner
Michigan

GINA
FERRIS

FAIR AND WISE

Silhouette®

SPECIAL EDITION®

Published by Silhouette Books New York
America's Publisher of Contemporary Romance

SILHOUETTE BOOKS
300 East 42nd St., New York, N.Y. 10017

FAIR AND WISE

ISBN: 0-373-09819-7

First Silhouette Books printing June 1993

Books by Gina Ferris

Silhouette Special Edition

GINA FERRIS

declares that she is Southern by birth and by choice, and she has chosen to set many of her books in the South, where she finds a rich treasury of characters and settings. She particularly loves the Ozark mountain region of northern Arkansas and southern Missouri, and the proudly unique people who reside there. She and her husband, John, live in Arkansas with their three children, Courtney, Kerry and David.

Monday's child is fair of face.
Tuesday's child is full of grace.
Wednesday's child is full of woe.
Thursday's child has far to go.
Friday's child is loving and giving.
Jared Saturday's child has to work hard for its living.
jintsey But the child that is born on Sabbath Day
is fair and wise and good and gay.

—Anon.

Prologue

Private investigator Tony D'Alessandro knew the moment he heard his operative's voice that the call was important. "Are you still in Little Rock?" he asked, leaning back in his comfortably worn leather desk chair.

"Yeah. And I think I've found your wife's youngest sister, Lindsay. I'm not a hundred percent sure yet—there are a few things I want to do to confirm her identity—but gut instinct tells me she's the one."

Tony's left eyebrow rose in interest. Chuck Johnson had been with him since he'd started his agency, and wasn't one to follow hunches without fairly solid evidence. "Sounds good, Chuck."

"Yeah. I need to do some more checking around, but I should have our proof within a day or two."

Tony smiled, anticipating his wife's pleasure with the information. "Call me back as soon as you've got confirmation, you hear?"

"Will do. Then what?"

"Then we'll let the family decide how to contact her."

"Okay, you got it. Talk to you in a couple of days, Tony."

"Right. And, Chuck—good job."

"Thanks, boss."

Tony hung up with a smile, knowing how excited Michelle would be when he told her the news. Michelle Trent D'Alessandro had been orphaned and separated from her six siblings when she was only a toddler. Several months ago, she'd hired Tony to find them for her. During the early stages of the search, Tony and Michelle had fallen in love, and he'd wasted no time making her his wife.

They'd located an older sister and brother, both of whom had been happily reunited with Michelle. They'd learned that yet another brother had died as a teenager, which left only twin brothers and the baby sister, Lindsay, unaccounted for. And now it appeared that Lindsay had been found. Michelle, Layla and Jared would be delighted.

Tony only hoped they could accept it if Lindsay chose not to be reunited with a brother and two sisters she couldn't possibly remember. Twenty-five now, she'd been only eight months old when her biological mother's death had made her a ward of the state. She had been adopted soon afterward—presumably happily. There was always a chance that she wouldn't want to complicate her life now with these strangers claiming kinship, nor could Tony really blame her if that was the case. Still, he knew Michelle couldn't help but be disappointed, though she professed herself perfectly content with the brother, sister, nieces and nephews she'd found so far.

Pushing those doubts to the back of his mind, Tony picked up the telephone again and dialed his home number. The melodious voice at the other end of the line brought back his smile. "Hi, darling. I just heard from Chuck. He thinks he may have found Lindsay."

Chapter One

Lindsay Hillman glanced up from her lunch when her mother, looking dazed, returned from answering a telephone call. "Mother? Is something wrong?"

Evelyn Hillman rejoined her adopted daughter at the tiny kitchen table where they'd been sharing a light Saturday lunch of tuna-stuffed tomatoes. "You'll never believe who that was."

Lindsay waited impatiently for a moment. And then, when her mother didn't immediately explain, she sighed and said, "Okay, I give up. Who was it?"

"Nick Grant. *Dr.* Nick Grant."

Now *there* was a name from the past! "Nick Grant? A *doctor?* You're kidding!"

Evelyn laughed and shook her head. "No. He's a pediatrician—and he's moved back to Little Rock to accept a partnership with a pediatrics clinic here. He called to ask if he could stop by for a visit sometime."

As surprised as Evelyn, Lindsay set down her fork and propped her elbows on the table. "This is really amazing. Have you ever heard from Nick since he left here—what, fifteen years ago?"

"Fourteen. And I haven't heard a word from him since he left to take that college scholarship."

"Not just any college scholarship," Lindsay corrected dryly. "Harvard. I remember how stunned everyone was when he announced that he'd been offered a full scholarship there. We knew he was smart, but..." She left the rest unspoken.

Evelyn nodded with a reminiscent smile. "I know. Your dad and I were so proud of him. I threw my arms around him and squeezed half the air out of him, I was so excited. He even hugged me back that time."

Which, in itself, was somewhat memorable, Lindsay mused. Though she'd only been nine when Nick joined her family, and eleven when he'd left, she remembered him clearly. He'd been a slim, quiet, complex boy boiling with repressed anger when he'd arrived, reserved and intense when he'd departed after two years with Lindsay's warm, loving, demonstrative family.

As hard as everyone had tried to pull him into the center of the family's activities, Nick had always remained on the sidelines, polite, apparently interested, but never fully involved. And, if he'd had any deep emotions, he'd never openly expressed them.

Lindsay could still remember hearing Evelyn voice her frustration that she just couldn't get through to the deepest part of the young man, the part that had been so badly hurt and so ruthlessly hidden after nearly sixteen years with his abusive, dysfunctional biological family. She had seen so much potential in the boy, she'd said. So much promise. If only she could reach him....

But he'd left with a high school diploma and a small bag of his few belongings, apparently without ever looking back. Until now.

Evelyn shook her head, still looking dazed by the call. "So many times we've thought of him, spoken of him, wondered what happened to him. But for him to call out of the blue like this, and to tell me he's a doctor now...well, I'm just so happy for him."

"When's he coming?" Lindsay asked, knowing her mother would have eagerly offered an invitation.

"Dinner tomorrow night," Evelyn answered with a smile. "He hesitated at first, but it didn't take me long to talk him into it. Oh, I'm so looking forward to seeing him again. Of all our foster boys, there was something special about Nick. I always had a soft spot in my heart for him."

Lindsay thought with an affectionate smile how typical the statement was of her mother. Evelyn's heart was a big one, and she'd loved each of the many foster sons who'd passed through her large, rambling home over the years, almost as much as she'd loved her own two sons and adopted daughter.

Evelyn Hillman and her husband, Earl, had devoted their lives to providing a home and guidance to boys with nowhere else to go, no one else to care for them. Their success rate had been phenomenal, their reputation in the foster care field a glowing one. They had rejoiced in the boys who'd left to build productive lives of their own, grieved for the few who'd chosen the wrong paths after leaving. And most of the young men had kept in touch over the years, sending Christmas cards and letters, photographs that covered nearly every wall of the Hillman home, occasional copies of newspaper articles detailing accomplishments or honors obtained in later years.

Nick had been one of the few who'd left without a backward glance. And yet Evelyn didn't seem at all hurt or resentful of the years of silence. Instead, she was delighted to hear from him again, looking forward to seeing him.

Lindsay shook her head in familiar bewilderment, knowing she couldn't have been as understanding. If she'd poured that much time and effort into a boy's life, she'd expect an occasional Christmas card at the very least!

"You'll join us tomorrow evening, won't you?" Evelyn interrupted Lindsay's thoughts to ask. "I'm sure Nick will want to see you again."

"I doubt that Nick even remembers me," Lindsay replied with a shrug.

"Of course he remembers you, Lindsay. Why, you were one of the first people he asked about when he called."

"You're kidding."

Evelyn shook her head and smiled. "No. His very words were, 'And how is Princess Lindsay doing?'"

Lindsay groaned.

"Princess Lindsay" had been a nickname that had haunted her from childhood. She'd been the pampered, adored, precocious adopted daughter of this couple who'd had two older sons of their own and dozens of foster sons over the years. Lindsay had satisfied the family's craving for a daughter and a sister, and in return, she had been indulged and coddled and brought up with love and laughter and perpetual companionship.

She'd been a pretty, bright teenager—cheerleader, homecoming royalty, honor society—and popular, as much for her outgoing personality as for the many good-looking boys she claimed as honorary brothers.

Yet she couldn't help wondering if anyone had ever known that pretty, pampered, popular "Princess Lindsay" sometimes felt as though she were performing for an audience, filling a role by reciting all the right lines, making all the right moves. Feeling secretly guilty because sometimes, even with all the love and advantages she'd been given by her adopted family, she'd been plagued by a sense that there was something missing in her life. Something important. Something that made her just a little different from the others.

Maybe that vague, haunting feeling of being different had been the reason she'd been so drawn to Nick Grant from the day he'd arrived; the reason he'd fascinated her throughout the two years he'd lived with them, though he'd never shared with her anything more than the polite smiles and careful conversation he'd given the others. Maybe she'd sensed a kindred spirit, though he had expressed his alienation by being aloof and reserved, whereas she had denied her own by being outgoing and enthusiastic, surrounding herself with friends and honorary brothers as determinedly as Nick had held others at a distance.

And maybe she'd been working too hard lately, she thought with a sudden scowl, turning back to her lunch. She was getting ridiculously fanciful.

"Sure, Mom," she said casually. "I'll be here for dinner. It sounds like fun."

Evelyn smiled her pleasure. "I'll call everyone else," she murmured. "This should be so interesting."

Nick Grant sat behind the steering wheel of his car, staring at the big, two-story colonial house at the end of the long driveway. The sun had set over an hour earlier, throwing the middle-class neighborhood into darkness, and lights burned brightly from nearly every window of the house. The lights seemed appropriate, somehow. He'd always remembered the Hillman home as a bright refuge in what had previously been a very dark childhood.

Unaccountably nervous, he tugged at his tie, feeling as though it were tightening to choke him. A tie. He chuckled with little humor. How things had changed. How *he* had changed since he'd left this home, clutching his meager bag of belongings and fighting a prickle of tears he would never have allowed anyone to see.

He drew a deep breath and reached for the door handle. Maybe he'd made a mistake coming here tonight. Hell, maybe he'd made a mistake moving back to Little Rock after all these years. But he'd never been able to forget the one place where he'd been almost happy—nor the family who'd made it possible for him to believe in himself. If it wasn't for the Hillmans, he'd probably be dead or in jail by now, he reflected, striding briskly toward the front door. He sure as hell wouldn't have been a successful, respectable physician.

He pushed the doorbell button without giving himself time for further introspection.

The doorbell's melodic chime cut into the moderate pandemonium that usually reigned in the Hillman household when everyone had gathered there. Sitting in a rocking chair with her youngest grandchild in her lap, Evelyn looked up in excitement. "That must be Nick! Lindsay, will you let him in, please?"

Since no one else made a move to do so, Lindsay headed for the entryway, automatically smoothing the rose-and-gray patterned sweater she wore with dark gray slacks, and then running a hand over her shoulder-length, toast brown hair. She wondered if Nick would recognize her after so many years. She wondered if she'd recognize him.

She opened the door.

The man illuminated by the bright porch light was tall and broad shouldered, wearing a dark suit that had apparently been hand-tailored and a silk tie that had probably cost more than Lindsay's entire outfit. His tawny hair was precisely cut and he wore thin-rimmed, young-professional-style glasses.

No, Lindsay thought in answer to her own question, she wouldn't have recognized him. She'd remembered Nick Grant as a slender boy with shaggy, sun-streaked brown hair and inexpensive clothing that had always appeared slightly disheveled. This impressive young man on the doorstep was someone she didn't know at all.

She managed a smile, wondering what in the world to say to a stranger who'd once been almost a brother to her. "Hello."

He studied her intently for a moment before responding. "Lindsay?"

His voice was deep, just a little gravelly. Her immediate response to it startled her. "Yes. Come in, Nick. It's good to see you again."

He stepped past her, then turned to watch as she closed the door behind him. "You were just a little girl when I left," he commented, his firm mouth tilting into the beginning of a smile.

She nodded, a bit self-conscious beneath his close regard. "Yes. I—uh—I've grown up now," she said, then almost winced at the inane reply.

His blue-gray eyes swept her at leisure from the top of her head down the full five feet five inches to the tip of her toes. "So I see."

She hid her blush by turning toward the den where the family waited to greet him. "Everyone's looking forward to seeing you again," she murmured, sensing that he followed closely as she led the way.

"Everyone?" he repeated cautiously, just as they entered the den.

Lindsay watched Nick out of the corner of her eye as he took in the number of people waiting for them. She noted that his mouth tightened almost imperceptibly at the corners—as though he was annoyed. Or nervous? But why should he, a Harvard-graduate doctor, be nervous about being reunited with the decidedly informal family with whom he'd lived for two years?

Evelyn had given her grandson back to his mother, freeing her to greet Nick with outstretched hands and a beaming smile. "Nick! How wonderful to see you again."

Lindsay noticed the softening in Nick's eyes only because she was still watching him so very closely, though she tried to be discreet about it. She was rather annoyed with herself for reacting to him now with the same fascination that she'd felt as a child. Was it only habit—or was there really something utterly fascinating about Nick Grant?

He took Evelyn's hands, returning her smile with a somewhat more restrained one of his own. "It's good to see you, too, Evelyn. You look great. Why haven't you gotten any older since I left?"

She laughed softly, though she was obviously pleased with the compliment. "I see you still know how to turn on the charm when you choose," she admonished him fondly, slipping a hand under his arm. "And we both know I look every day of my sixty years. But thank you, anyway. Earl, come say hello to Nick," she added in the same breath.

Earl Hillman, a big, gruff-talking marshmallow-hearted, retired insurance company executive, stepped forward to give Nick a hearty slap on the back that almost made the younger man stagger. "Look at you, boy! Slicker than spit. And Evelyn tells us you're a doctor now. How about that?"

Lindsay watched as a grin spread across Nick's face. "Yeah," he returned. "How about that."

He extended a hand to Earl. "I owe a lot of it to you, Earl. Thanks."

Earl ignored the proffered hand and slung an arm around Nick's shoulders, giving him a casual, unselfconscious hug. "You made your own decisions, son. Evelyn and I simply tried to expand your options."

The faintest tinge of color touched Nick's lean cheeks in response to the hug. Her lower lip caught between her teeth, Lindsay eyed him thoughtfully, wondering if he was quite as detached and imperturbable as he tried to appear.

"Nick, you remember our sons, don't you?" Evelyn asked as two men approached for their turn to greet the prodigal foster son.

"Yes, of course."

Nick extended his hand to the neatly bearded man who reached him first. The Hillman brothers both had their father's red hair and stocky build and their mother's gray eyes, in marked contrast to Lindsay's brown hair, dark blue eyes and slender frame. "Hello, Greg," Nick said, then glanced at the shorter, clean-shaven redhead. "Hi, Steve."

Steve, who at thirty-one was four years younger than his brother and only a year younger than Nick, pumped Nick's hand enthusiastically. "How's it going, Nick? Hey, remember the time we sneaked into that adult theater on Asher Avenue to see a girlie movie and got caught?"

Nick chuckled and glanced at Earl. "I remember. We spent the next two weeks stuck in our rooms with our choice of studying our textbooks or the Bible."

Earl nodded in satisfaction. "And you both turned out okay, didn't you? Steve's a high school administrator now. And Greg's a computer analyst."

Nick didn't seem surprised by either revelation. "You always did like high-tech equipment," he commented to Greg. "Are you still fascinated by aviation?"

Greg smiled. "I'm a private pilot," he admitted. "Got my own plane—a dual-engine Cessna Golden Eagle. I'll take you up in it sometime."

"I'd like that." Nick turned to Steve. "So you're a school administrator. You always did like school, even though you were the bane of all your teachers."

"I'm still the bane of teachers," Steve admitted cockily. "Only now *I'm* the boss. I love it."

Evelyn continued the introductions, from Steve's pretty, very pregnant wife, Kim, to Greg's wife, Paula, and their two children, three-year-old Tricia and six-month-old Zane. And then she turned to a skinny, shaggy-haired boy of about fifteen.

"This is Scott Driskell," she said, "our new foster son. Scott's been with us for three weeks. Scott, this is Dr. Nick Grant. He lived with us for a while when he was a teenager."

Lindsay all but held her breath when Nick extended his hand to the boy. She wondered, as everyone else in the room probably did, whether Scott would acknowledge the polite overture. So far, no one had been able to make much headway with Scott, a boy who'd been so neglected during childhood that he simply didn't know how to respond to kindness.

Scott cast a glance at Nick's expensive clothing, ignoring the outstretched hand. "Doctor, huh?" he grunted. "Guess you did all right for yourself."

Nick's hand fell to his side. "I did okay," he agreed coolly. "I took full advantage of the opportunities I had after I came into this household."

Scott shrugged and turned away. Lindsay noted that Nick watched the boy for a moment with a thoughtful expression before he turned back to Earl.

She pulled her attention away from Nick with surprising difficulty. "Can I help you with anything in the kitchen, Mom?"

"Yes, thanks, honey. Dinner's almost ready to be served," Evelyn accepted gratefully, turning to lead the way.

Lindsay wondered if she was imagining that Nick watched her as she left the room. She couldn't quite relax until she was in the kitchen with her mother, completely out of Nick Grant's sight.

Chapter Two

Nick couldn't stop watching her. From the moment she'd opened the door to him, he'd felt as though someone had kicked him square in the chest—and he still hadn't quite caught his breath.

He'd remembered Lindsay Hillman as a little girl with big, dark blue eyes and glossy brown hair, smiling like the princess they'd called her as she was surrounded by her loving family and admiring friends. She'd only been eleven when he'd moved out, but already he'd seen evidence of a heartbreaker-in-the-making.

It wasn't that she'd had any cruelty in her, he'd decided at the time; it was simply that she didn't realize exactly how deeply everyone cared for her. She returned affection easily, warmly, wholeheartedly, but she treated everyone the same, playing no favorites even among those who'd tried to be special to her. Little girls who'd wanted to be her best friend, little boys who'd wanted her to be their girlfriend—

Lindsay simply hadn't seemed capable of showing favoritism, to their disappointment.

He couldn't help wondering, as he watched her during dinner, if anyone had ever succeeded in becoming number one in her affections.

There was little chance for him to talk to her during the noisy, laughter-spiced meal. Nick responded politely and attentively to the questions Evelyn and Earl asked him, yet half his attention remained on Lindsay.

She'd been a pretty girl, but she was a beautiful woman. The dark blue eyes were still framed by impossibly long dark lashes, but now gleamed with the intelligence and awareness of maturity rather than the joyous enthusiasm of childhood. Her face was a delicate oval, her skin fair and almost flawless, her mouth full and temptingly curved. She wore her shining brown hair loose to her shoulders. He wondered if it could possibly feel as soft as it looked.

A chair clattered against the floor as it was shoved abruptly back from the table. Scott Driskell stood, obviously finished with his meal and on his way out. Earl stopped him with a quiet, "Haven't you forgotten something, Scott? Rinse your plate and utensils and stack them in the dishwasher if you've finished eating."

Scott scowled at the dirty dishes he'd left at his place. And then he lifted his sullen gaze to the eight adults looking back at him. "Why should I have to do that with all these women here to do dishes?" he muttered, giving Earl a warily rebellious look.

Earl didn't even blink. "You know the rules of the house, Scott. Take your dishes to the kitchen and rinse them, please."

Nick could almost see the debate going on in the young man's head. Hell, he could almost *hear* it. How many times had he weighed the odds of winning a battle of wills with this big, determined, utterly patient man?

Nick bit the inside of his cheek against a faint smile when Scott finally gave a deep sigh and grudgingly cleared his place at the table. The others quickly turned back to their desserts and their conversations, almost as though they hadn't noticed the brief contretemps. Nick felt Earl's gaze on him, and turned to face the man at the head of the long table.

"Familiar scene?" Earl asked, his eyes glinting with humor.

Nick chuckled and nodded. "Yeah. Real familiar. How does he feel about making his bed every morning?"

Earl grinned. "Same way you did. Thinks it's about the dumbest custom anyone ever invented, particularly since he's only going to crawl back into it every night."

"Bet he does it, though."

"If he wants to leave the house, he does," Earl agreed. "The rules around here have worked for a long time. I don't see any need to go changing them now."

Nick finished the last bite of his apple pie and washed it down with the last sip of his coffee. "You might like to know that I still rinse my dishes after every meal and make my bed every morning," he said.

Earl's smile broadened. "Glad to hear it. You turned out all right, boy."

It was the first time anyone had ever said that to Nick. He swallowed hard, wondering how to respond. He finally settled for a mumbled, "Thanks, Earl."

Whatever Earl may have said in return was cut off by a gasp of fright from the other end of the table. "Tricia? *Tricia!*"

Evelyn leaped from her chair, her eyes on her three-year-old granddaughter. "Paula, she's choking!"

The child was immediately surrounded by frightened family members, all of them babbling instructions. Instantly going into doctor mode, Nick tried to push through, only to be frustrated by a wall of concerned bodies. He was just about to shout to get attention when Lindsay beat him to it. "Would everyone move back?" she demanded loudly. "We have a doctor here! Let him help her!"

Nick was immediately given access to the child, who lay in her mother's lap, her eyes huge and tear-filled, her lips already turning blue. Nick noted at a glance that Tricia wasn't breathing, her air passage totally blocked by whatever had lodged in her throat.

"On the floor," he ordered, stripping off his coat. He was aware that Lindsay reached to help him, taking the coat out of his hands almost before he'd removed it, but he didn't take time to acknowledge her as he knelt beside the child.

Everyone in the room sighed in unison a few brief moments later when Tricia gasped, coughed, then burst into noisy tears, her throat cleared by an efficient sweep of Nick's finger. Relieved to see the color returning to the little face, Nick was grateful that the chunk of meat had been within reach and that more drastic measures hadn't been necessary.

He resisted Tricia's efforts to throw herself into her mother's arms only long enough to make sure that no lasting damage had been done. And then he stood back as the child was petted and pampered by her parents, grandparents, aunts and uncles.

Sensing that someone was watching him, he glanced around, only to have his gaze collide with Lindsay's. She stood a few feet away, his jacket still draped over her arm. Seeing that she had his attention, she held the jacket out to him. "Does this sort of thing happen to you often?"

He gave her a half smile and shrugged into his jacket. "Not very often, fortunately," he replied. "Strangely enough, it happened in a Mexican restaurant only last week. A boy at the table next to mine choked on a nacho chip. He couldn't speak or cough to get attention, and his family was busy talking about something and didn't notice his distress until he was close to passing out. I chanced to look up from my meal and saw what was going on in time to get to him and administer the Heimlich."

Lindsay cocked her head in interest at the story, and Nick realized it was the most he'd said at one time all evening. He remembered now that it had always been easy to talk to her when they were kids; apparently, he still felt that way about her, though he couldn't have explained why. She'd only asked one short question.

"You really love your work, don't you?" she surprised him by asking.

"Yeah," he admitted with a self-conscious nod. "I do."

Her brilliant smile went directly to the pit of his stomach with an almost physical punch. "I'm glad," she said softly.

Oh, man, he thought, rather dazed. *This woman could be dangerous.*

Before he could stop to analyze why that thought had popped into his head, he found himself being heartily slapped on the back by Greg, who thanked him for taking care of Tricia. And then the child's mother thanked him, followed by Earl and Evelyn. Steve made a teasing comment about how it was hard to believe the boy who'd once sneaked into girlie movies with him was now saving lives on a daily basis, to which Nick responded with a smile and a self-deprecatory quip.

By the time the conversation returned to the easy camaraderie of earlier, whatever spell had fallen between Nick and Lindsay was broken. She went into the kitchen with

Evelyn and her sisters-in-law, the women gravely excusing the men from K.P. duties "just this one time." Nick spent the next half hour in the den with Earl, Steve and Greg, feeling more relaxed and at home than at any time during the past fourteen intense, work-filled years.

"He's gorgeous!" Kim pronounced with a giggle. "Why didn't anyone tell me Nick Grant was such a hunk?"

Paula shook her head repressively. "Why, Kim Hillman. You're a married, pregnant woman."

"Since when do either marriage or pregnancy cause blindness? Admit it, Paula, he's prime meat."

Paula hesitated only a moment before grinning. "You're right," she conceded. "The man is a major babe."

Evelyn looked from one daughter-in-law to the other before turning to Lindsay. "Am I to interpret that Paula and Kim find Nick attractive?"

Lindsay smiled, hoping none of the others would notice that she had to make quite an effort to do so. She understood all too well what Paula and Kim were saying about Nick. "Yes, Mom, that's what they're saying in their rather dated teen vernacular."

Still giggling, as she always had a tendency to do, Kim shook a finger at Lindsay. " 'Teen vernacular'?" she repeated. "Honestly, Lindsay, one would think you were a hundred years old rather than twenty-five. You English teachers all sound just alike."

"And you and Paula resembled a couple of my students a moment ago, rather than respectable married women," Lindsay retorted, sliding a clean platter into a cabinet.

"Is that right? So, how would *you* describe Nick Grant?" Paula challenged.

Lindsay hesitated only a moment. "Okay, you're right," she conceded with a smile. "He's a babe. A serious, major babe."

Evelyn shook her head and muttered something about never understanding modern slang, but she was obviously amused by the younger women's foolishness.

Lindsay's smile vanished abruptly when Kim commented, "I think Nick's interested in you, Lindsay. Maybe he'll ask you out."

"Don't be ridiculous," Lindsay answered quickly, avoiding the others' eyes as she reached abruptly for a freshly washed plate. "He treated me exactly the same as he did everyone else."

"Not exactly," Paula mused. "He *does* seem interested, Lindsay. He watched you all through dinner."

Cheeks flaming, Lindsay shook her head. "The two of you are at it again—trying to pair me off with someone. You just can't stand it that I'm twenty-five and still not involved with anyone, can you? Nick and I hardly even know each other. I was just a little girl when he left, for heaven's sake."

"I think he noticed that you're not a little girl now," Kim murmured daringly, her voice ripe with suppressed amusement at Lindsay's obvious embarrassment.

Evelyn quickly came to her daughter's rescue, expressing her admiration of how competently Nick had handled Tricia's choking. "I'm so glad he was here," she added tremulously. "I don't know what we would have done if he hadn't been."

Paula nodded fervently. "I've studied first aid and CPR since the kids were born, but I have to admit I panicked when I realized what was happening," she said. "I think I could have handled it, but I'm glad Nick was here so I didn't have to put it to the test."

"You're sure that fine young doctor was once a rebellious delinquent like Scott?" Kim asked skeptically.

Evelyn smiled and nodded. "Oh, yes. As a matter of fact, we had more trouble with Nick at first than we've had with Scott so far. Nick was such an angry, bitter boy. Thank God they sent him to us in time to make a difference."

"What was his home life like?" Paula asked curiously.

"Oh, I don't think he'd want us to gossip about his past," Evelyn replied gently. "Let's just say his childhood wasn't a happy one."

Lindsay couldn't help wondering if Nick had finally found happiness now. He still seemed to be as emotionally guarded as she'd remembered him, slow to smile, careful with his words. He obviously loved his work, but what about his personal life? He'd said he'd never married, but had he ever been in love? Was there anyone special to him now? A woman who was allowed beyond the polite facade he'd erected for the rest of the world? Someone who knew what lay behind the imaginary shutters in his eyes?

Lindsay blamed Kim and Paula for her discomfort when Nick's gaze met hers as she entered the den a few minutes later with the other women. She assured herself that it was only coincidence that he looked up at the exact moment she walked in.

"Nick was just saying that he has to go," Earl announced.

Nick nodded. "I've got some paperwork to go over tonight and an early appointment tomorrow," he explained. "Evelyn, the dinner was delicious. Thank you for inviting me."

She beamed at him. "We loved having you here, Nick. Please say you'll come back soon."

"I'd like that," he answered, and again Lindsay noted that his voice warmed and softened when he talked to Evelyn. He must have been very fond of her mother, Lindsay thought, still trying to understand the puzzle that was Dr. Nick Grant.

She watched as the others took their leave of Nick. Greg and Paula thanked him again for his assistance with Tricia, and Steve challenged him to a round of golf, which Nick accepted with apparent pleasure. He added jokingly that golf was one of the required courses at medical school.

The others laughed; Lindsay studied Nick's smile, which didn't quite reach his eyes. Did he ever allow any emotion to show in those inscrutable eyes of his? she found herself wondering. Amusement? Passion? Love?

What would Nick Grant be like when—or if—he finally lost that formidable control?

She was still watching him when he glanced her way, their gazes locking again. Lindsay felt her cheeks warm, though she ignored the sensation when she spoke. "It was good to see you again, Nick."

He nodded, his eyes still holding hers. "Yeah. You, too."

"Where do you live, Nick?" Kim asked suddenly.

"I bought a house in west Little Rock," he replied, breaking eye contact with Lindsay to turn to Kim.

Kim smiled brilliantly. "Really? Lindsay has an apartment in that area. Steve and I will be taking her home this evening. She doesn't drive at night if she can help it."

Annoyed with Kim, because she knew exactly what her matchmaking sister-in-law was up to, Lindsay tried to change the subject by saying lightly, "My family still tends to be overprotective of their little sister, I'm afraid. I have trouble convincing them sometimes that I'm quite capable of *taking care of myself.*" She stressed the latter words just slightly, frowning repressively at Kim as she spoke.

"Do you still suffer from night blindness?" Nick startled her by asking.

"You remembered that?" she asked. Then she immediately answered, "Yes, I do. It's only a mild case, more inconvenient than debilitating, but I do try to avoid driving at night if I can help it."

"I'd be glad to drive you home, if you're ready to leave now," Nick offered.

Ignoring Kim's smug smile, Lindsay swallowed a groan of embarrassment. "Thank you, Nick, but—"

"That's a good idea," Steve injected quickly, giving Lindsay a cocky grin. "It'll give you and Nick a chance to get to know each other again, Lin."

"Oh, but—"

"No trouble at all," Nick assured her, his smile just this side of mocking.

Lindsay glared at him, deciding on the spot that Nick could probably tempt her to violence on occasion if she spent much time with him. There was something about the way he looked at her—as though he was taunting her, seeing just how much it would take to rile her. She wondered if he remembered that it didn't usually take all that much. Her bouts of temper had been as frequent as her laughter during her childhood, to her older brothers' wicked delight.

She called on all the dignity required of a junior high school English teacher to reply without providing her brothers further grounds for future teasing. "In that case, I'll accept. Thank you, Nick. Just let me get my purse."

"Take your time," he murmured, and for just a moment she caught a glimpse of genuine emotion in his eyes.

It annoyed her greatly that the breakthrough was due to his obvious amusement at her expense.

Nick's car was low, sleek and expensive. Lindsay couldn't help remembering the battered old Mustang he'd bought as a teenager with money he'd earned working after school at a fast-food restaurant. Picturing that younger, shabbier boy in his jeans and leather jacket, she glanced sideways at the elegantly groomed man behind the wheel now. Odd how clearly she remembered him as a teen, she mused. She'd been so young, and it had been so long.

"Your family hasn't changed much," Nick commented, as though he'd read her thoughts. "It was almost like old times."

"My family may be very much the same, but you've changed quite a bit since those old times."

Nick shrugged. "On the outside, maybe."

"Well, you never gave us much chance to see the inside," Lindsay replied candidly.

He lifted an eyebrow, but said merely, "Maybe not."

When it was obvious that he didn't intend to say anything else, Lindsay shook her head. "See what I mean?"

Nick drove for a moment longer in silence, then commented, "You're very lucky to have such a close family. It's easy to see that you all care very much for each other."

"Yes, we do. And yes, I am lucky," Lindsay conceded. "I've often thought how fortunate I was that Mother and Dad were the ones to find me and give me a home."

"I remembered that you were adopted," Nick said, glancing at her. "But I never knew the details. Were you a newborn when they got you?"

"No. I was almost nine months old. Obviously I don't have any memories prior to my adoption."

"That's probably for the best," Nick muttered.

Lindsay wondered if he referred to his own unpleasant early memories. "At least I always knew I was adopted," she went on, trying to continue the conversation. "My parents were very open about it. I knew adopted kids who found out traumatically when they were teenagers or later. That's very hard news to take at that age.

"It also helped for me to know from the beginning that my biological parents had both died. I never had to wonder if they were out there somewhere looking for me, or why they gave me up, all the questions my few adopted friends had to deal with. I always considered myself lucky that when my natural parents died, from whatever the causes, Earl and Evelyn Hillman were there to take me in and give me all the love I could ever have asked for."

"They're good people."

"Yes." Lindsay took a deep breath, then asked daringly, "Do you ever hear from your own biological family, Nick? Are your parents still living?"

His voice was clipped, utterly without emotion. "My father was killed when I was eight. I was informed that my mother died while I was in college."

"You never heard from her after you left her home when you were sixteen?" Lindsay asked, wishing she could read his expression.

"No."

Though she knew she shouldn't press him for details he obviously wasn't eager to give, she couldn't help asking another question. "You didn't have any brothers or sisters, did you?"

"No."

He was so very alone. "Don't you have anyone in your life now?" she asked sympathetically.

He shrugged again. "I have my work, my patients. A few friends from med school, though they've scattered across the country. I've made a good life for myself, Lindsay. Don't start feeling sorry for me."

"I don't," she assured him, though she knew she lied. She felt sorry for anyone who didn't have the kind of loving, caring, supportive family that she had found with the Hillmans.

Lindsay didn't quite have the nerve to look at him when she asked the next question. "Have you ever been in love with anyone, Nick?"

He sounded startled when he responded after a momentary pause. "Why?"

"I don't know. I just wondered."

She thought he wasn't going to answer. Finally he did. "I lived with someone for a couple of months during my residency. It didn't work out."

Lindsay chewed her lower lip, finding herself strangely reluctant to picture him living with a woman, sharing a bed and a life with her. Still, she couldn't help observing, "I'd bet you broke her heart."

"The hell I did. She left me. Moved out one day while I was at work."

That didn't surprise her. Nor did it change her opinion. "I have a feeling she couldn't reach you, that she needed more than you were able—or willing—to give her."

Nick made an involuntary movement that confirmed her suspicion that he'd heard those words before. "She said something to that effect," he admitted after a moment. "Truth was, she wasn't willing to make the concessions required of anyone involved with a doctor. I gave her all I had left to give. It wasn't enough to satisfy her."

Lindsay guessed that Nick's work had been a convenient excuse for him to avoid making the type of commitment the unfortunate woman had hoped for. She suspected that a woman who truly loved him would be willing to make the sacrifices required by his career if she knew that she was as important to him as the job, and that he needed her in some way.

But even after the short time she'd spent with him this evening, Lindsay thought that Nick Grant would resist making himself vulnerable to anyone, admitting a need for anyone. He'd had to learn early to depend on no one but himself. A woman who loved him would either have to learn to accept the emotional walls he'd built around himself—or she'd break her heart trying to hammer through them.

Which meant that Lindsay would be wise to ignore the attraction she'd felt for Nick Grant since she'd first opened her parents' door to him. She knew herself well enough to understand that she'd need much more from a man than an occasional pat on the head or superficial affection. She longed for the passion and spiritual communion described in the best romantic novels. A connection that went far beyond the physical and lasted for an entire lifetime.

Perhaps that was why she'd always found it easier to treat the men in her life with the same easy affection she gave her brothers, to the intense frustration of several of her erstwhile suitors. She'd always known that when she finally met a man she *couldn't* treat like a brother, she'd have found the one who held the power to break her heart.

Keeping that thought in mind, she decided she'd better start trying to think of Nick Grant as another honorary brother. Quickly.

Nick interrupted her thoughts with a gusty exhalation. "How did we get on this conversation, anyway?" he demanded. "I don't like wasting time thinking or talking about the past."

"We're almost at my apartment," she assured him. "Turn right at the next intersection."

He nodded. "Did I hear someone mention that you're an English teacher?"

"Yes. Steve's principal of the junior high school where I teach."

"How does that work out? Having your brother for your boss, I mean."

She chuckled. "We've had our moments. I usually manage to treat him with professional respect in front of the others, but when I get him alone I don't mind telling him what I really think."

"I'm sure you don't. You were never shy about expressing your opinion."

"No. I certainly told you what I thought of that girl you dated your senior year in high school, didn't I?" she remembered with a grin. "The one who treated me like a mindless child. I couldn't stand her and didn't hesitate to tell you at every opportunity. What was her name?"

"I don't remember," he replied rather shortly. "As I said, I rarely think about the past."

"You obviously haven't completely forgotten the past," Lindsay retorted, frustrated with his reticence. "After all, you were the one who called Mother and wanted to see us again."

He pulled the car into a parking space she'd indicated to him. "Yeah. I was, wasn't I?"

He sounded as though the action puzzled him almost as much as it did her, Lindsay thought in exasperation. Any woman who'd get involved with this man would have to be a masochist. Who could ever hope to fully understand him?

"Good night, Nick," she said, one hand already on the door handle. "Thanks for bringing me home."

"I'll walk you to your apartment."

"That's not—"

But he was already out of the car. Lindsay muttered a disgruntled curse and opened her door.

Nick took her arm when she reached his side. She started to tell him with some asperity that the excellent security lighting of the apartment complex took care of her annoying problem with mild night blindness. But something about

the feel of his hand on her arm, even through the thin
sweater she wore in deference to the late October chill,
completely took away her ability to speak.

Not the way she'd respond to a brother, she reminded
herself irritably, forcing herself to breathe normally and relax. She subtly removed her arm from his grasp by digging
in her purse for her keys.

"This is my apartment," she announced, approaching the
third door on the right. A bright light blazed from beside the
door, illuminating her entryway as well as the flight of stairs
that led upward to the second floor. The security of the
apartment she'd chosen had been closely scrutinized by her
parents and her brothers before they'd given Lindsay their
approval of her choice.

Nick didn't seem as satisfied. He looked around the unusually deserted complex, shaking his head. "Doesn't look
very safe," he said. "No guards? No intercom system at
your door?"

"I have a peephole," she pointed out. "And there is a
full-time security guard who patrols at night. He must be
walking around one of the other buildings at the moment."

"That wouldn't do you much good if you needed him
now," Nick replied curtly.

She managed to hold on to her smile. He was sounding
more like a big brother by the moment. Now if only she
could make herself think of him as one. "Trust me, Nick,
I've learned to take care of myself. I've had self-defense
training, and Steve says I've got a scream like a steam engine. I'm perfectly safe here."

Not visibly reassured, Nick took her key from her hand
and efficiently unlocked the door. "I'll check inside for you
before I leave."

"No, that's—" But he was already inside. "Dammit, I *wish* you'd let me finish a sentence occasionally!" Lindsay complained, following him in.

Nick gave her a half smile, though he finished his quick tour of the one-bedroom apartment before he seemed content to leave her alone there. "Nice place," he commented, handing her the keys when he returned from his inspection of the bedroom.

"I'm so glad you approve," Lindsay answered dryly.

He chuckled. "Sorry. Guess there's something about you that brings out my latent protective instincts."

"You and everyone else, apparently," she grumbled, crossing her arms in front of her. "When is everyone going to realize that I am no longer a little girl?"

"Trust me, Princess," Nick murmured, his voice suddenly husky. "I noticed that the moment I saw you tonight."

Her eyes going wide, Lindsay looked at him in question. Only to find him looking back at her with an expression that made her mouth go dry. Before she could think of anything to say in response, Nick headed for the door. He opened it, then glanced back over his shoulder. "Lindsay?"

"Yes?" she asked in little more than a whisper.

"You seeing anyone? Anyone special, I mean."

She was startled into giving him a candid answer. "No."

He smiled. "Then you'll be hearing from me. G'night. Lock the door behind me."

"I always lock..."

But, again, he didn't give her a chance to finish her automatic reply. He was already gone.

You'll be hearing from me, he'd said.

Her hand at her throat, Lindsay knew that he hadn't been talking about resuming the semisibling relationship they'd had fourteen years earlier.

And she wasn't at all certain it would ever be possible for her to treat him like a brother, no matter how hard she might try.

"Oh, damn," she murmured, her eyes still focused on the door through which he'd disappeared. "I don't think I'm ready for this."

Chapter Three

Lindsay had never been more nervous dressing for an evening. It wasn't just that she'd be attending a ritzy affair in a home in the most exclusive neighborhood in Little Rock, when she was more accustomed to chaperoning school parties. It wasn't just that some of the most important community and society leaders in town would also be in attendance. Nor was her nervousness due solely to the fact that the society reporters from the local newspaper would be in attendance with their cameras and notepads.

No, she could handle all that. Though she had attended few such gatherings, she'd managed to acquit herself well enough at other social events. The most unnerving aspect of the evening, as far as Lindsay was concerned, was that she'd be attending the party as Nick Grant's date. And she was highly annoyed with herself for allowing that to disconcert her so intensely.

She was even more annoyed when it took twenty minutes to arrange her hair to her satisfaction. Her temper finally flared and she slammed the brush down on the countertop with a muttered curse.

"Would you stop it?" she demanded of the flushed, harried-looking young woman in her mirror. "You're acting like an idiot!"

And she had been ever since Nick had called two days before—over a week since the dinner at her parents' home—and invited her to go as his date to this cocktail party being given by his medical associates to welcome him to Little Rock. She'd accepted with reservations, then had promptly gone into a panic at the realization that she had absolutely nothing to wear. It had taken her an entire day of shopping to find just the right dress—and now she wasn't at all sure it was the right dress, after all.

She sighed.

"This really isn't the way to start thinking of Nick as just another honorary brother," she muttered, walking away from the vanity to don the dress.

Ten minutes later she was ready—sort of. The dress consisted of an off-the-shoulder, long-sleeved white bodice and a black skirt that began just below her breasts, fit tightly to her hips, then swirled about the knee. Her shoulders rose bare and creamy above the fabric, exposing just a hint of cleavage in the dip at the front of the low neckline. She debated adding a necklace, then decided her diamond-drop earrings—a college graduation present from her family— were all the ornamentation she needed.

Studying the full-length cheval mirror in one corner of her bedroom, she decided with cautious approval that she looked very different from the eleven-year-old girl who'd told Nick goodbye so many years ago. The woman in the mirror looked mature, competent, poised. Fully prepared to attend a glitzy cocktail party on the arm of an attractive man.

The doorbell rang, startling her almost out of her black heels. She put a hand on her pounding heart and wondered in exasperation if she was having some sort of breakdown. She'd never completely lost her composure over any man before. Why was she doing so now? It was, after all, only Nick.

Satisfied that she had herself under control now, she took a deep breath and opened her door. Then nearly forgot how to breathe at the sight of Nick Grant in impeccably tailored evening clothes.

Only Nick? That seemed to be exactly the problem!

For just a moment, she caught a glimpse of something in his eyes, behind his thin-rimmed glasses, that shook her down to her toes. A glimpse of genuine, volatile emotion that just might have been a deep, masculine hunger. But almost as quickly as she'd seen it, he'd pulled down those imaginary shutters again, leaving her to wonder if she'd only been fantasizing, perhaps trying to convince herself that he was as deeply affected by the attraction between them as she was.

"Lindsay," he said, his rough voice low and apparently quite calm. "You look lovely. Are you ready to go?"

She nodded, hoping she'd be able to speak as composedly. "Yes, I'm ready. Just let me get my purse."

"You may want a wrap. It's a bit cool out."

She shook her head. "I haven't anything that matches this outfit. I'll be fine."

"Vanity," Nick mocked gently, holding the door for her as she passed him on the way outside. "You'd rather risk hypothermia than be accused of not matching."

"Exactly," she replied with a smile, more comfortable with his teasing than with whatever emotion she might have glimpsed in his eyes. Teasing she could handle. Anything else would be too much with this man.

Determined to keep the evening light and unthreatening, Lindsay kept up a brisk, airy conversation as Nick drove her the short distance to the home where the party would be held. She didn't give him much chance to contribute anything more than an occasional comment or question. Not that he probably would have said much more, anyway. He seemed content just to listen to her talk. Nick never had been much of a talker, as Lindsay remembered.

She found out during the first hour or so of the party that, despite his natural tendency to quietness, Nick had certainly learned to interact socially during the years since she'd known him. He shook hands, made introductions, air-kissed cheeks, chatted and mingled with the skill of a born politician. He had cultivated a smooth, sophisticated public persona—urbane, witty, charming. And though he didn't talk a lot, the other guests tended to listen carefully to what he did say. Lindsay could tell that Nick had made quite a favorable impression on Little Rock society.

She wondered if she was the only one to notice that his smiles rarely reached his serious eyes, that his polite words didn't always ring true. She wondered if anyone would ever really know Nick Grant. Something about that unyielding reserve of his bothered her. She found herself watching him with growing irritation...and a building desire to do something crazy—ruffle his hair, crumple his tie, taunt him into losing his temper—anything to threaten his thorough, daunting control.

"He's a fascinating man, isn't he?" a feminine voice sighed into Lindsay's ear at one point during the evening.

Lindsay turned to find a tall, curvaceous redhead in a clinging emerald dress sipping champagne from a crystal flute and watching Nick with visible lust. Lindsay had met the woman earlier, but couldn't remember her name. Bitsy? Tippi? Cissy? Something unbearably cute like that.

"Yes, Nick is a very interesting man," she agreed, her voice cool.

"Have you known him long?" The woman gave Lindsay a speculative look as she asked the question, obviously measuring the competition.

"Yes, for several years," Lindsay found some pleasure in saying.

"I see. No one seems to know much about Nick's background. I understood that he's just moved here from Boston?"

"Yes, but he's originally from this area."

"So you knew each other when you were just kids?"

"Yes."

The redhead began to smile again. "A brother-and-sister relationship, I suppose?" Her tone implied that she couldn't imagine there would be anything else between Lindsay and "fascinating" Nick Grant.

Lindsay gritted her teeth and smiled. "Not exactly." She only wished it *were!* Things would be much more comfortable all around.

A hand fell on Lindsay's waist, making her look quickly around. Nick gave her a bland smile, then glanced at the other woman. "I believe your husband is looking for you, Buffy."

Buffy immediately looked bored. "Oh, I'm sure Howard will get along fine without me for a while."

She placed a perfectly manicured hand on Nick's arm, totally ignoring Lindsay. "I was hoping to show you Debbie's solarium, Nick. It's really spectacular. She raises tropical plants, you know. I think you'd find them fascinating."

"I'm sure we would. We'll have to see them before we leave, won't we, Lindsay? But I promised Howard I'd send you his way if I saw you, so perhaps you'd better find him, Buffy. I'd hate to be in hot water with my senior partner so early in our professional relationship."

Nick spoke genially enough, but his message was unmistakable. He had no intention of having anything more than a passing acquaintance with his senior partner's wife, whatever her own blatant hints may have suggested to the contrary.

Buffy's sigh was rich with regret. "No, we couldn't have that, could we?" she murmured. "But if you change your mind, I'm available—to show you the solarium," she added with a coy smile.

"Of course." Nick gave her a nod, then turned deliberately to Lindsay. "I haven't introduced you to Sam and Betty Levin yet, have I? They're a nice couple—I think you'll like them."

He leaned close to her ear as they moved out of Buffy's range. "Was Buffy giving you a hard time? She can be a bit much."

"I can handle Buffy," Lindsay replied, piqued that he'd seemed to feel she needed rescuing. Hadn't she held her own quite well this evening, mingling with the rich and powerful with an outward ease that she was far from feeling on the inside? This overprotectiveness Nick tended to display around her could get tiresome in a hurry.

"I could handle Buffy, too," Nick murmured, rolling his eyes.

Lindsay giggled despite her irritation with him, as they approached a distinguished-looking, middle-aged couple standing near one of the canapé tables. Sometimes his sense of humor surprised her.

Overriding Lindsay's protests, Nick insisted on checking her apartment yet again when he took her home, having already irked her by pointing out that he'd told her to wear a jacket when she shivered in the cool October night air.

"This really isn't necessary," she complained, watching him open the bathroom door to look inside. "It's as though you expect to find a mad rapist lurking beneath the bed or something. Honestly, Nick."

He shrugged. "You can't be too careful. There are too many crazies running loose these days."

"Anyone ever tell you you're just a bit too compulsive, Dr. Grant? Not to mention more than slightly paranoid?"

For just a moment, she thought she detected annoyance in his expression in response to her gibes. He masked it swiftly. "Everything looks okay here."

Lindsay crossed her arms. "I can't tell you how much safer that makes me feel."

He looked at her with a lifted eyebrow. "Does it really annoy you that I'm concerned about your safety?"

"It annoys me to be treated like a helpless little girl," she retorted. "I've been living on my own for several years. I'm quite capable of looking under my own bed for things that go bump in the night."

"Of course you are," he assured her, and the hint of patronization in his voice made her long to hit him.

She settled, instead, for trying yet again to penetrate that almost palpable reserve of his. "You seemed to fit in quite well tonight, Nick. Very yuppie and upscale, one of the crowd. You've come a long way since high school."

"I've learned to make small talk when it's necessary, if that's what you mean."

"Oh, it's more than that. Why, you worked that room like a gubernatorial candidate. If there'd been any babies there, you'd probably have kissed them. Aiming for a senior partnership for yourself, Nick?"

He frowned a little in response to her tone, but answered evenly enough. "It never hurts to make a good impression with one's business associates. Being successful these days involves more than being good at one's job."

"One has to be equally good at kissing up, is that it?"

"I prefer to call it socializing," he replied, still infuriatingly unruffled by her deliberate digs.

"Yes, I'm sure you do," Lindsay muttered, glaring at him.

He suddenly looked amused. "Lindsay, are you trying to make me lose my temper?"

She tossed her head defiantly. "Maybe."

His smile deepened, pushing intriguing dimples into the corners of his nicely shaped mouth. "Want to tell me why?"

She was stung into answering with total honesty. "I just want to see if you're even capable of genuine emotion. I haven't seen a glimpse of anything real since you picked me up this evening. You're like a...a facade of an up-and-coming young doctor who's no more sincere than an attractive cardboard cutout."

He chuckled with a patient indulgence that made her hands clench, the urge to hit him growing even stronger. "At least you called me attractive," he murmured.

"Dammit, Nick, what does it take to make you mad?"

His smile faded abruptly. "Trust me. You wouldn't want to know."

She lifted an eyebrow and eyed him curiously. "What are you, the Incredible Hulk? You think I wouldn't like you if you got angry?"

He only shrugged and looked away.

"Nick, it's okay to be yourself around me. I know where you came from, remember? I was there when you were a rebellious kid in a foster home and I know how hard you've worked to put that behind you. I'm not afraid of what I might find beneath the surface you've manufactured for yourself during the past few years.''

"No?" He looked at her again, his expression so closed to her it might as well have been carved in granite. "Perhaps you should be."

"Why? It's only natural that I'd want to know more about your past if we—well, if we're going to be seeing each other. Your past is what made you the man you are today."

"I don't talk about the past. How many times do I have to tell you that before you'll believe it?" he asked roughly.

She studied the finality in his expression. "You don't intend to ever tell me about it, do you? No matter what may happen between us."

"No. It's over. It has nothing to do with us."

Her arms lifted and then fell to her sides in defeat. "I don't understand you."

Nick stepped closer and placed his hands on her bare shoulders. Gazing up at him, she shivered, though not with cold this time. "Maybe you'll understand *this,*" he muttered, just before he lowered his head to hers.

Lindsay was thoroughly shaken by Nick's kiss, staggered by a wave of emotion more powerful than anything she'd ever experienced before. Her lips parted in surprise, and Nick took immediate advantage of the opportunity. Lindsay could only cling to his broad shoulders in dazed reaction, unable to pull away, not even wanting to do so. She'd never been kissed like this, never felt these emotions with any other man. How did he *do* that to her?

Any fleeting hope she'd had of regarding Nick as another honorary brother vanished forever during that kiss. She and Nick could end up as lovers or enemies—maybe cautious friends—but her feelings for him would never be the platonic affection of siblings.

She'd always known that someday she'd meet a man she couldn't pinhole so neatly. She'd always known that when she did, she'd be completely vulnerable to him, in danger of having her heart broken for the first time in her life. And Nick Grant was, most definitely, that man.

Very slowly, Nick lifted his head, though he didn't release her from his arms. Gasping for breath, Lindsay stared up at him. "Why?" she asked in a husky whisper, knowing she didn't need to elaborate.

"I've been wanting to do that since the first time I saw you again," he answered, his own voice rougher than usual.

And then he kissed her again—skillfully, passionately— and she melted willingly into the embrace. She couldn't think when Nick kissed her, could only feel. Could only want, as she'd never wanted before.

He wanted her, too. He made no effort to hide his desire from her, particularly when he pressed a hand to the small of her back and held her more closely to him. And yet even in his passion she sensed that he held something back. Something deep inside himself that she suspected no one had ever been able to reach.

That thought gave her the strength to pull out of his arms. "That's enough," she said, taking several steps away, needing the distance between them. "It's too soon, Nick. I don't know you well enough for this."

"You know all there is to know," he answered, though he made no effort to detain her.

"I can't believe that. There are depths to you that you don't allow anyone to see—not friends, not associates, not even . . . lovers. And those are the depths I'd have to know before we go any further with this."

Nick sighed impatiently and ran a hand through his hair. "Do you never stop digging? There are depths to everyone that no one else needs to know. It's called privacy. Everyone deserves some—me, you, everyone."

"It's called intimacy," she corrected him defiantly. "And true intimacy is based on total communication."

He gave a snort that sounded suspiciously derisive. "The problem with you is that you've been spoiled, Princess. You're much too accustomed to manipulating people, having them fall all over themselves to accommodate you. But I'm afraid I don't play those games. I don't believe in wasting time. When I see something I want, I go after it—no games, no ritual dances. You take me as I am, or not at all."

Lord, the man was arrogant! Stung by the accusation that she was spoiled—she knew he was probably right, though she wouldn't have admitted it if he'd shoved needles under her toenails—she narrowed her eyes and glared at him. "Fine. I won't take you at all."

"Your choice." He gave her a taunting, skeptical, outright challenging bow. "For now."

"For always."

"We'll see. Good night, Lindsay. Thank you for a delightful evening." He made no effort to disguise the mockery this time.

The name Lindsay muttered beneath her breath as he left was hardly flattering to Nick's ancestry. If he heard, he gave no sign, merely closing the door firmly, quietly behind him.

Lindsay glared at that closed door for a long time, her lips still tingling from his kisses, her body still throbbing from his touches.

Was that how Nick had worked his way from destitute foster child to successful young doctor? With total unwillingness to admit the possibility of defeat, an arrogant refusal to compromise? Maybe she *was* spoiled, maybe she did expect too much from him, but Lindsay had no intention of allowing herself to fall for a man who felt she had no right

to know his thoughts, no reason to want more than the bits
of himself he allowed her to see.

Had the woman who'd once lived with him fought those
emotional barriers of his? Had he arrogantly assured her
that what she saw was all there was to him, even when both
of them had known he was lying? Had she left with her
heart broken, her confidence shaken, defeated and frustrated by her inability to break through to him? Or was
Lindsay only predicting the outcome if *she* were to be so
foolish as to fall for the infuriatingly reticent Nick Grant?

She knew herself too well to believe she'd ever be content
with a superficial relationship, an affair based on no more
than physical attraction. She hadn't waited this long for so
little, hadn't spent years looking for something so shallow.

She wanted more. She needed more. And, like Nick, she
didn't believe in wasting time. If he couldn't convince her
from the outset that he would be willing to share himself
with her, at least eventually, then there was no need to start
anything that could only end unhappily.

Okay, so she'd never be able to look at him as a brother.
She'd probably never be able to forget the way he'd made
her feel in his arms. Maybe never feel quite the same way
with anyone else. But that didn't mean they couldn't be
friends, of a sort, did it, as long as Nick was willing to cooperate?

If only she could convince herself that she didn't still want
him so badly her teeth ached, so badly she still trembled just
at the memory of his kisses.

She groaned in frustration and whirled on one high heel,
anxious to get out of the dress that made her look like
someone she didn't know at all. Someone as shallow and
superficial as Nick Grant was pretending so hard to be.

Wandering around his house in the middle of the night,
Nick thought of Lindsay and debated a cold shower. Damn,

but he ached for her. More than he'd ached in a very long
time. It couldn't all be attributed to the lack of female
companionship in his life during the past few busy months.
There'd been women available, had he been interested.
Problem was, no one had interested him more than pass-
ingly—until he'd seen Lindsay again.

He wanted her. Maybe it wasn't wise—after all, she was
younger, more impulsive and spontaneous than he was.
They didn't seem to have a great deal in common. And then
there was her family, who'd always been so protective of her
and probably wouldn't hesitate to interfere should they decide she was in danger of being hurt—even by Nick, whom
they treated almost like a son. No, an affair with Lindsay
wouldn't be easy. But still he wanted her.

She wanted him, too. She hadn't been able to hide her re-
sponses to him, hadn't developed his skill at masking
thoughts and emotions. Her expressions had been so open,
so transparent. She'd wanted him, but she was afraid of
him. Afraid of her feelings for him.

He didn't understand why she couldn't just accept their
attraction and enjoy it. Why she felt it necessary to keep
digging, prodding at him, trying to uncover emotions within
him that would be uncomfortable at best, dangerous at the
worst. She didn't know what she was asking, couldn't understand how important it was that those deeper, darker
emotions remain buried inside him. He'd worked too damn
hard and too damn long to keep them there to allow Lindsay—or anyone—to dig them up now.

So she had a choice. She could accept him on his terms,
enjoy the feelings between them, take a chance that what
they could have would be truly spectacular—and Nick suspected it would be—or she could take the coward's way out
and refuse to have anything to do with him. He'd give her a
little time to think about it—and then he was going after her

with the same single-minded determination with which he'd pursued his medical degree.

His mouth tilted upward in a slow smile. Lindsay Hillman was in for the challenge of her life if she thought she could just walk away from him without a backward glance, the way Sheila Greene had done a few years ago.

Nick hadn't cared enough to fight for Sheila, had been more annoyed than distressed when she'd stormed out of his life. But Lindsay was different. Lindsay was special. And he had no intention of letting her slip away without making one hell of an effort to convince her to give them a chance.

Chapter Four

Maybe it was because Lindsay had been trying so hard not to think of Nick for the past week that she reacted so dramatically when her sister-in-law said his name on the following Saturday afternoon. The plastic tumbler she'd been holding clattered noisily against the enamel sink when it slipped from her fingers. She made an effort to laugh lightly.

"I've been such a klutz lately," she complained, retrieving the tumbler and refilling it with ice cubes before turning on the water. "What were you saying, Kim?"

Sitting at the kitchen table behind a large glass of milk, Kim didn't seem particularly curious about Lindsay's clumsiness. "I was just saying that Steve is out playing golf with Nick. Steve's delighted to have found a new golf buddy, though I warned him that doctors are supposed to be real masters of the game. Even Nick said golf is a required course at medical school."

Lindsay slipped into a chair across the table from her sister-in-law. "I think he was teasing, Kim."

"I know. But I'd still bet he's pretty good. Nick strikes me as the type who'd be good at anything he does."

Lindsay choked on another sip of water, her mind suddenly filled with memories of how very adept Nick had been at kissing. She shivered to think of how good he might be at other things.

"You okay, Lin?"

"Yes, of course. I'm just a real klutz today."

Kim sighed, her dark eyes looking rueful beneath her fringe of black bangs. "Join the club. I've always been one, but now that I'm as big as a Mack truck, it's getting ridiculous. Steve makes fun of me for walking into walls and stumbling over patterns in the carpet. I told him *he* should try navigating with an enormous watermelon strapped to his stomach, totally blocking his view of anything below it."

"I think you're getting around just fine," Lindsay said, defending her loyally. Then she grinned. "You waddle more gracefully than anyone I've ever known."

Kim made a face. "Thanks so much."

"You're welcome."

"I just hope I get somewhere close to a size six again after this kid's born. Looking at this enormous belly, it's becoming very hard to believe I'll ever fit into my old clothes again."

"Sure you will. Don't you remember how huge Paula got with Zane? And she's already back to her original size. It only takes a little discipline after the baby's born—exercise, watching what you eat."

"Says the woman who's never had to count a calorie in her life," Kim accused. "Just wait until *you're* in this condition someday!"

Which, of course, only led Lindsay to wonder whether she ever *would* be in that condition. And suddenly she found herself thinking of Nick again, to her intense discomfort.

To distract herself, she changed the subject. "How are things going at work?"

An investment counselor for a large Little Rock bank, Kim planned to work until four weeks prior to her due date, which would make her maternity leave begin around Thanksgiving. "Everything's fine," she assured Lindsay. "I get a little tired at midafternoon, but management has been very supportive. They usually encourage me to take a half hour break to put my feet up and have a protein snack. I'm lucky to have such understanding supervisors."

"Yes, you are. I've heard such horror stories about the way pregnant women are treated in the workplace. Your bosses, however, know what a treasure they have in you. They wouldn't want to risk losing you after the baby comes."

"Thanks. It'll be hard going back to work when the baby's only six weeks old, but I still plan to try it for a while."

"Is Steve accepting that decision any better now?" Lindsay asked carefully. She didn't want to pry, but she knew Kim's decision to return to work after the baby's birth had caused some friction in the otherwise happy marriage.

Steve had always fully supported Kim in her career, but he'd hoped she would take more time off after their child's birth. Reluctant to lose the seniority and responsibility she'd earned in her job during the past few years, Kim had been afraid to risk having to start from the bottom again if she took too much time off.

"Steve still wishes I'd take a few years off," Kim admitted, "but he has accepted my right to make my own decision. I think he finally understood when I said it would be perfectly all right with me if he left *his* job for a few years

and allowed me to support the family financially. He said
he'd love to spend that time with our child—but what would
it do to his future career? I said, 'Exactly. Now you know
how I feel.'"

"Very logical of you. My brother is stubborn, but not
totally unreasonable." Lindsay took another sip of her water. "By the way, have the two of you ever agreed on
names?"

Kim smiled and nodded, her hand unconsciously going to
her stomach. "Yes. Michael Gregory, if it's a boy."

Lindsay was pleased. "Greg will like that," she said ap-
provingly. The Hillman brothers had always been close—
Greg and Paula had named their son Zane Stephen.

"And if it's a girl, her name will be Catheryn Lindsay."

Touched, Lindsay bit her lower lip. "Oh, Kim. I would
love that. It means a lot to me that you and Steve would
consider naming your child after me."

"We love you," Kim answered matter-of-factly.

"I love you both, too. And I can't wait to be an aunt
again."

"Mmm. So when are you . . ."

But whatever Kim had intended to ask was interrupted
when the kitchen door suddenly flew open and Steve burst
noisily through, talking rapidly and laughingly to the man
who followed him inside. Lindsay caught her breath when
Nick's eyes met hers from across the room. For a moment,
he seemed almost as startled by this unexpected encounter
as she was, though—of course—he swiftly masked his expression. She found that trick of his as frustrating today as
she had on their date.

"How was the golf game?" Kim asked, eyeing Lindsay
and Nick as though sensing undercurrents she couldn't quite
understand.

"He stomped me," Steve admitted cheerfully. "Never take a doctor on a golf course."

"A vicious stereotype, of course," Nick replied with a smile. "Not all doctors play golf—and I know some who play very poorly. I just happen to be good at the game."

"He says modestly," Steve muttered from the depths of the refrigerator as he pulled out two cans of cola.

Nick chuckled. "This from the man who has already boasted that he'll totally humiliate me next time we play?"

"Consider yourself warned," Steve agreed gravely. "Today I was just being kind to a newcomer to our town. I let you win."

"Yeah. Right."

Kim laughed. "Enough of the macho posturing already. Would either of you like anything to eat?"

"We had sandwiches at the club," Steve answered, leaning back against the countertop as he looked from his wife to his sister. "You two been up to anything interesting?"

"Just visiting," Lindsay answered, determined not to sit like a paralyzed lump just because Nick Grant was in the room. "I bought something for the baby while I was shopping this morning and I couldn't wait to bring it over."

"Oh, Steve, it's the sweetest little yellow playsuit," Kim enthused. "You wouldn't recognize the designer name on it, but trust me, it's a famous one. I told Lindsay she's already spoiling the child, just like she does Greg and Paula's kids."

"That's what aunts are for, isn't it?" Lindsay demanded teasingly. "We spoil them and then Mom and Dad have to unspoil them. Besides, the playsuit was on sale. I saw it and couldn't resist it."

"A woman of little willpower, hmm?" Nick murmured, eyeing Lindsay over the top of his cola can.

She gave him a sugary smile. "*Only* when it's something I just can't resist."

"I'll keep that in mind."

Steve cleared his throat. "Am I missing something here?"

"Nothing important, Steve." Lindsay stood and carried her water glass to the sink. "I've gotta run. I have a dozen things to do this afternoon. See you guys later."

"Thanks again for the baby outfit, Lindsay. I love it."

"I was hoping you would, Kim. I'll see you at Greg's to-morrow, okay?" Lindsay kissed her brother's cheek as she passed him, then gave Nick a polite smile. "Nice to see you again, Nick."

"Yeah. See you tomorrow, Lindsay."

"Tomorrow?" Lindsay repeated, frowning in sudden suspicion.

He confirmed her fears with a glint of humor in his eyes. "Yes. Greg's invited me to lunch at his house with the rest of you. Wasn't that nice of him?"

Lindsay swallowed hard, holding on to her smile with some effort. She didn't bother to answer Nick's question— he hadn't really expected her to, anyway, she was sure—but slipped outside without further delay, all but running to her car.

How was she supposed to put Nick Grant out of her mind when her family seemed to be doing everything possible to throw him back into her path? She muttered in frustration as she started her car, annoyed that her hands hadn't quite been steady ever since Kim had mentioned Nick's name.

As always when the Hillman clan got together—which they did as often as possible—there was a great deal of chatter and laughter during the lunch at Greg and Paula's house on Sunday. Lindsay was grateful for the noise, hop-ing it would distract the others from how little she had to say that afternoon. For some reason, Nick had all but glued himself to her side since they'd arrived. He hadn't said much, but kept giving her smiles that curled her toes and fleeting little touches that made her constantly, vividly aware of him. As though she wouldn't have been, anyway.

She didn't know what he was trying to prove today. Whatever it was, she wished he'd stop. The others were beginning to notice how closely he'd stayed by her side, how much attention he was paying her. He even mentioned—oh, so casually—the party he and Lindsay had attended together. Lindsay wasn't sure why she hadn't already said something about that date to anyone in her family. At Nick's comment, Evelyn looked at Lindsay questioningly, obviously wondering about the oversight herself.

Looking as though he'd rather be anywhere else, Scott Driskell picked at the food on his plate and participated even less than Lindsay in the general camaraderie around him. When he did speak, it was to voice a question that caused a sudden, awkward silence to fall around the table.

"How come you're the only one in the family that don't have red hair? Steve and Greg look just alike, but you don't look like anyone. You adopted or something?" he asked Lindsay. He sat across the table from her, and although she'd been aware that he'd been studying her for several minutes, she hadn't expected this.

Lindsay felt Nick tense beside her at Scott's deliberate rudeness, but she had never been self-conscious or defensive about her adoption. She answered the boy's question with a smile. "Why, yes, Scott, I am. I thought you knew."

"Nah. No one told me."

"I suppose no one thought to mention it," Evelyn said as evenly as Lindsay had spoken. "Lindsay came to us when she was less than a year old."

"So did your real parents beat you or something?" Scott persisted.

"As far as I'm concerned, my 'real' parents are right here at the table with us," Lindsay returned, trying to keep in mind that Scott had little experience with a close, loving family, that he was still feeling his way with the household who'd taken him in. "My biological parents died when I was a baby."

"Lucky you," Scott muttered.

Though Kim looked a bit startled by the boy's bitter words, no one else reacted to them. After years of experience with foster care, the Hillmans all knew that some parents didn't deserve the love or respect usually expected from their children.

Steve looked as though he was about to change the subject when Scott spoke again, this time addressing his question to Nick. "What about you? How did you end up with this bunch?"

"I guess I just got lucky," Nick answered with a shrug, adroitly evading the details—as he always seemed to do. "So are you, Scott. A lot of foster homes aren't nearly as pleasant as this one. Trust me, I've been there."

Scott looked down at his plate. "Tell me about it," he muttered. "The last one I was in stunk. But at least," he added with a touch of his usual defiance and a glance at Earl, "I didn't have to wash my own dishes there."

Earl chuckled. "Guess no place is perfect, Scott."

Steve did change the subject then, launching into a story that had nothing to do with the former conversation but soon had everyone laughing. Lindsay noticed that even Scott had to fight a smile at one point. Maybe, she reflected, the boy's questions meant that he was trying to adapt, trying to learn how to better fit in with his foster family, as Nick had eventually learned to do. She wondered if Scott, like Nick, would always keep a part of his past bottled up inside him, locked away even from those who would someday care the most about him.

After dinner, the family gathered in Greg's large den to talk and watch a football game on television. Again, Nick managed to position himself close to Lindsay, as though he belonged at her side. Lindsay took advantage of the first opportunity to talk to him in private, when the others were distracted with a particularly exciting play in the football game.

"What are you doing?" she rasped. It wasn't necessary to raise her voice, since he was standing so very close.

Nick looked confused by her question. "Just standing here."

"No, I meant why *here?*" She gestured to indicate the very short distance between them.

"Because—it seemed like a good place to stand?"

Lindsay swallowed a sigh at what she knew must be deliberate obtuseness. "Nick. You passed your medical exams, so you must be relatively bright. Try to stay with me here, okay? Why are you staying so close to my side that everyone's beginning to think we're a couple or something?"

His mouth tilted into a deliciously lopsided grin. "Maybe because we are a couple. Or something."

"The hell we are."

"When are you going to admit that you're fighting the inevitable, Lindsay? When are you going to acknowledge that there is something between us and it's not going away until we do something about it?"

"All I want between us now is some distance," she replied from between clenched teeth. "Back off, Nick. I mean it."

"Whatever you say, Lindsay."

"Whoa, Nick. That's no way to begin a relationship," Steve chided from behind them, his voice full of wicked laughter. "Gotta start out with the upper hand with women. Start giving in to them at the beginning, and before you know it, you'll be wearing an apron and scrubbing floors."

"Don't be ridiculous, Steve," Lindsay snapped. "Nick and I aren't beginning a relationship, so we hardly need your tasteless, sexist opinions."

"Thank you so much for that valuable advice, Steve," Nick murmured, ignoring Lindsay's protest. "I'll keep it in mind."

"You do that, buddy. I'm telling you, I know what I'm talking about." Steve shot Lindsay a look that reminded her of when they were kids and he used to tease her about the little boys who went out of their way to get her attention. "Forget all that sensitive, modern male business. We guys gotta show 'em who's in charge. Gotta keep 'em in their place. You know?"

"Steve." Kim's voice interrupted him from the other side of the room. "Honey, I left my purse in the car. Would you mind running out to get it for me?"

"Yes, dear," Steve called back obediently.

Nick laughed, though Lindsay seemed to have lost her sense of humor.

Steve shrugged sheepishly. "Didn't I mention that I was speaking from bitter experience?" he asked before turning and heading for the front door.

"Now look what you've done," Lindsay accused Nick the moment her brother was out of hearing. "You've got Steve talking about our 'relationship,' for pete's sake."

"Yes, I understand completely," Nick assured her. "You want to keep our relationship private. Intimate."

"No, that is *not* what I—"

Perhaps fortunately for the peacefulness of the remainder of the afternoon, they were interrupted again when Earl approached them with his reluctant-looking foster son in tow. "Nick, I was just telling Scott that you were a pretty good dirt-bike racer when you lived with us. Scott's interested in dirt-bike racing himself. Thought you could give him a few pointers about getting started."

Nick turned away from Lindsay after giving her a smile that promised they were a long way from finishing what he'd started. "I'd be glad to, Earl. It's been a while since I participated in the sport, but I really enjoyed it when you got me into it. It takes a lot of discipline and a lot of practice, Scott. Have you raced yet?"

Lindsay noted that Scott reacted positively to Nick's matter-of-fact, totally unpatronizing tone. Always on the defensive—and with good reason to be, considering his abusive background—Scott hated it when he thought anyone was talking down to him or trying to humor him.

Suddenly, though, he was talking to Nick—slowly, warily at first, and then with more enthusiasm as he described the few times he'd taken borrowed dirt bikes on wild and daring runs. And Nick was interacting beautifully with the boy, listening, encouraging, subtly giving warnings of the dangers of carelessness, promising to give him some lessons with the used dirt bike Earl had provided for Scott's use as long as he kept his grades up at school.

Though Nick's attitude toward Scott couldn't exactly be called warm, his prosaic, equal-to-equal manner was exactly what Scott seemed to want. Not another father or brother figure, but just another guy with a common interest. Because he'd been so angry and withdrawn, Scott had been sadly short on friends the past few years.

During the next hour or so, Lindsay watched Nick with Scott, watched the boy open up to the man. And found herself wondering why it seemed so much easier for Nick to share himself with a troubled teenager than with the woman with whom he claimed to want a "relationship." Would she ever understand him? And would he ever allow her to really try?

Lindsay was sleeping soundly when the telephone rang in the middle of the night on the Friday following the family gathering at Greg's. Groggy, disoriented, still only partially conscious, she slapped the alarm clock before realizing what was making the noise. Frowning—*This had better not be another drunk reaching a wrong number!*—she pulled the receiver to her ear and croaked, "H'lo?"

"Lindsay, it's Greg. We're at the hospital with Dad. I think you might want to be here." Her brother's voice was grim, so serious that Lindsay's chest clenched.

"What's wrong with Dad? Why is he in the hospital?"

"We're not sure, but—we think he's had a stroke, Lindsay."

"Oh, God."

"I know. Listen, I just called Nick. He's going to pick you up in a few minutes, okay?"

Lindsay's hand tightened on the receiver. "Greg, why did you do that without calling me first?"

"Honey, I knew you'd want to be here, and none of us wanted you driving at night and upset. Don't be angry with me—I just didn't want to waste any time."

She bit her lip, disturbed by the implication that time may be critical. "I'm not angry, Greg. Thanks for being concerned about me."

She was out of bed almost before she had the telephone back in its cradle, frantically reaching for jeans and a sweater, pulling a brush ruthlessly through her sleep-tousled hair, sliding her feet into the running shoes she'd left lying beside the bed earlier. She didn't bother with makeup. She'd just tied her shoelaces when her doorbell rang. She didn't even pause to check the peephole or ask who was calling as she pulled open the door, her purse in one hand, a jacket in the other.

"Nick. Thank you for coming for me...though I could have driven myself," she felt compelled to mention.

"I'm sure you could have," Nick agreed gruffly, looking a bit rumpled himself, "but Greg wanted to make sure you arrived safely. It's hard enough to drive when you're worried without having to deal with night blindness."

"Nick." Lindsay put her hand on his arm as she stepped through her door, appealing to him now as a doctor rather than the man who had kept her so confused since he'd come back into her life. "Do you think Dad really had a stroke?"

He covered her hand with his own, leading her quickly toward his car. "There's no way for me to know without seeing him, Lindsay. The few symptoms Greg mentioned when he called could indicate any number of problems."

"But it could be a stroke?" she persisted.

He hesitated. "It's possible. But I think we should wait and talk to the doctors before we start trying to make diagnoses."

She nodded and climbed soberly into the passenger seat, automatically buckling her seat belt, anxious to be with her family at the hospital.

Evelyn, Steve, Kim, Greg and Scott were gathered in the waiting room when Lindsay and Nick arrived. Lindsay rushed straight into her mother's open arms. "Mother? What happened? What's wrong with Daddy? Have you heard anything from the doctors?"

"Only that he's stable, though he hasn't regained consciousness since we arrived," Evelyn answered, obviously trying to remain calm for her family's sake, though her eyes reflected her deep worry. "They're running tests now to try to determine what's wrong with him."

"But what happened?" Lindsay repeated, searching her mother's haggard face for answers.

"He couldn't sleep. He complained that he was thirsty and got up for a glass of water. He'd taken only a step or two when he collapsed," Evelyn explained. "When I couldn't revive him, I called an ambulance, and then Greg. Greg arrived at the house at almost the same time as the ambulance."

Nick, who'd been having a low-voiced conversation with Steve and Greg, stepped to Evelyn's side and put a hand on her shoulder. "Are you all right?"

"I'll let you know when we hear something," she answered, trying to smile for him, though the result was heartbreaking. "Nick, can you tell what's wrong with Earl?"

"Not without seeing him, Evelyn. Will it make you feel any better if I go back and check on him?"

She nodded. "Oh, yes, please. We've been told so little since we arrived."

"Only because the staff is very busy," Nick assured her. "This is an excellent hospital. Earl is getting the best of care."

"But you'll check for me, anyway, won't you?"

"Yes, of course. I'll be right back," he promised. He touched Lindsay's shoulder as he passed her. The fleeting gesture warmed her.

"I'm so glad Nick's here," Evelyn murmured, watching as he strolled purposefully toward the emergency room doors.

Lindsay was watching him, too. "Yes. So am I," she agreed thoughtfully.

The family waited anxiously for Nick's return, or for any word about Earl's condition. Evelyn sat on the edge of a vinyl bench, wringing her hands in her lap, Lindsay on one side of her, Kim on the other. Greg and Steve sat on another bench, talking a little, both wearing worried frowns. Scott paced restlessly around the room, silent, withdrawn, resisting the brothers' attempts to include him in their conversation. They waited for what seemed like hours, growing more and more tense as the minutes crawled by.

All of them surged to their feet when Nick finally returned, accompanied by the tall, gray-haired woman who'd been taking care of Earl and Evelyn Hillman for several years.

"Dr. Carmical!" Evelyn rushed forward, one hand on her throat. "How is Earl?"

Dr. Carmical took Evelyn's free hand in both of her own, patting reassuringly. "He's going to be fine, Evelyn. We'll be keeping him for a few days to make sure, but he's conscious now and out of danger."

"Was it a stroke? Will there be any permanent damage?" Evelyn asked, obviously relieved, yet still worried.

"It wasn't a stroke," Dr. Carmical assured her, glancing around to make sure the rest of the family heard her. "He had a severe reaction to the new medication we put him on last week. Sometimes reactions like this happen when we least expect them, as is true with Earl. The symptoms did mimic a stroke, and I won't try to convince you that it wasn't a terribly close call. Earl was in critical condition when he was brought in. We've stabilized him with other medications and there should be no lasting side effects from this incident, though we will, of course, watch him very carefully for a while."

"Oh, thank God," Evelyn murmured, sagging into the curve of Greg's supportive arm.

Lindsay closed her eyes and silently repeated the prayer, her hands clenched tightly in front of her. She didn't have to open her eyes to know whose hand fell gently on her shoulder. "You okay?" Nick asked quietly.

"Yes," she said, looking up at him through a film of tears. "I'm just so very relieved. You're sure he'll be okay, Nick?"

"He'll be fine," he answered bracingly, slipping his arm around her. "He's conscious now—he knew me when I went in. He's already starting to complain about the IVs and monitors they've connected him to."

Lindsay tried to smile, though the result was tremulous. "That sounds like him. Oh, Nick..." She allowed herself to bury her face in his comfortingly broad shoulder, needing to feel the warmth of his arms around her. His arms tightened, his heart thudding reassuringly beneath her cheek. She savored only a moment of his embrace before slowly, reluctantly pulling away. "Thank you."

"Anytime," he replied, and his voice seemed just a bit huskier than usual, his sharp eyes a bit brighter behind the lenses of his glasses.

She made herself turn away, back to her family, all of whom looked so relieved that Earl would be all right. Even Scott looked pleased, proving that he'd had little more success resisting Earl's gruff charms than most of the boys who'd preceded him in the Hillman household.

It was several hours later before Lindsay could be persuaded to leave the hospital. Only when everyone had spent a few moments with Earl to see for themselves that he was improving would the family consent to leave him in the care of the hospital staff. Greg finally insisted on taking his mother and Scott home to rest. Expressing concern that Kim had been on her feet too long, Steve swept her out of the hospital right behind the others. Lindsay found herself back in Nick's car soon afterward, her head resting wearily against the back of the leather seat as they rode in silence toward her apartment.

They didn't speak until Nick turned off the car in her parking lot. "You really don't have to walk me to the door," Lindsay felt obligated to say, though she suspected she was wasting her time. "You're tired. You should go home and try to get some rest before you head for your office in the morning."

"It *is* morning," he reminded her indulgently, reaching for his door handle. "And I am walking you to your door."

Lindsay was too drained to argue with him, even when he went through his by-now-familiar routine of checking every room of the apartment the moment they entered the door— which, of course, had still been safely locked. "Everything secured?" she asked with one tired attempt at sarcasm when he returned from his inspection.

"Seems to be." As usual, he didn't appear to notice her facetious tone. "You look beat," he added, studying her closely.

She made a face and lifted a hand to her hair. "Thanks so much," she muttered.

He smiled faintly and reached out to touch her cheek. "It wasn't an insult. You're still beautiful. But you could use some rest."

Startled by the matter-of-fact compliment, Lindsay blinked at him and tried to think of something to say.

He didn't give her a chance to say anything. Instead, he leaned over to kiss her lingeringly before pulling back. "Good night, Lindsay."

She stopped him just as his hand touched the doorknob. "Nick?"

He looked over his shoulder. "Yes?"

"You're pushing me again."

"Am I?"

"Yes," she answered huskily, her lips still tingling from the kiss. "You are."

"Sorry." But he wasn't—and they both knew it. "I'll talk to you tomorrow," he promised before slipping out the door. He closed it firmly behind him.

Lindsay sighed and pushed both hands into her hair, feeling utterly exhausted, both mentally and physically. Though part of her thoughts were still focused on her father's near-tragic collapse, she couldn't put Nick out of her mind. He'd been so helpful, so supportive of her and the rest of the family. She couldn't help but be grateful that he'd been available to them when they'd needed him—and they *had* needed him, Lindsay as much as the others.

He'd responded quickly, unselfishly, uncomplainingly. And yet, she thought gravely, during the entire evening, Nick hadn't once revealed a glimpse of his own feelings about Earl's brush with disaster. He'd appeared worried, but always in full control, a bit distanced from the others. Perhaps he'd automatically reacted to the crisis as a doctor—sympathetic, competent, efficient, yet professionally detached from the feelings of the family. Even when he'd comforted Lindsay in his arms after she'd learned that her father would recover, Nick had held a part of himself back.

Lindsay hadn't needed another doctor—there'd been plenty of those at the hospital. She'd needed Nick. Needed him in a way that troubled her deeply—mostly because she wasn't sure he'd ever be willing to offer her the depths of him she most longed to reach. She had his interest, his desire, but would she ever have his heart?

Chapter Five

Lindsay saw Nick several times during the next week, running into him twice at the hospital when she visited her rapidly recovering father, once at her parents' house after Earl was allowed to go home. Through warning glances and her polite but cool manner, she made it clear to him on those occasions that she wanted him to do nothing in front of her family that would lead to further speculation about whatever might be going on between them.

Nick cooperated, but with a glint in his eyes that let her know he was only humoring her, biding his time until she finally acknowledged "the inevitable," as he'd termed it.

It irritated her that he seemed so confident she wouldn't be able to resist him in the end, whatever her justifiable concerns about their differences. Was he so accustomed to having women fall at his feet? So spoiled by their attentions? His attitude only fueled her willpower, gave her more reason to proceed very slowly in deciding whether she was interested in anything more than friendship with him.

After all, she assured herself bracingly, she'd resisted more handsome men than Nick. Not that she could remember any of them at the moment. And she'd had more charming admirers. Perhaps.

Lindsay had waited twenty-five years to become involved with a man, determined she wouldn't settle for anything less than the loving, exclusive, mutually supportive lifelong commitment Earl and Evelyn Hillman had maintained through the years. She'd never even imagined herself in that sort of relationship with any of the men she'd known before, so it hadn't been so very hard to withstand their attempts at seduction, to eventually induct them into her ranks of close friends and honorary brothers.

But she'd known from the beginning that Nick was different, that he wouldn't be as easy to placate with friendship. Just as she'd known that she would grow to want so much more from this man. For the first time in her life, Lindsay found herself the one frustrated by wanting more than a man was willing to give—perhaps it was her penance for disappointing so many hopeful suitors during the past ten years or so.

If only Nick would give her some sign that he was willing to try, that he cared enough to let down some of his barriers with her. That the distance he maintained even from Evelyn and the other members of the Hillman family wouldn't be necessary between himself and Lindsay.

Despite his innate reserve, it was soon glaringly apparent that Nick had completely won over Lindsay's brothers and their families. Steve and Kim, Greg and Paula all seemed delighted by the possibility that Lindsay and Nick were showing interest in each other. Lindsay couldn't talk to any of them without hearing what a great guy Nick was, how helpful he'd been during Earl's illness, how good he was with children, what a fine husband and father he'd make.

She'd tried ignoring them, arguing with them, begging them not to mention any of this to her parents, who hadn't yet said anything on the subject. But still they persisted—as though, Lindsay thought in frustration, she were an aging spinster with one last chance at marital bliss if only she'd cooperate.

Lindsay received a message at work one rainy afternoon to call Paula when she could. Hoping nothing was wrong, she took the first opportunity between classes to call her sister-in-law from the teachers' lounge. "Paula? What's up?"

"I was hoping you'd do me a favor on your way home from work," Paula replied. "Do you have any extra time this afternoon?"

"Sure. I'd planned to go straight home from here. What do you need?"

"Zane's cold doesn't seem to be getting much better, so I called Nick. He said he had some medicine samples for us to try. Greg's out of town on business, and I hate to take the baby out in the rain, so I was hoping you'd drop by Nick's clinic for me."

Feeling trapped—after all, how could she refuse to pick up medicine for her sick baby nephew?—Lindsay reassured herself that she probably wouldn't even see Nick. He'd probably have the medicine waiting at the front desk for her. She hoped. "All right, Paula, I'll pick it up for you."

"Thanks, Lindsay. I knew I could count on you. And if you see Nick, tell him thank you again for me, will you?"

Lindsay promised she would, shaking her head in exasperation at the eagerness in Paula's voice. Why couldn't her family understand that she was perfectly capable of making her own decisions where Nick was concerned? That she didn't need their less-than-subtle attempts to push her toward him?

Lindsay was beginning to feel as though fate had it in for her. She'd hardly stepped into the large, successful clinic in which Nick was a partner when she spotted him—and he saw her. He was standing behind the reception desk, looking over a chart with a nurse, when Lindsay pushed through the glass doors. Nick smiled a greeting and motioned for her to join him.

"Paula said you'd be by. I was hoping I'd have a chance to see you for a minute."

"Did you want to give me a message for Paula?" Lindsay asked, aware that his office staff was watching them curiously.

"No," he replied, his smile deepening. "I just wanted to see you."

Lindsay swallowed. "Oh."

He chuckled and took her arm. "C'mon. I'll show you my office. I've had a last-minute cancellation, so I've got a spare minute." He handed the file back to the nurse. "Call me when my next patient arrives, Kaye."

"Yes, Dr. Grant."

"Dr. Grant?" another young woman said quickly, seeing that he was about to move away. "Dr. Walcott asked me to tell you he'd like to meet with you this afternoon before you leave the clinic."

"Thanks, Sharon. Tell him I should be free around five."

"Yes, sir."

Hearing the respect in the voices of his employees, Lindsay couldn't help but think back a few years to a ragged, angry, sullen teenager whose chances of future success had looked slim indeed when he'd arrived on the Hillman doorstep. Nick Grant had come such a long way since that time, had obviously worked very hard to leave his past behind. But, in doing so, had he also lost a part of himself?

Lindsay and Nick had taken only a few steps down the hallway when they were greeted by a pigtailed little girl skipping toward the waiting rooms from the other end of the hall. "Hi, Dr. Nick!" she greeted him cheerily. "Got my allergy shot. That new nurse is pretty good. I didn't even feel it."

"I'm glad you approve of her, Tiffany. I suppose I won't fire her, after all," Nick replied gravely, making Tiffany giggle.

A woman carrying a sleeping baby passed them a few feet later. "He fell asleep while I was putting his clothes back on," she explained with a smile for Nick.

"The medication will make him drowsy for a few days," Nick explained with a glance at the infant. Then he smiled for the mother. "You could probably both use the rest."

"I'll rest a lot easier now that I know he's getting better," the child's mother admitted. "Thank you, Dr. Grant."

"I'll see you in five days, Mrs. Keane. Be sure and make an appointment with Joyce on your way out."

"You're a busy man," Lindsay observed unnecessarily as Nick escorted her into a large, leather-and-mahogany-furnished office, its wood-panelled walls covered with official-looking diplomas and documents.

"Mmm." Nick leaned back against his desk, his long legs crossed at the ankles, hands resting on the desk at either side of his lean hips as he looked at her. "You look very nice today."

Instinctively, she smoothed her hand-knitted sweater over the band of her pleated slacks. "Thank you." He himself looked good enough to eat, in his dark dress slacks, pale blue shirt, floral silk tie and white lab coat. She decided not to tell him so. "You have the medicine for Paula?" she prompted him.

"Right here," he answered, gesturing toward a small white paper bag on the desk beside him. His eyes laughed at her from behind their lenses. "You in a hurry?"

"Well—um—" She cleared her throat self-consciously. "I'm sure Zane needs the medicine as quickly as possible."

"A few minutes won't make much difference. He only has the sniffles."

"That's your scientific diagnosis?" Lindsay asked, trying to tease.

"Yeah. Why are you always so nervous around me, Lindsay?"

She blinked at the blunt question. "I'm not—"

"Yes. You are. You're not like this with anyone else."

Lindsay sighed and nodded in resignation. "Okay, you're right. You do make me nervous."

"Why?"

"I don't know."

His smile turned just slightly smug. "Don't you?"

"Nick." She glared at him. "Stop it."

"Have dinner with me tonight."

"No."

"Why not?"

"Because."

He shook his head, still smiling. "Not good enough. Because why?"

Tossing her head, she reminded herself that she didn't owe him any explanations if she chose not to go out with him. Still, she heard herself saying, "Maybe it's because you make me so nervous."

He pushed himself away from the desk and caught her shoulders in his hands. "Nervous isn't always bad," he murmured, his voice low, seductive, his mouth only inches from hers. "Sometimes it just adds a bit of excitement between a man and a woman."

"And sometimes there's a very good reason for being nervous," she whispered, staring up at him.

He brushed her lips with his own. Just hard enough to make her ache for more. "When are you going to stop fighting me, Lindsay?"

"When—or if—you stop pushing me away," she replied as evenly as possible under the circumstances.

His arms slipped around her. "I'm not exactly pushing you away. Have dinner with me tonight."

"And if I do, will you tell me about your childhood?" she asked daringly.

Nick stiffened. "No."

She tried to hide the extent of her disappointment with his nonequivocal answer. "Then I guess you have your answer."

He exhaled impatiently, holding her a few inches away to glare down at her. "Dammit, Lindsay. I don't know why you—"

A tap on the office door interrupted him. "Dr. Grant?" a woman's voice spoke through the door. "Your next patient is in room two."

Lindsay pulled away from him, snatching the paper bag from the desk. "I'd better be going. Are there any instructions you want me to pass along to Paula?"

"No. I told her everything she needs to know on the phone. Lindsay—"

"'Bye, Nick. Paula said for me to tell you thanks." She slipped out of his office before he could detain her further, avoiding the curious eyes of the nurse still waiting in the hallway. She thought she heard Nick say her name again, but didn't wait to make sure. Taking care not to run down

any of his tiny patients, Lindsay left Nick's clinic as quickly
as possible.

She delivered the medication to Paula without lingering,
unwilling to subject herself to any more probing from her
well-intentioned family. Claiming that she had dozens of
term papers to grade that evening, she escaped rapidly,
anxious for the lonely—but safe—refuge of her own apartment, where she could brood about her apparently hope-
less feelings for Nick Grant in private.

Nick dined alone that evening, unenthusiastically polish-
ing off a frozen entrée he'd cooked in the microwave.
Though he never touched alcohol—having seen firsthand
the unpleasant results of alcohol addiction—he almost
wished he had such an escape tonight. An escape from increasingly frustrated desire, from resentment at Lindsay's
stubborn refusal to acknowledge what they both knew lay
between them, from vicious, barely suppressed memories
that prowled so close to the doors of the mental cages Nick
had locked them in so many years ago.

Wandering around his large, professionally decorated
home, he tried to draw comfort from the pleasant sur-
roundings, from the soothing, harmonious colors the dec-
orator had chosen at his request, but instead found himself
obsessed with thoughts of Lindsay. Why was she so determined to pry into his past? Why did she think it so important to know all the ugly details? What was she hoping to
prove? That she could manipulate him at will, make him
jump through hoops in hope of winning her favor?

Well, she could forget that. Nick had long since learned
to live life on his own terms. He'd held control of his emotions, his actions, his future since the day he'd struck out on
his own at eighteen—and damned if anyone was ever going

to take that control away from him again. Not even Lindsay.

He told himself to give up on her, to find someone who'd be satisfied with the things he was willing to offer. Lindsay would never give up. She'd been too spoiled, having her own way with the family who'd always catered to her so lovingly. She wanted some malleable, spineless guy willing to bare his heart and soul to her, someone with an uncomplicated, spotless past he didn't mind discussing with her. Well, that wasn't Nick. He should wish her luck in finding a man like that and go on his way.

The problem was, he *didn't* wish her luck. Didn't want her finding anyone else. Couldn't stand the thought of anyone else touching her, holding her, tasting her.

Realizing the direction his thoughts had taken, he looked down at his clenched fists, appalled at the violence of his sudden, unprecedented possessiveness toward Lindsay. Jealousy was another of the dangerous emotions he'd locked away—and yet he couldn't deny that he was feeling decidedly jealous now, just at the thought of Lindsay with another man. Which only went to prove that he'd been right all along to resist her efforts to make him release the past.

He wanted her, but it was still on his terms or none at all. Remembering the way she'd responded to his kisses, the temptation in her eyes when he'd held her in his arms, he still believed he'd have her on those terms if he just persisted long enough. And Nick Grant was never short on persistence, as Lindsay Hillman was soon to discover for herself.

Lindsay wasn't expecting anyone when her doorbell rang a few days later, not long after she'd arrived home from a parent-teacher conference at school. She'd been in her kitchen, looking through the pantry for something for dinner, and she patted her stomach ruefully as she crossed the living room toward the front door. She'd had only a small salad for lunch and she was hungry!

Though she hadn't really expected to find Nick on her doorstep, neither was she greatly surprised. Even though she hadn't heard from him since she'd bolted from his office, she'd known all along he hadn't yet admitted defeat. "Hello, Nick," she said in resignation.

He looked tired, she noticed, his shoulders slumping just perceptibly beneath his impeccable suit jacket. Had he had a rough day? But he made an effort to smile and say teasingly, "Try to restrain your enthusiasm, will you, Princess? You'll inflate my ego."

"I think your ego is quite full of hot air now," she answered tartly, though she found she couldn't close the door in his face when he looked so tired and dispirited. Sighing at her own gullibility, she gestured him inside. "Why are you here?"

"Call it an impulse," he replied, entering her apartment quickly, as though concerned she'd change her mind if he dawdled. "I was on my way to my big, lonely house when I passed your apartment, and I thought maybe you'd take pity on me and offer me something cold to drink. I'm very thirsty."

Lindsay rolled her eyes at the obvious play for sympathy. "All right, you can have a drink. I'll even make you something to eat—as long as you behave yourself," she added sternly.

"I'll make an effort," he promised, slipping out of his jacket and loosening his tie.

"Make yourself right at home," Lindsay murmured, watching him drape the jacket over the back of the couch.

"Thanks. I will. What's for dinner?"

"I'll let you know as soon as I decide. Want to watch the news or read the paper while I cook something?"

He shook his head. "The news is too depressing. I'd rather watch you cook."

"If you come into my kitchen, be prepared to help, not just watch," she warned.

"I can handle that, too. What would you like me to do?"

She led him into the kitchen. "First I'll make your drink. There's a bottle of cheap wine in the fridge, maybe a bottle of Scotch in the pantry, if you want something stronger."

"Got any fruit juice?"

She opened the refrigerator and looked inside. "Apple or grapefruit?"

"Apple, thanks."

Though she was a bit surprised that he'd opted for a juice, she obligingly poured him a glass. "I guess I shouldn't be surprised that a doctor prefers healthy beverages. Do you ever drink alcohol?"

"No." He didn't elaborate, but took a long drink of the cold apple juice, proving he really had been thirsty.

"Oh." She searched the freezer for something healthy to offer for dinner. "You like broiled fish?"

"Very much."

"Good. That won't take long to prepare."

"What can I do to help?"

Lindsay set him to work chopping vegetables for a salad while she thawed the fish and seasoned it with butter, lemon and freshly chopped herbs. They chatted sporadically while they worked, Lindsay responding to Nick's casual questions, telling him a little about her day at school, biding her time until he felt like disclosing the real reason he'd stopped by that evening. She sensed that something was wrong, something more than a hard day at work, but she knew Nick well enough by now to understand that she'd have to wait until he was ready to talk. If he decided to talk at all.

They'd almost finished eating when the breakthrough came. Nick had gone quiet a few minutes before, his expression distant, his eyes shuttered. Though he'd said he liked the food, he ate mechanically, his mind obviously on something else.

Lindsay waited.

When he spoke, it was so softly she almost had to strain to hear him. "I lost a patient today."

Her throat tightened. "I'm sorry. Was there an accident?"

"No. Spinal meningitis. It's not always fatal, but this case was a bad one. His mother let it go too long, I'm afraid, trying to treat him with over-the-counter medications, thinking it was just the flu. By the time I started treating the boy, it was too late to do anything more than hospitalize him, throw everything we had at him, and pray. It didn't help."

Lindsay searched Nick's face, trying to read his expression. She couldn't. His eyes, his features, were all schooled to blankness, hiding whatever emotions he may have felt. Only his voice had changed, going just faintly rougher than usual so that she might not have noticed had she not been trying so hard to understand him. "How old was he?"

Nick cleared his throat. "He'd just turned two."

"Just a baby," Lindsay whispered, laying down her fork as the remainder of her appetite fled. "His poor parents."

"He only had his mother—she isn't married. Barely twenty herself. She didn't mean to neglect him, she simply didn't know any better and didn't have anyone to guide her. Her pastor's the one who brought the child to me two days ago. The mother was devastated when the child died this afternoon."

"Did you have to break the news to her?"

His jaw tightened just enough for a muscle to jump there. "Yes."

Lindsay reached across the table to lay her hand over his. "I'm so sorry, Nick. That must have been very hard for you."

Though he didn't move his hand away, he didn't return the pressure of her fingers. "It's part of the job," he said brusquely, avoiding her gaze. "It's never pleasant, but I'm getting used to it."

"I can't imagine you'd ever get used to something like that," she argued. "Nor should you want to. You're a man, not a machine. How could you ever learn not to grieve over the loss of a child?"

"A doctor who gets too deeply involved with his patients loses his edge. Can't perform to his patients' best interests."

"Bull. The best doctors I ever knew were the ones who cared the most. And don't try to tell me you don't care, Nick. I could tell there was something bothering you as soon as you arrived."

"I didn't say I don't care. Just that I can handle it."

She longed to take him in her arms and soothe the pain she knew he was trying to hide from her. Despite his efforts to convince her otherwise, it was obvious that Nick was grieving for his tiny patient, tearing himself up over the mother's pain. He hadn't wanted to be alone tonight, had needed to be with someone. With her. He just wouldn't admit it.

As much as she ached to comfort him, she wanted almost as badly to take him by the shoulders and shake him until his teeth rattled—until he'd finally acknowledge that he had feelings and emotions just like everyone else. That sometimes he needed someone else to lean on, someone else to turn to.

Had his childhood been so terrible that he'd never completely trust anyone again? And how could she understand if he wouldn't talk to her about it?

She sighed. "Nick, why *did* you come here tonight?"

He looked surprised at the question. "I wanted to see you," he answered simply.

Which, of course, left her nothing to say in return.

Nick helped Lindsay clear away the dishes after dinner, saying no more about his work or his loss that afternoon. Resigned that the subject was now closed to her, Lindsay made no further reference to it, either. She was taken by surprise when he stepped up behind her and slid his arms around her waist. "How about some dessert?" he asked, his mouth very close to her ear.

She moistened her lips, which had suddenly gone dry in response to his nearness. "Um—I think I have some ice cream in the freezer."

He touched his lips to the side of her throat, and she knew he had to feel the pulse that pounded wildly there. "I had something warmer in mind," he murmured. He pressed a series of fleeting, moist kisses from her ear to the curve of her shoulder. "Sweeter."

Her knees melted. She stiffened them with an effort. "Nick. Stop that."

"Still fighting, Lindsay?"

"Still hiding, Nick?" she returned tartly, though she wanted desperately to turn in his arms and press her mouth and body to his. It would be so easy to give in, so convenient to persuade herself that she only wanted to offer him comfort and affection. But as much as she wanted to take care of Nick's needs, she knew she had to think of her own, as well.

Nick exhaled noisily and rested his forehead against the back of her head. "Lord, you're stubborn."

Since he sounded more rueful than angry, she managed a shaky smile. "I was raised by Earl Hillman," she reminded him. "I was taught by the best."

"I'll keep that in mind." He dropped his arms and stepped away, leaving her oddly bereft without his touch. She wrapped her own arms at her waist in a vain effort to assuage the emptiness there.

"I'd better go," Nick said, running his hand through his hair as Lindsay turned warily to face him. "Thanks for the meal, Lindsay."

"You're welcome."

He reached out to cup her face in his hands. "Don't try to deceive yourself that I'm giving up. I'm only taking time out to reevaluate my strategy."

She didn't smile. "This isn't a game, Nick."

"No," he agreed. "But I intend to win, anyway."

He kissed her thoroughly before she could utter a scathing comment about his incredible arrogance. And then he left her standing in the middle of her kitchen, her mouth throbbing, her body on fire, her heart aching for everything that could be between them if only Nick could learn to trust her with his true emotions.

Chapter Six

"You're sure you'll be okay driving home? You don't want me to follow you?" a friend and fellow teacher asked Lindsay at the end of a particularly long-running teachers' meeting. It was well after 9:00 p.m. and most of Lindsay's friends knew of her problem seeing after dark.

"No, thanks, Tina," Lindsay declined graciously, touched by the other woman's consideration. "It's really not that far, and the streets are well lighted between here and my place. I shouldn't have any problem."

"Then I guess I'll see you at school tomorrow."

Lindsay made a face. "Don't remind me. Thanksgiving holidays can't get here quickly enough, as far as I'm concerned."

"Need some time off, do you?" Tina asked with a laugh.

"Desperately."

"What you need is a social life," another friend told Lindsay sternly, joining the conversation after seeing several other guests to the front door.

Carole Packer, in whose home the meeting had taken place, was a blissful newlywed who'd been trying to match Lindsay up for months with various of her new husband's friends. "Why won't you let me arrange a meeting between you and Tommy's friend from work, Stan Jackson? Trust me, Lindsay, he's a great guy. Good-looking, successful, polite—and he's completely over his divorce, I'm sure."

"Carole, please, no more matchmaking," Lindsay begged. "I'm really not interested right now."

"So when are you going to tell us about the guy you were in the society pages with a few weeks ago?" Tina demanded, as she had several times since spotting Lindsay's photograph in the newspaper following the reception for Nick. Lindsay had firmly maintained that Nick was only a friend of her family's, despite her friends' skepticism.

"There's nothing to tell," Lindsay answered, but even she heard the lack of conviction in her own voice.

Tina and Carole both raised their eyebrows. "Is that right?" Carole murmured speculatively.

Lindsay sighed. Whatever happened to a person's right to privacy? she wondered in frustration. If it wasn't her family prying into her personal life, it was her friends. And it didn't help much to know that all of them were interested only because they truly cared about her. "I'd better be going. I'll see you both later."

Her friends accepted the hint reluctantly, saying no more about Lindsay's social life as they gathered coats and purses and headed for the door, Carole seeing them off from the front porch. Lindsay climbed behind the wheel of her car with a sigh of relief that the interrogation was over. It was hard enough not dwelling on her problems with Nick Grant without everyone else bringing him up all the time!

She turned up the volume on her radio in an attempt to drown out her thoughts. She drove slowly, carefully, never taking her eyes off the road ahead, grateful for the bright streetlights that illuminated the potential dangers. She'd never have attempted driving this late on rural roads or for long distances, but occasionally she needed the independence of not depending on anyone else for her transportation. Her condition was more annoying than debilitating, as far as she was concerned.

She'd eaten out with her friends before the meeting, so she hadn't been home since leaving for work that morning. Gathering an armload of books and papers from the passenger seat of her car, Lindsay balanced them precariously in the crook of one arm as she walked toward her apartment, fumbling in her coat pocket with her free hand in search of her key. Most of the cars in the parking lot were empty, though she thought she saw someone sitting in a dark brown pickup truck parked close to her own space. She could almost feel eyes trained on her as she stepped onto the sidewalk leading to her apartment.

She noticed that the compound seemed quieter and more deserted than usual, which made her uncomfortable since there'd been several rapes and muggings reported in her area during the past few months. Little Rock, unfortunately, was catching up with larger cities across the country in terms of crime. As usual, the security guard seemed to be on the other side of the large compound.

Cautiously, she watched the bushes along the walkway as she sped up her pace, peering into the shadows to make sure no one was there. She wasn't the overly nervous type, but like most women she knew, Lindsay didn't take unnecessary chances with her safety. Her fingers closed around her keys, automatically sliding them into position to be used as weapons, if necessary, as her brothers had taught her years earlier.

She was so intent on watching the bushes—the most obvious place for someone to be lurking—that she was taken completely by surprise when a large male body suddenly loomed before her from the inset doorway of her own apartment.

"Where the hell have you been?" he demanded at the same moment Lindsay gasped and dropped everything she'd been carrying.

It took her only a moment to realize who he was. "Dammit, Nick!" she scolded, one hand pressed to her pounding heart. "You scared me half to death jumping out at me like that! Look what you made me do. I'll never get these papers back in order."

He stood over her as she bent to retrieve her belongings. "It's nearly ten o'clock. What are you doing out driving by yourself at this hour? And then walking across a deserted compound without giving a thought to your own safety?"

She glared up at him in response to the unfairness of the accusation. "I was being careful! I was fully prepared to defend myself, if necessary."

He snorted derisively. "Yeah, right. Which explains why you never even saw me standing here until I stepped out and scared you half out of your wits."

Lindsay surged back to her feet with a firm grip on her papers—and her temper. "I was watching the bushes, not my own doorway. Would you move, please, so I can open the door?"

Nick took the keys out of her hand and turned to unlock the door himself, his movements too quick for her to stop him. "I've been worried sick about you," he grumbled, shoving the door open and preceding her inside without waiting for an invitation.

Still griping loudly enough to be clearly heard from every room, he began his usual inspection, to Lindsay's vexation. "I called your number half a dozen times after I realized you were out in your own car after dark. I even called your family, and no one knew where you were. I've been waiting here for you for nearly an hour.

"I don't suppose it occurred to you," he went on as he emerged from the bedroom, "that someone might worry when you stay out so late without telling anyone where you are?"

Lindsay was rapidly losing control of her temper. She set her things on a table with a thud, taking several deep breaths before turning to him.

"If I had thought it was anyone's business," she said icily, "I would certainly have given out my itinerary for the evening. Since I am an adult, perfectly capable of taking care of myself, I didn't think it necessary. And what do you mean, you called my family? How could you do that? You've probably worried them for nothing. Now I'll have to call them and assure them that I'm okay, that you were just indulging in hysterical overreaction for some incomprehensible reason."

"Hysterical overreaction?" Nick repeated silkily, his fists on his hips as he faced her, fire in his eyes. It was the first time she'd seen him really angry, anything less than totally in control.

She realized then that he looked different than usual—less polished, less civilized. He was dressed in faded jeans, a black sweatshirt and a well-worn pair of running shoes. He wasn't wearing his glasses, and his hair looked as though he'd been running his hands through it with little consideration for his customary neat style. For the first time since he'd come back into her life, Nick looked more like the rather dangerous adolescent he'd once been than the sophisticated, upwardly mobile physician he'd become.

He took a step closer and she swallowed, automatically backing a step away before refusing to retreat any farther. Her chin lifted in defiance. She would not allow him to intimidate her with his tantrum!

"You heard me," she retorted boldly. "Why are you here, anyway? Since you've been so anxious to locate me, I assume you must have wanted something important."

He ignored the gibe, speaking again in that low, rough voice that made involuntary shivers course down her spine. "Where were you, Lindsay? Who were you with tonight?"

"That," she told him coolly, "is none of your business. We do not have a relationship, Nick, no matter how arrogantly you've tried to convince me we do. I haven't decided whether I *want* to get involved with a man who won't share his feelings with me—a man who won't even give me credit for being capable of driving myself home after a professional meeting!"

She hadn't meant to tell him where she'd been, but she saw that her verbal slip hadn't escaped him. Some of the tension left his face, though he looked no less daunting as he dropped his hands on her shoulders. "The decision has already been made, whether you like it or not," he growled, pulling her closer. "We *are* involved—and it's high time for you to admit it!"

"You—" But her furious words were smothered in the depths of his angry, avid kiss. And within moments, Lindsay had forgotten what she'd intended to say.

He'd never kissed her like this. Wild. Deep. Desperate. And she'd never responded like this. Hot. Demanding. Frantic.

His hands gripped her hips, dragging her against him, making her fully aware of his arousal. She clutched his back through the soft sweatshirt, wanting to be even closer to him.

Nick tore his mouth from hers with a gasp for air. "Lindsay," he groaned, lowering his head to her throat. "I've been going out of my mind."

She closed her eyes and tilted her head back when his warm, parted lips pressed hungrily to the pulse in her throat. Shuddered in pleasure when his hand slipped between them, closing around one aching, swollen breast. His thumb rotated around her taut nipple, and she moaned. "Nick. Oh, please..."

She'd wanted to make him lose control—wanted to know the real emotions behind the social facade. Now she wondered rather dazedly if she knew what she'd unleashed. Nick wasn't in control now, but neither was Lindsay. Both were lost in the madness of passion—and she was no more anxious to reclaim sanity than Nick seemed to be.

Suddenly he was tugging at the hem of her sweater, seeking the smooth skin beneath, and she was pulling just as greedily at his shirt, longing to feel him against her. She couldn't hold back an exclamation of startled pleasure when she first felt herself pressed against him. He was so warm, so strong...so pulsingly, virilely *alive!*

When her achingly sensitized nipples brushed the crisp hair of his chest, her knees weakened and she was forced to cling to his broad, bare shoulders for support. Even that didn't help when he tugged her nipple into his mouth, his tongue deliciously rough against her tender skin. Lindsay's knees buckled. Nick's arms went around her, lowering her carefully to the carpet, his knee sliding between her legs as he half covered her, still paying thorough, lavish attention to her breasts.

She arched into his mouth, and he increased the pressure of his knee, making her moan and clutch her fingers more tightly in his hair. She wanted him, ached for him—*hurt* for him. So badly that she made no effort to stop him when he tugged impatiently at the button of her waistband.

Nick moved down her body, his mouth investigating the pale skin he revealed as he slid the slacks down her legs and tossed them aside. Lindsay quivered helplessly beneath the onslaught, unable to think, unwilling to resist, incapable of doing anything more than follow Nick's lead. He left her only long enough to throw off his own clothing and then he returned, fitting his mouth to hers. As his hair-roughened legs tangled with her smooth ones, she realized that nothing separated them, nothing prevented them from finishing what they'd started.

She moistened her lips nervously when he lifted his head. She was trembling uncontrollably—willing, but apprehensive. This was a big step for her—bigger than Nick probably suspected. Should she tell him?

"Lindsay." It was little more than a rough growl, bearing little resemblance to his normal voice. His hands were locked in her hair, holding her still, her face tilted up to his. His eyes were searching, intent, his jaw rigid as he spoke with some effort. "I've wanted you from the moment you opened the door that first night at your parents' house. But if you want to stop, tell me now."

"No," she whispered, surrendering to the inevitable. "I want you, too, Nick. I have from the beginning. But—"

He silenced her with the tips of his fingers—and she realized in wonder that he was trembling almost as hard as she was. "You want me?"

Her gaze locked with his, she nodded.

"Then that's all that matters now," he muttered, and covered her mouth with his again at the same moment his body covered hers.

Instinctively, Lindsay wrapped her legs around his hips and arched upward just as he thrust forward. Her choked cry of momentary discomfort was lost in the depths of his mouth. Nick stiffened, his hands tightening in her hair, but she urged him on with her hands on his back, afraid he'd stop before showing her where this could lead.

He groaned deep in his chest and began to move, less forcefully now, soothing her even as he drove her higher. She quickly discovered that this new, gentle side of him was just as seductive as his turbulent passion had been. His mouth was warm, tender, moving swiftly from her lips to her throat to her breasts and back again, tasting and pleasuring every inch in between. His hands moved over her, leading, encouraging, seeming to be guided by instinct to the very places where she most wanted him to touch her.

Lindsay responded to his patient tutelage with an innate aptitude, until it was no longer necessary for him to guide her, until she was moving as eagerly, as confidently as he, until both were swept into a frenzied race to the finish. Rocked by waves of sensation, she bowed upward with a cry of pleasure when her climax overtook her. Nick's raw groan followed closely, his damp body shuddering in her arms as he gave in to his own release.

Lindsay closed her eyes and buried her face in his throat, fighting back tears at the perfection of what had transpired between them. He wasn't hiding from her now, hadn't held anything back in their lovemaking, and she wanted to cling to the intimacy, knowing that reality would return all too soon. That Nick would do his best to repair the damage their passion had done to the emotional barriers he'd spent so many years building.

* * *

Both of them jumped when the telephone rang, intruding jarringly into their privacy. Still trying to regain control of his breathing, Nick rolled out of the way as Lindsay scrambled to her feet. She snatched a colorful afghan off the couch and wrapped it hastily around her as she reached for the phone—almost, Nick thought with a fleeting smile, as though she had to conceal herself from whoever was calling.

His smile faded immediately when she spoke, her voice sounding a bit higher than normal. "Hi, Mom. Yes, I'm fine. I had a teachers' meeting tonight which ran later than usual."

She glanced at Nick, then flushed and immediately looked away. "Yes, Nick knows I'm home. I told him there was no need for him to have worried. I'm sorry he bothered you."

Maybe it was something in the way Lindsay had looked at him. Nick suddenly realized exactly where he was, exactly what he'd just done. He'd taken Lindsay on the floor, with little more care than an oversexed adolescent—and, damn, he hadn't even thought about any form of birth control! It had never even crossed his mind.

He groaned and rubbed a hand over his face, still trying to understand exactly how the events of the evening had gotten away from him. He'd been worried about Lindsay's safety—hell, he'd been damned near distraught by the time she'd shown up—concerned that something had happened to her, disturbed that she might be on a date with another man in an attempt to deny the involvement with Nick she'd been fighting so stubbornly. When she'd finally appeared, looking distant and beautiful and defiant . . . well, he'd lost it.

He took little comfort in the memory that he'd given her a chance to stop him at the last moment if she'd wanted to do so. His fleeting attempt at chivalry had been too little, too late.

She'd been a virgin. Though part of him gloried in the knowledge, he was appalled that her first sexual experience had been so frenzied, so lacking in romance or finesse. Had he known, he would have— No. It probably wouldn't have made any difference. He'd never been so totally out of control as he'd been tonight, never so totally lacking in consideration or responsibility.

What was Lindsay Hillman doing to him?

Dragging a deep, steadying breath into his burning lungs, he reached for his scattered, embarrassingly tangled clothes and began to dress, only half-aware that Lindsay had finished talking to her mother. By the time she hung up, he'd managed to convince himself that the lapse had only been a temporary one, brought on by the stress of worrying about her and by the past weeks of frustrated desire for her. The powerful, dangerous emotions he'd learned to fear as a child—jealousy, anger, violent passion—were now firmly, safely locked away. He wouldn't risk setting them loose again.

That decided, he turned back to Lindsay—and felt his heart clench in his chest. Still wrapped in the oversize afghan, she watched him shyly, her toast brown hair tousled, her blue eyes huge in the pale oval of her face. She looked young and vulnerable and sweet, and it was all he could do not to throw her over his shoulder and carry her into the bedroom, to spend the rest of the night showing her how much more there could be to lovemaking than the frantic coupling they'd just shared. He resisted only by telling himself that they both needed time to recuperate, time to clear their minds and regroup their defenses.

"Are you all right?" he asked, more gruffly than he'd intended.

She nodded. "Yes."

He shoved his fingertips into the back pockets of his jeans. "Lindsay—" Damn, but this was awkward! "—I'm sorry about what just happened. I didn't mean to...well, to be so rough."

She flushed. "I know."

"It won't happen again."

Her eyes widened, and he realized what she'd thought he meant. "I didn't say I wouldn't make love to you again," he clarified. "I only meant that I won't lose control like that again. It shouldn't— I don't usually— Hell, I don't know what happened tonight. But it won't happen again," he repeated firmly.

"I've told you that you don't always have to be in control around me," Lindsay murmured, drawing the afghan more tightly around her bare shoulders. "It isn't necessary to hide anything from me."

He hoped she wasn't going to start that rather naive perfect-communication bit again. He held up a hand to forestall her. "It was more serious than lack of finesse on my part. I didn't use anything to protect you, Lindsay. Since you weren't taking any precautions yourself, we have to face the fact that you could be—"

"Who said I wasn't taking any precautions?" Lindsay interrupted to ask.

He frowned. "I know that was your first time, Lindsay. You couldn't hide that from me."

Her cheeks went even pinker, if possible, though she held her chin high. "As it happens, I've been taking birth control pills for several months to alleviate menstrual cramping. Of course, I *would* have expected you to find that out sooner."

Stung by the justifiable criticism, Nick scowled. "Look, I've admitted things got out of control tonight. You're right,

I should have asked sooner... and if you're worried about whether I've been that careless in the past, don't be. I haven't.''

"I suppose I should be relieved to hear that," she murmured.

"Damn right you should." He exhaled impatiently and shook his head, realizing that the conversation was getting away from him again. Why were they standing here sniping at each other now, when they'd just shared the most incredible lovemaking he'd ever experienced in his life? He should be cuddling her, complimenting her, not getting defensive over everything she said.

They definitely needed some time alone.

"It's getting late. I'd better go." He crossed the room to where she stood and reached out to tuck a stray strand of hair behind her ear. "You'll be all right?"

"Yes."

He wasn't satisfied with the guardedness of her response, but he didn't know what else to do tonight. "I'll call you tomorrow, okay?"

"All right."

"Lindsay..." He cupped her face in his hands, wishing he could think of something to say to tell her how much their lovemaking had meant to him, how special she was to him. The words eluded him, leaving him tense and frustrated. "I'll talk to you tomorrow," he said finally, conceding defeat for now.

"Good night, Nick," she whispered.

He brushed her lips with his own, exerting an effort to keep the caress light. "Good night, sweetheart."

The endearment surprised him almost as much as it seemed to startle her. Without allowing himself to look back, he left her standing by the telephone, wrapped in her afghan and her thoughts.

* * *

Lindsay watched Nick leave, standing without moving for several long moments after he closed the door behind him. Her gaze fell to the floor, where her scattered clothing lay as though mocking her for her foolishness.

She'd made love with Nick Grant. Without forethought, without regard for the consequences, without any reassurance that he wanted anything more from her than this. Yet, at the moment, she found it impossible to be sorry. It had been wonderful. Spectacular. Beautiful.

And her life would never be the same again.

He'd given so much—yet taken so much away afterward. Just as she'd anticipated, he'd retreated in near panic almost immediately after they'd returned to their senses. She'd gotten too close, seen too deeply inside him—and she wasn't sure he'd ever forgive her for that.

He was willing to give her only passion—but passion would never be enough for her.

Stalemate.

One of them would have to give. And Lindsay sadly suspected she knew who'd be the first to stop fighting.

Chapter Seven

It surprised Lindsay that, of all her family, only her mother seemed to have reservations about Lindsay becoming involved with Nick. She'd have thought Evelyn would have been very much in favor of her daughter dating the successful young doctor who'd once been almost a member of the family.

"Have you been seeing much of Nick?" Evelyn asked over coffee the next afternoon, when Lindsay dropped by to visit on her way home from work.

Lindsay hoped she didn't blush at the errant thought of exactly how much she'd seen of Nick the night before. Did she look any different today? Could Evelyn somehow tell that Lindsay's life had changed irrevocably less than twenty-four hours earlier?

"Um . . . yes, I've seen him quite a bit lately," she managed, avoiding her mother's eyes as she diligently stirred sweetener into her coffee.

"I assumed that was the case when he called last night, worrying that he didn't know where you were."

"Yes, well, he overreacted. He seems to think my night blindness is worse than it really is, that I shouldn't be driving at all after dusk. I think I set him straight."

"He also seemed to think you should let him know where you're going to be in the evenings—as though the two of you have a commitment."

Lindsay stirred her coffee more vigorously. "I tried to set him straight on that, too." Not that she'd had much success. Just the opposite, in fact. She'd given Nick every reason to believe that there *was* something extremely significant between them now.

"So you aren't seriously interested in Nick?"

Something in Evelyn's voice made Lindsay stop stirring and look up at her mother. "Would it bother you if I were?"

Evelyn cleared her throat delicately. "Yes," she admitted after a moment. "I think it would."

Lindsay set her spoon down with a frown. "But, Mom— I thought you loved Nick. You said yourself that he was always special to you."

"Yes, I did. And, if you'll remember, I also said that I nearly broke my heart trying to get through to him. I'd hate for you to do the same."

Stunned that her mother was voicing the concerns Lindsay had had from the beginning, she clenched her hands in her lap and swallowed hard. "You don't think he's changed very much?"

"Oh, he's changed. Outwardly. He's made something of himself, and obviously worked very hard to do so. He's a fine, upstanding young man. An excellent doctor, I'm sure."

"But...?"

Evelyn sighed. "There's still a . . . a darkness in him. An inability—or perhaps a refusal—to express his deepest emotions. He still holds himself back, as though he chooses to stand on the outside and watch life from the safety of the sidelines. I know you so well, Lindsay. I can't imagine you ever being content with only being given the part of Nick he'd allow you to have—not if you really loved him."

Lindsay chewed her lower lip. "I don't know if I could ever be content with that, either," she confessed. "Not if I . . . if I loved him."

"Lindsay? You *don't* love him, do you?"

Meeting her mother's eyes across the small kitchen table, Lindsay stopped trying to hide her confusion and distress. "I don't know. Maybe."

"Oh, dear." Evelyn set her coffee cup down carefully, as though concerned she'd spill it if she didn't move very slowly and deliberately. "Then it's more serious than I'd thought."

"Yes."

"I see." Evelyn was silent for a long time, looking at her hands as though trying to prepare what she wanted to say. She began hesitantly. "There's one more thing I think you should know about Nick, Lindsay. Your father and I had several long, serious discussions about whether we should take him in when we were told about him so many years ago. We always worried a bit about the influence of our foster sons on our first family, but we truly believed we had so much more to gain than to risk from sharing our home and our love. Nick worried us more than most."

"Nick? But why?"

"We hadn't yet met him. All we knew about him was what the social worker had told us. And he indicated that Nick was—well, that Nick could be violent. Even dangerous, perhaps."

"Nick?" Lindsay repeated, shocked. "Sullen and withdrawn, perhaps, but violent? I can't believe that."

Evelyn took a deep breath. "Neither could I, once I saw him. Your father and I had agreed to meet the boy before making our decision. As soon as I looked into Nick's eyes and saw the pain and loneliness there, I knew I couldn't turn him away. During the two years he stayed with us, he never gave me a reason to regret that decision—and yet, that darkness, that unknown part of him, was always there. Always simmering just beneath the surface. And, I confess, it always worried me a bit. It worries me now."

Lindsay shook her head firmly. "No. I don't believe Nick would ever hurt me—not physically, anyway. He's much too controlled, much too cautious. Mother, I've seen him with his patients. He's so gentle and caring and careful. I've seen him grieve over the ones he can't save. Nick's real problem is that he just doesn't know how to express the feelings inside him, how to unlock the emotions that make him most vulnerable. I don't know if he'll ever learn to open up, and I worry that he and I can never really be together unless he does, but I've never for one moment worried that he would ever be violent with me."

Reaching across the table, Evelyn took both Lindsay's hands in her own. "I'm sure you're right, Lindsay. I've always wanted to believe the best of Nick. I just thought you should know why I'm a bit concerned, based on things I was told in the past.

"As for your relationship with him, I didn't say it *couldn't* work out, dear. Maybe, if you love him and he loves you, you'll be able to teach him to fully share himself with you. He's had so little experience with real love. I don't really know the details of his early life, other than that his family was abusive and uncaring, but I know he still bears emotional scars from those early years."

"The question is whether Nick would ever allow himself to love anyone—and, if he does, to make himself vulnerable enough to admit it."

"I'm afraid that is something valid to worry about with him," Evelyn agreed. "He's so...guarded."

"So skittish," Lindsay seconded glumly.

"So adept at masking his true feelings."

"So hard to resist," Lindsay groaned, hiding her face in her hands.

"I suppose he is that," Evelyn murmured with a touch of amusement. "If I were your age and single, I'd probably fall for him myself, despite my better judgment."

Lindsay dropped her hands to her lap. "What am I going to do, Mom?"

"You could stop seeing him. Break it off now, before it goes any farther."

"I don't think I can do that." She'd already tried to hold Nick at a distance. It hadn't worked. Maybe because she'd wanted him too much to try hard enough. Still wanted him that badly.

"Then all I can suggest is that you do everything you can to encourage Nick to open up to you. Nick doesn't know how to meet you halfway, so you'll have to be the one going most of the distance. There's a chance you'll succeed where I failed. Few people have been able to resist you when you really set your mind on something."

"And if I can't get through to him, either?"

Evelyn smiled rather sadly. "Then I'll be here for you when you need a shoulder to cry on."

"I love you, Mother."

"Oh, sweetheart, I love you, too. And I only wish I could protect you from ever being hurt or disappointed."

Lindsay shook her head, managing a faint smile of her own. "I'm afraid that's not possible. It's called growing up—and I think it's time I did that. 'Princess Lindsay' has been sheltered and protected for too long."

Evelyn's eyes glowed with love. "It's been our privilege to do so."

And then, as though sensing that Lindsay needed time to think about what they'd said, she changed the subject, telling an amusing story about little Tricia. They spent the next hour swapping family gossip, neither of them mentioning Nick again that afternoon, though Lindsay knew he was very much on both their minds.

The sun was just setting when Lindsay pulled into her parking space after the visit with her mother. As she climbed out of her car, she noticed a brown pickup truck—one she didn't recognize as belonging to any of her neighbors— parked across the lot. A man in dark glasses and a baseball cap sat in the truck, smoking, looking prepared to stay where he was for some time. He seemed to be watching Lindsay. Could this possibly be the same truck she'd noticed the evening before, when she'd had this same uncomfortable feeling of being watched?

She looked away and hurried toward her door, chiding herself for the ripple of apprehension that coursed down her spine. He was simply waiting for someone, she assured herself, and was watching her for lack of anything else to do during his wait. It wasn't as though she was totally unaccustomed to masculine attention. The only reason she was nervous now was because Nick had shaken her so badly by stepping out of the shadows unexpectedly last night.

She made sure she locked her front door behind her when she entered her apartment. After all, it never hurt to be too careful. Feeling safe again now that she was home, she put away her things, changed out of her teaching clothes into a comfortable black-and-hot-pink nylon running suit, and

snapped on her television to watch the news before deciding about dinner.

It wasn't easy to concentrate on crime reports, political
updates and weather forecasts when her eyes kept wandering to the carpet in the middle of the living room, her memory replaying the events that had taken place there the night
before. She and Nick had made love. Even more signifi-
cantly, Lindsay had been forced to realize that her feelings
for him were more than attraction, more than fascination.
That they could very well haunt her for the rest of her life.

Somehow she knew who rang her doorbell. Nervously
smoothing her hands over the legs of her black running
pants, she wondered what she should say to him. What he'd
expect her to say.

Though she was almost certain she'd find Nick on the
other side of the door, a fleeting thought of the man in the
brown pickup made her ask, "Who is it?"

"Nick."

The sound of his voice set her heart to tripping again. She
pressed a hand over it in exasperation, wishing that just once
she could respond to him with her common sense rather
than her hormones. Thinking of her mother's concerned
warnings, she reached for the doorknob, determined to be
more cautious this time. She refused to reveal the full extent of her feelings for Nick without being given more clues
about the depth of his feelings for her.

Nick hadn't quite known how to expect Lindsay to greet
him this evening, not after everything that had happened
between them the night before. Cautiously, perhaps. De-
fensively, maybe. It was even possible that she'd try to send
him away, though he had no intention of leaving meekly.
They needed to talk, needed to define the relationship that
had finally begun between them last night, and which Nick

had no intention of denying. As far as he was concerned, Lindsay had given herself to him last night. She belonged to him now.

What he *hadn't* expected was that she'd usher him in as courteously as though she'd invited him for tea, politely inquiring about his day, offering to take his jacket, asking if he'd like a cold drink. For the first time, Nick looked into her lovely blue eyes and found them completely shuttered, her thoughts effectively hidden from him.

"Lindsay?" he asked, after declining the drink. "What's wrong?"

"Why, nothing," she replied, though she avoided his gaze. "Are you hungry? I don't have much to offer, but I could make you a sandwich or something."

"I thought I'd take you out for dinner tonight. You don't have other plans, do you?"

"No. But I hope you don't mind going someplace casual. I don't really feel like dressing up again," she answered, gesturing toward her brightly colored, fashionable-looking outfit. Nick didn't think she looked any more casual than he did in his cream sweater and brown dress slacks, not that he was an expert on women's fashions.

"You look very nice." It was an understatement, of course. She looked wonderful.

Her smile didn't quite reach her eyes. "Thanks, but I wasn't fishing for compliments."

"You don't have to. You must know by now that I think you're beautiful."

Her cheeks darkened. "You're embarrassing me."

He smiled. "How about if I feed you, instead?"

"I'll get my purse."

Nick caught her arm as she passed him. "I haven't even kissed you today," he murmured, his attention suddenly focused on her soft, moist, unpainted mouth.

She went still, looking up at him, obviously waiting for him to correct that oversight. He brushed his lips over hers, once, then twice, so lightly he hardly tasted her. He wanted more—much more—but he suddenly found himself needing some sign that he wasn't the only one who wanted. He touched his lips to hers one more time, and was delighted when Lindsay impatiently rose up to meet him, pressing her mouth to his for a deeper, more satisfying embrace. Nick gave it to her willingly, his tongue slipping between her invitingly parted lips to be warmly welcomed by hers.

Lindsay could hide her thoughts for a time, but she couldn't disguise her physical response to him. He'd be content with that—for the moment.

Because he was watching her so closely, Nick noticed that Lindsay glanced rather nervously around the parking lot when they walked out to his car, almost as though she was looking for something—or someone—in particular. "What's wrong?" he asked, his gaze following hers. He saw nothing out of the ordinary, just apartment residents going to or from their cars on this average Friday evening. Had someone been bothering Lindsay? he wondered with a return of the uncharacteristic possessiveness he'd felt before with her.

Lindsay shook her head. "Nothing. Earlier I thought— No, really, there's nothing wrong. Where would you like to eat?"

Sensing that she was evading his question, Nick wanted to persist, but gave in because he didn't want to argue with her now. They needed to get this relationship on a more natural footing, he reasoned. A pleasant dinner, an unthreatening evening together. As deeply as they'd suddenly become involved, they'd had only one date so far. The rest of their time together had been marked by defensive sparring. Tonight he intended to show her that he could be as charming and entertaining as any other guy she'd dated!

"How about Shorty's?" he suggested, casually slipping an arm around her waist as they approached his car. "I could really go for a big, sloppy burger right now."

"A burger?" Lindsay repeated with a smile. "Hardly health food, Doctor."

"Sometimes even doctors have dietary lapses," Nick returned gravely. "I'm even going to have fries. Maybe with cheese and chili."

"Might as well live really dangerous and have fried onion rings with that," she teased.

Pleased that she was responding to his light tone, Nick grinned. "Maybe I will."

Nick decided later that most people would have called the casual dinner date a success. He and Lindsay talked easily enough over the high-calorie meal, smiling often, even laughing aloud a few times. Anyone watching them would most likely have thought they made an attractive, quite suitable couple.

Yet, as much as he enjoyed the evening in some ways, Nick still found himself growing increasingly frustrated by his inability to read Lindsay's expression. Her thoughts had always been so open to him, her feelings so close to the surface. Had she learned so quickly from him to mask her emotions behind an affable facade?

He didn't like it. Not at all.

He waited until they'd returned to her apartment before trying again to reach her. "I suppose I don't have to ask whether you've thought about what happened between us last night," he began, watching as she made coffee in her small kitchen.

Lindsay's fingers seemed to tighten around the measuring scoop she held, but that was the only sign of reaction when she answered. "I've thought about it."

"And...?"

She turned her attention back to the coffeemaker. "And what?"

"Any regrets?"

"No."

"That's good." He leaned one elbow against the counter, still watching her closely. "I have a few."

She looked momentarily startled. "You regret that we—that we—"

"Made love," he supplied when she seemed at a loss for the right words. "And, no, I don't regret that. How could I? I only wish I'd been more gentle with you, that I'd given you more time, taken more care. I didn't mean to hurt you, Lindsay."

She wiped a spot of water from the countertop with a paper towel, her hair falling over her face to conceal her expression from him. "You didn't hurt me," she said a bit gruffly. "It was...very nice."

He winced at the tepid description of what he'd considered to be uniquely magnificent. Making love with Lindsay had been the most delightful experience of his life—and yet she called it "very nice"?

His passion must have made him even more clumsy than he'd guiltily imagined. He made a mental vow to make it up to her, to devote himself to making it as perfect for her as for himself next time. Which—he hoped—would be tonight.

"Lindsay, what we have, what I feel for you is—" He hesitated, frustrated with the words, knowing she expected them. "Well, it's special."

She gave him a look that told him absolutely nothing about her own feelings. "Is it?"

Annoyed, he frowned. "Of course, it is. Do you think I've ever made such a fool of myself over any other woman as I have with you?"

Her eyebrow lifted. "I wouldn't know."

"Dammit, Lindsay, talk to me! What's with you tonight?"

"I don't know what you mean, Nick. We've talked quite a bit tonight."

"You *do* know what I mean," he refuted fiercely. "You're shutting me out, Lindsay. Why?"

She pulled two coffee mugs out of a cabinet. "I haven't done anything you haven't done often enough to me, Nick," she pointed out reasonably.

That took him aback. "Is this some sort of retaliation?"

"No. I just haven't felt like arguing with you this evening."

"Why are you so certain we'd argue?"

"We always do," she answered simply. "Every time we try to talk about anything important, I start pushing and you get prickly and defensive and before long we're quarreling. I don't want to quarrel with you, Nick."

"I don't want to quarrel with you, either."

She handed him a steaming cup of coffee. "Then there's no problem, is there?"

Thoroughly frustrated by her apparent logic, he exhaled impatiently and took a sip of the coffee. Maybe she was right, he told himself. Maybe he should stop pushing her to reveal her true feelings. After all, hadn't he refused to cooperate each time *she'd* been the one asking questions?

Not that it was at all the same, of course. Nick had good reasons for declining to discuss the details of his past, while he strongly suspected that Lindsay *was* simply getting back at him with her own stubbornness this evening. Still, maybe it would be best—at least for tonight—if he humored her.

Lindsay wouldn't be able to keep this up indefinitely. She hadn't had nearly as much practice as Nick had.

"Good coffee," he said, his decision made.

If she was surprised that he didn't persist, she didn't allow it to show. "Thanks. Why don't we take it into the living room."

"Fine."

They debated watching television while they lingered over their coffee, but decided to turn on some music, instead, when Nick admitted that he wasn't particularly interested in the network programming. He found it so much more appealing to watch Lindsay. It wasn't long before he realized that watching wasn't enough. He needed to touch.

Sitting beside her on the couch, Neil Diamond's silky voice crooning from the stereo speakers, Nick loosely cradled his nearly empty coffee cup in his right hand as he reached out with his left to brush a strand of hair away from her cheek. Her hair was so soft, so shiny. Always smelled so nice. He wondered idly if it was her shampoo—or just Lindsay.

He traced the curve of her cheek with his fingertips. Her skin was like velvet—smooth, fair, flawless. She usually wore makeup—as most women did—but she was subtle with its application. He'd never cared for the heavily painted look.

He touched the tip of one finger to her full lower lip, feeling her warm breath brush over his skin. Her mouth made him crazy. An enticing combination of innocence and sensuality. A taste that was somewhere between heaven and sin.

The coffee cup clattered against the coaster when Nick set it on the low table in front of the couch. Her own hands empty, Lindsay turned to him just as he reached for her, going into his arms as if she'd only been waiting for him to make the first move. He murmured his pleasure and captured that heavenly, sinful mouth of hers beneath his own.

Already he was on fire for her, his pulse racing, his body clamoring for release. But tonight he was determined to do this right—even if it killed him.

He pushed himself off the couch and held one hand out to her. Lindsay placed hers in it. He noticed the tremble in her fingers, and was well aware that his own hadn't been quite steady. Together, silently, they walked to her bedroom. Nick didn't bother to turn on the lights, leaving the room in shadows, illuminated only by a soft glow caused by security lights filtering through the window curtains. He wished for a moment for candles and roses, all the sentimental trappings he hadn't provided the last time. Yet there were other ways to give her romance.

Pausing beside the bed, he turned her to face him, cupping her face tenderly in his hands. "You're so beautiful," he murmured, stroking his thumb across her lower lip. "You make me ache, Lindsay."

She rested her hands on his chest, her eyelids going heavy as she tilted her head back to invite his kiss. He caught her lower lip gently between his teeth, running his tongue across it to savor the taste. And then he delved deeper, finding more sweetness, more pleasure. Her tongue touched his, shyly at first, and then more eagerly as she gave herself fully to the embrace.

For long, lazy minutes, they did nothing more than kiss, exploring textures, angles, pressures, pausing only occasionally for quick, ragged breaths. He touched her with no more than his hands on her face, not wanting to tempt himself to hurry when he had all night to love her.

His willpower lasted until Lindsay slid her arms around his neck and crowded closer. "Nick," she whispered between kisses. "Touch me. Please."

He moaned and hoped he'd be able to survive with his sanity intact. "I'm trying to take this slowly, Lindsay. I don't want to rush you tonight."

"Just make love to me," she urged, pressing feverish kisses to the side of his throat.

His low laugh was ragged. "I intend to, sweetheart. Every perfect inch of you."

As he'd promised himself, Nick proceeded very slowly, excruciatingly slowly. He undressed her with gentle hands, taking time to explore and pleasure every part of her he revealed. When Lindsay tried to return the favor, he stopped her with husky whispers and long kisses, until finally she surrendered, willingly putting herself into his hands. Next time he'd want her to participate, would show her how to please him. This time was for Lindsay.

The room was quiet, the only sounds, their labored breathing and the soft echoes of the music still playing in the other room. Nick dedicated himself to pleasuring her with his mouth and hands, leaving no inch of her undiscovered, untouched. Lindsay gasped and trembled, her hands clenching and unclenching at his shoulders as he knelt before her, concentrating on nothing but her satisfaction.

It was Lindsay who finally urged him to the bed, whose hands reached out avidly to pull him down to her. Lindsay who arched upward as he finally moved to make them one, who wrapped her legs tightly around his hips to hold him to her. Lindsay who bowed upward and cried out brokenly when the waves of climax coursed through her. And it was Lindsay who made sure afterward that Nick's pleasure was just as thorough.

Nick surrendered to his release with the deep satisfaction of knowing that he'd given her everything he had to give, that this time he'd taken her with him to ecstasy.

Long after Lindsay had fallen asleep, Nick lay awake, cradling her protectively against his shoulder, listening to the music and remembering Lindsay's passion. At least in bed, she'd been unable to hold back from him. Hadn't been able to hide from him. But he didn't like wondering if she'd withdraw again in the morning—and he understood now how frustrating it had been for her when he'd withheld so much of himself.

He'd worked so hard to build a future, to make a success of himself. He'd been satisfied with his progress, satisfied that, in Lindsay, he'd found someone with whom to share that promising future. Yet now he wondered bleakly if his past would rear up, after all, to destroy him, despite his best efforts to keep it buried. Would Lindsay ever accept that there were things he simply couldn't tell her, or would she finally grow tired of trying, as the woman he'd once lived with had done? Would Lindsay, too, throw up her hands and walk away from him?

His arm tightened involuntarily around her at the thought of living without her now that he'd found her, now that he'd discovered how special they could be together. He wouldn't be able to allow Lindsay to leave without a fight—and yet how could he hold her if she couldn't be happy with him?

The only alternative was to tell her everything, as unpleasant as the memories were, as reluctant as he was to dig them up again. But then he realized that he was afraid of what Lindsay would think of him if he revealed the ugliness he'd lived with for so long, the potential for violence still lurking deeply inside him. He knew he'd never hurt her, never turn that violence against her—but how could Lindsay be sure of that if she ever heard the full story of his youth?

Either way—truth or silence—he risked losing her.

No. He couldn't tell her. The risks were too great. She'd simply have to learn to trust him, to believe that he knew what was best for them in this.

Somehow he had to make her understand.

It took Lindsay a moment to orient herself when she woke the next morning to discover Nick sleeping beside her. She'd never awakened with a man in her bed before, so she wasn't exactly sure of the protocol. Should she wake him? Let him sleep? Slip out of the bed and make breakfast for him? It was Saturday, so she had the day off, but what if Nick had to work? Should she rouse him and ask?

Before she'd decided which course to take, he opened his eyes to find her watching him. He smiled, the expression softening his beard-shadowed face. "Good morning."

"Good morning." Even tousled, heavy-eyed and be-whiskered, he looked wonderful. She couldn't imagine anything she'd rather see every morning than Nick's smile. "It's almost nine o'clock. I hope you don't have any early appointments this morning."

"No. I have the day off. Two of the other partners are on call this weekend."

"That's nice for you."

"Mmm." His smile turned wicked. "It means we don't have to leave this bed for hours yet," he said, reaching for her. He paused with his mouth an inch above hers. "Unless you had other plans this morning?"

"If I did, I've forgotten them," Lindsay answered truthfully, sliding her arms around his neck. "Just what did you have in mind, Dr. Grant?"

He demonstrated quite nicely. And he'd been right. It *was* several hours later when they finally left the bed.

* * *

It was too late for breakfast when hunger finally drew them out of the bedroom, so Lindsay made sandwiches and a dip for fresh raw vegetables while Nick used her shower. He'd offered to scrub her back while she showered, but she'd told him they'd *never* get anything to eat if he did, with which he'd laughingly agreed. He'd been a perfect gentleman—almost—while she'd bathed and then dressed in jeans and an oversize cotton sweater, piling her hair up in a loose knot on top of her head and adding just enough makeup to satisfy her vanity. He'd only distracted her ten or twelve times during that process with kisses and wayward touches.

She'd just set the table and filled glasses with ice for tea when Nick joined her. His hair was still damp, but neatly combed, his face clean-shaven with a borrowed disposable razor, and he'd donned his slacks and sweater, which were only a little wrinkled after a night on her floor. He'd left his glasses on the nightstand, and his eyes were bright and contented when he bent to kiss her on the way to the table. "This looks good, Lindsay."

"We're having sandwiches, Nick. Lavish praise is not expected," she said dryly.

He chuckled. "Trust me, I'm hungry enough to lavish praise on sandwiches."

"If you'll remember, I suggested breakfast several hours ago."

"I enjoyed breakfast very much, thank you. Now I'm hungry for food."

She sighed and shook her head, though inwardly she was delighted with his teasing. Nick didn't laugh enough. Maybe showing him how to play was a step in teaching him how to love, she thought wistfully.

They'd just finished eating when the doorbell rang. Nick looked up in question. "You expecting anyone?"

"No. It's probably someone from the family," Lindsay answered in resignation, knowing Nick's presence in her apartment would raise eyebrows. "No one else drops by without calling first—no one except you, of course."

The slight dig didn't appear to perturb him. He only shrugged and followed her into the living room to see who was ringing her doorbell. Since Nick was with her, Lindsay didn't bother to ask the caller to identify himself before she opened the door. She'd been so sure it would be one of her family that she was surprised to find a total stranger on the other side.

The man was tall and slender, dark-haired, dark-eyed, olive-skinned. He looked Italian. He wore a sport coat, dress shirt and a casually knotted tie with jeans and white running shoes, and he had a smile that Lindsay couldn't help returning.

"May I help you?" she asked, thinking that if this guy had appeared on her door a few months earlier—before Nick had come into her life—she might have been tempted to think he was there in answer to her dreams, at least until she'd spotted the gold band he wore on his left hand. Now, however, she found that she admired his attractiveness only with a rather distant appreciation, preferring Nick's somewhat more conservative good looks.

The man was studying Lindsay's face with a rather odd expression. "Miss Hillman? Lindsay Hillman?"

"Yes?"

"My name is Tony D'Alessandro. I'm a private investigator from Dallas, Texas. I wonder if I could come in for a moment to talk to you."

A private investigator? Lindsay stared at him in surprise. She'd never even met a P.I. before, much less had one show up on her doorstep and ask to come inside!

Her life had been full of firsts lately, she thought rather dazedly, wondering what in the world this was all about.

Chapter Eight

Before she had a chance to speak, Nick abruptly moved to Lindsay's side, glaring at the other man suspiciously. "You're a private investigator?"

D'Alessandro nodded, looking a bit cautious in response to Nick's tone. "Yes."

"You have identification?"

"Of course." As though he'd been prepared for the question, the man held out a leather wallet. Rather than glancing at it from a distance, Nick took it and studied it closely. "D'Alessandro Investigations," he murmured. "Your firm?"

"Yes. And you are...?"

"This is Dr. Nick Grant," Lindsay answered when Nick made no effort to do so. "Please come in, Mr. D'Alessandro. What's this all about?"

Nick blocked the way when D'Alessandro would have entered the apartment. "Wait a minute. Why don't you just tell us why you're here first?"

"Nick!" Annoyed with him for trying to take charge again, Lindsay grabbed his arm and tugged firmly. "This *is* still my apartment, and I've asked the man in. Now will you please stop being so rude and move out of his way?"

Nick didn't look pleased, but grudgingly did as she asked. Lindsay smiled at the wary-looking P.I. "Sorry. He tends to be overprotective. Please have a seat, Mr. D'Alessandro. May I get you something to drink?"

"No, thank you. And the name's Tony."

"All right. I'm Lindsay." She dropped into a chair and waited until he was seated on one end of the couch. Nick chose to hover behind Lindsay's chair like some sort of overanxious bodyguard, and she ignored him as she asked, "Now, perhaps you'd tell us why you're here, Tony?"

"Yes, of course. I'll start from the beginning."

"Good idea," Nick muttered.

Tony didn't react to the comment. "Twenty-five years ago, Hazel Walker, a twenty-nine-year-old widowed mother of seven, died from complications of pneumonia in Texarkana, Texas. Because there were so many of them, and there were no other relatives willing to take them, her children—ranging in ages from eleven to less than a year old—were separated and sent to various foster homes and orphanages."

Lindsay swallowed hard as she was struck by the suspicion that she was more intimately involved in this story than she'd thought when he started speaking. Her fingers clenched in her lap. "How does this involve me, Mr.—Tony?" she asked, though she believed she already knew.

"Just over six months ago, a young woman, Michelle Trent, came to my office and hired me to locate her long-lost siblings. She'd been adopted as a toddler and raised as an only child. Her adoptive mother died earlier this year and left a letter for Michelle, telling her about the six brothers and sisters she'd never known she had. Michelle wanted a chance to meet them."

"You're saying you think Lindsay is one of your client's siblings?" Nick asked, voicing the question Lindsay had been holding back.

"I'm positive that she is," Tony replied, still looking at Lindsay. "I've found documentation. But even if I hadn't, I would have known. I can't get over how much you look like her," he added, shaking his head in wonder. "It's—rather startling. We've located an older sister who bears a strong resemblance, but you—well, you could be Michelle's twin."

Lindsay stiffened. "I'm not, am I?" It was disturbing enough to hear that she had so many biological brothers and sisters she hadn't known about. But to think she might have been separated for so many years from a twin! She didn't know how she'd react to that.

Tony immediately shook his head, to her relief. "No, Michelle's almost two years older than you, not that she looks it. The only twins in the family were a set of boys, five years old at the time of the separation, and the only ones still left unaccounted for, now that we've located you."

"You've . . . found all the others?" Lindsay asked, still trying to comprehend everything he was telling her.

"Yes." He smiled sympathetically, obviously understanding her bewilderment. "Jared, the eldest, recently bought a small ranch in the Dallas area. One of my employees, Cassie Browning, located him and his teenage son, Shane, in New Mexico and told them about Michelle's search. During their three-day trip back to Dallas to visit

Michelle, Cassie and Jared fell in love. They were married only a few weeks afterward.''

''That's very touching, but what—''

Lindsay held up a hand to interrupt Nick's impatient question. ''What about the others?'' she asked, still watching Tony.

''Layla, the eldest sister, is married and has three children. She lives in Fort Worth. She was the first one we found, actually, since she'd registered years earlier with an organization that provides assistance in reuniting biological families separated for various reasons, such as adoption. Another brother, Miles, died in a car accident several years ago, which leaves only the twins, who haven't been seen since they were sixteen years old and ran away from the last of a series of unsuccessful foster homes.''

''Your client—Michelle—she's pleased to have found her brother and sister?'' Lindsay asked quietly.

''Very pleased. They've become good friends during the past few months, which means a great deal to Michelle. Since all of them live so close now, they get together often and have a nice time when they do. It's been good for Michelle. Despite her adoptive parents' wealth, she was a very lonely child who always longed for a large family.''

Lindsay studied the look in Tony's eyes when he spoke of Michelle. ''She isn't married?''

He smiled and lifted his left hand to display the new-looking gold band on his ring finger. ''She wasn't when she hired me, but she is now.''

Lindsay returned the smile. ''Congratulations.''

''Didn't waste any time marrying your wealthy client, did you?'' Nick muttered.

Appalled at his rudeness, Lindsay gasped and whipped her head around to glare at him. ''Nick! Honestly!''

His smile fading, Tony D'Alessandro gave Nick a long, cool look. "Believe me, you're not the first to accuse me of that," he said deliberately. "During my early search for Michelle's siblings, I stumbled onto the discovery that her longtime family attorney had been stealing from her for three years. He tried to cover his actions by making Michelle believe I was the one who was only after her money. Because I loved her and needed her trust, I proved myself to Michelle by producing evidence of her attorney's guilt, but I don't waste time defending my actions to people who don't particularly matter to me."

"Good for you," Lindsay approved, giving Nick a "so there" look. "I'm sorry, Tony."

"Dammit, Lindsay, don't apologize for me," Nick ordered curtly, slapping a hand down on the back of her chair. "We still don't know what this guy wants from you. We haven't even seen his so-called documentation that you have any connection with his client or her 'long-lost siblings.' "

Tony reached calmly into his jacket and pulled out a legal-size envelope. He laid it on the coffee table. "There's the proof you requested, Dr. Grant. As for what I want—Lindsay, I'd like you to consider coming to Dallas, at Michelle's expense, of course, to meet your brother and sisters. They'd really like to see you. Jared and Layla remember you as a baby, since they were eleven and ten when the family was split up."

"Oh, Tony, I don't know," Lindsay demurred, crossing her arms at her waist. "I have to admit I'm curious, but—well, you must understand that I *have* a family. Wonderful parents and two terrific older brothers, two sisters-in-law, a niece and a nephew and another on the way. I've always known I was adopted, but I can't imagine any family being more special to me than the Hillmans. I love them as if I really were born to them. These other people are strangers to me."

"I know, Lindsay. And I understand. So do Michelle and the others. That's why they sent me to talk to you—in case you decided you'd rather not complicate your life by meeting them. But please believe that they only want to meet you, to see how you've turned out as an adult. They don't want to replace the family you have now or to interfere in your life in any other way."

Tempted, Lindsay chewed her lower lip. "I don't suppose it could do any harm to just meet them," she murmured after a moment.

"She'll think about it and get back to you with her answer," Nick said, giving Tony a look that dared him to argue.

Tony didn't even try. "Of course. That's all we expected this time. I'll leave my card."

Deciding to have a long talk with Nick about this tendency of his to speak on her behalf, Lindsay ignored him again as she spoke to Tony. "I would like to think about this for a day or two, Tony. Maybe talk to my parents before I make a decision."

"I understand. I appreciate you making time to talk to me today."

"I'd say the pleasure was mine, but—" she shook her head in bemusement "—to be honest, I'm not sure, yet."

Tony chuckled and stood. "I'd better be going. I'm sure the two of you would like to—um—discuss this," he said wryly, with one quick glance at Nick. "It was very nice to meet you, Lindsay. I'll be expecting your call."

"It's nice knowing you, too, Tony. I guess we're in-laws, in a way, aren't we?" The thought dazed her.

"Yes, we are. And, by the way, I come from a huge family myself, Lindsay. Two parents, two brothers, dozens of aunts, uncles and cousins. We're all very close, but I've learned during the past year that there's no such thing as too much family. There's always room for more people who care about you.''

Nick snorted derisively, though he refrained from saying anything else.

Lindsay saw Tony off with a promise to be in touch with him soon. And then she turned on Nick, hands on her hips. ''I have never seen a more disgusting display of rudeness in my entire life! Not even from the angry, rebellious foster kids who've come through my family's home during the past twenty years or so. And don't tell me you don't know any better, *Dr.* Grant, because I've seen you work a snobby society affair with the skill of a professional politician, remember? Why in the world did you treat that poor man that way?''

''I don't trust him,'' Nick answered shortly, though he had the grace to look uncomfortable with her accusations.

''Why not? He told us exactly why he was here, left proof of his claims, didn't ask for anything except my consideration of his request. He was friendly, polite, pleasant.''

''Unlike me, right?'' Nick snapped.

''Right,'' she shot back. ''So, what is your problem, Nick?''

''He's going to mess up your life—he and his wife and those others. You don't need them, Lindsay. You've got everything going for you here—a close family, a good job, a life of your own. Why would you even consider complicating it with these strangers?''

Lindsay was doing her best to understand Nick's violent opposition to Tony's quest. She figured it had something to do with Nick's unpleasant past. She tried to speak more calmly, more conciliatorily. ''Nick, you know how much I love my family. I adore them, I really do. But, like all adopted children, I *have* always been curious about my biological family, in a detached sort of way. I can't imagine them ever becoming family to me, not in the same way my parents and my brothers are—but what harm could there be in just meeting them?''

Nick looked grim, more so than she'd ever seen him, his eyes haunted by the old memories she knew he would still refuse to share with her. ''There is always harm in digging up the past,'' he said. ''What happened twenty-five years ago is over and best forgotten. All that matters is the present and the future.''

''That's your opinion. I'll have to make up my own mind about this.''

''Lindsay, listen to me,'' Nick said urgently, reaching out to catch her shoulders in his hands. ''You've been so sheltered and protected—you don't know what people can be like out there. You don't know how they can hurt you or use you for their own gain. Why risk that when there's no need to do so?''

''Nick, you're treating me like a helpless child again! I'm not as naive as you seem to think I am. I can take care of myself, I can deal with strangers—I could even deal with your past, if you'd ever trust me enough to share it with me,'' she added daringly.

She could almost feel him withdraw from her, though he didn't take his hands from her shoulders. ''That has nothing to do with this.''

''Doesn't it?''

His jaw tightened. ''No. You're not going to listen to me about this, are you?''

''I've listened to what you said. But I plan to make up my own mind after I've given it more thought.''

"You'll talk to your family? Maybe you'll believe them if they tell you this is a lousy idea."

"I'll certainly pay attention to anything they have to say. But in the end, I'll still have to make up my own mind," Lindsay repeated stubbornly, determined to make him understand that she was an adult and ultimately accountable for her own actions. How could she and Nick ever have a successful relationship if he didn't start treating her as an equal? He still wouldn't open up to her about his own life, and she'd be damned if she'd let him start managing hers!

Nick nodded glumly and allowed his hands to fall to his sides. "When are you going to talk to them?"

"Later this afternoon, I suppose. I'd like to think about it for a while, decide what I want to say." She half turned away, depressed that the day that had started so nicely had deteriorated to this, and all because Nick still didn't trust her.

Maybe he felt threatened by the appearance of her long-separated siblings, or maybe he really was worried about her, but the bottom line was that he didn't give her credit for being a capable adult. And that hurt.

"I'd like to go with you to talk to your parents."

She looked over her shoulder, questioningly. "Why?"

"Because this is important! Dammit, Lindsay, I don't know what you think is going on between us, but we're more than casual acquaintances now. And it's a lot more than sex. We're lovers, we have a relationship, and that extends further than the bedroom, as far as I'm concerned!"

She flushed. "It does for me, too. But—"

"Don't shut me out of this, Lindsay. Please."

She closed her eyes at the uncharacteristic entreaty in his voice. "Oh, Nick," she said on a sigh. "You're being so unfair."

"Maybe," he agreed roughly. "And maybe I just need more time to understand your needs."

She was desperate enough to grab at any scrap of reassurance he could offer that everything would work out between them. She was willing to give him time, willing to give almost anything if only she could believe Nick was trying, too. Which only went to show how futile it had been to tell herself she hadn't been in love with him all along, she thought wearily. "All right, Nick. You can come with me to talk to my family. But, please, don't try to influence them. Please let me handle this my own way."

"I'll try" was the best he could seem to offer.

Only a few hours after his visit with Lindsay, Tony D'Alessandro walked into his Dallas home—the impressive Tudor-style Trent mansion in which Michelle had been raised—to be eagerly met at the door by his wife.

"Well?" she demanded, hardly giving him a chance to kiss her in greeting. "Did you see her? Did you talk to her?"

"Yes, to both questions."

"What does she look like?"

"Like you. So much like you I was startled when she opened the door."

"Younger, of course," Michelle remarked with a slight sigh.

"No one could tell it by looking," Tony argued loyally.

"What's she like?"

"We know from our research that she's a junior high English teacher, and that she's very close to her family. She's active in professional organizations and in her church and seems to lead a quiet, contented life."

"I know all that," Michelle interrupted impatiently. "What's she *like*?"

"From what I could tell, very nice. Polite, considerate, friendly. She welcomed me into her home, offered me a cold drink and very courteously listened to everything I had to say, even when her boyfriend—a preppy-looking doctor who appeared to be about my age—was ready to toss me out on my ear."

"Why was her boyfriend so belligerent?"

"Apparently, he didn't trust me. Thought I must have some ulterior motive for approaching Lindsay on behalf of strangers claiming kinship. He seems to be the possessive, overprotective type, though she didn't seem pleased by his attitude."

"D'you think it's serious between the two of them?"

"From what I saw—yes. Very serious. As aggressive as the guy was, I'd say he's crazy about her. And as irritated as she became with him, she's obviously in love with him."

Michelle nodded, trusting Tony's usually reliable instincts about people. And then she took a deep breath and asked the question Tony knew was the most important one to her. "Is she coming to visit us? Was she interested in meeting us?"

Tony caught his wife's hand in his own. "You knew there was a chance she wouldn't be interested, Michelle. After all, she doesn't remember anything about her life before the Hillmans adopted her."

Michelle's eyes dimmed visibly. "She isn't coming," she said, trying without much success to conceal the depth of her disappointment.

Tony squeezed her hands and shook his head. "I didn't say that. She hasn't given me an answer yet. Said she'd like to think about it, discuss it with her parents. She seemed somewhat interested, but I could tell Grant's going to do everything in his power to talk her out of it. If her parents agree with him—if they feel equally threatened by us—then chances are she'll go along with them. At least now she knows how to find us should she ever decide she wants to do so.''

Michelle nodded. "Yes. And we know that she's well and apparently happy. That's all that really matters. I'll call Layla and Jared and tell them.''

"She may still choose to come, Michelle.''

"I hope she does. But, if not, it's okay, Tony. You've done your best. And I love you for it.''

He caught her to him for a long, thorough kiss. "I love you, too," he murmured when it ended. And he knew, as Michelle probably did, that he'd try very hard to fetch her the moon if she asked for it.

Lindsay wondered if it was fate that her brothers were visiting at her parents' house when she and Nick arrived late that afternoon, after stopping by Nick's house so that he could change into fresh clothing. Steve and Greg had just returned from a nine-hole golf threesome with Earl—his first time on the course since his illness—and had stopped for a visit with Evelyn before heading toward their respective homes.

On one hand, it was convenient that the brothers were there, so Lindsay would only have to tell the story of Tony's visit once. On the other, she suspected that their reaction would be much the same as Nick's, and she rather dreaded the confrontation.

Though she wasn't quite ready to admit it, even to herself, she knew she'd already made her decision. She wanted to meet Michelle and Jared and Layla, names that hadn't stopped haunting her since Tony had said them. They were her sisters and her brother, and even if she never felt for them the same feelings she had for Greg and Steve, she still wanted to meet them, no matter how disapproving Nick or the others might be of her choice.

The family greeted Lindsay and Nick with barely veiled curiosity. Lindsay waited only until perfunctory small talk had been exchanged and cold drinks served in the den before taking a deep breath for courage. She would have preferred that Scott had been elsewhere, but she was reluctant to hurt the boy's feelings and further alienate him by sending him out of the room before beginning a family conference. "There's something I want to discuss with all of you," she began.

Steve's eyes went wide as he looked quickly from Lindsay to Nick. "Does this mean you and Nick have an announcement to make?"

Realizing what Steve thought—and probably the rest of them, too, judging by the way they were staring at them—Lindsay flushed and shook her head. "This has nothing to do with Nick," she said firmly. He frowned, but she ignored his obvious displeasure as she continued. "I had a visit from a private investigator from Dallas today. Nick just happened to be there, which is why he's here with me now."

"Why would a private investigator visit you, Lindsay?" Evelyn asked, looking a bit nervous. Lindsay thought her mother was probably picturing a television P.I., storming into Lindsay's life and bringing danger and disaster in his wake.

Lindsay linked her fingers in her lap. She couldn't think of any way to break the news except bluntly. "His name is Tony D'Alessandro. He—um—he's representing my biological sisters and brother, who hired him to find me and see if I wanted to meet them, at my convenience."

Taut silence followed her announcement. Glancing around the room, Lindsay noted that her parents had gone stiff and her brothers had started to frown. Typically, Steve was the first to speak. "Your *biological* sisters and brother? Who are these people? What makes them think they're related to you?"

"The P.I. had a copy of my original birth certificate," Lindsay answered quietly. And then she opened the envelope she'd been holding in her lap and pulled out a copy of an old black-and-white photograph. "He also had this."

Earl took the photograph and held it where the others could look over his shoulder. They gasped almost in unison.

Lindsay knew how they felt. She'd gasped, too, when she'd looked at the photo and seen herself as a baby, sleeping in the arms of a pale, drawn young woman surrounded by six other children—all of whom bore a startling resemblance to Lindsay now. Even Nick hadn't argued that the baby in the photo might not be Lindsay. Both of them had seen enough of the dozens of pictures Earl and Evelyn had taken of Lindsay as a baby to recognize another one.

"They look so much like you," Evelyn said, her voice a bit shaken. "The resemblance is . . . uncanny."

Lindsay felt the same way. So many times during her childhood she'd been aware of how different she looked from her redheaded, gray-eyed brothers. And now, to see these children with her features and, probably, her coloring—well, it had shaken her. She hadn't been able to look long at the woman in the old photo, knowing the woman— her mother—had died only months after it had been taken. She looked at Evelyn, her heart aching as she thought of how much she loved the woman who'd so eagerly and competently taken over the mothering of an orphaned baby girl.

"All of the rest of these kids are still together after all these years?" Greg asked. "Why weren't they separated?"

"They were," Lindsay answered. "Only three of them have been reunited—the oldest brother and sister and the

girl closest to my age. One of the other brothers has died and
the twin boys are still unaccounted for."

"Why do they want to meet you?" Steve demanded,
hands on his hips as though he were prepared to defend
something that belonged to him. "What do they want from
you?"

"They don't want anything from me," Lindsay replied,
aware that Nick had shot her an isn't-that-exactly-what-I-
asked look. She continued to disregard him as she concentrated on her family. "They only want to meet me, see how
I turned out. The oldest ones claim to remember me as a
baby. Tony assured me they won't pressure me to meet
them, or for anything else afterward. I suppose they're just
curious. To be honest, so am I."

Greg's frown deepened behind his neat beard. "You're
going to meet them?"

"I'm thinking seriously about it," she admitted.

"I don't know that that's such a good idea," Steve muttered. "What do you think about this, Nick?"

"I don't like it," Nick answered frankly. "I've already
told Lindsay that I think it's best to leave the past alone. She
doesn't know these people, doesn't share their memories. I
see no point in complicating her life with them."

"I'm inclined to agree with you," Greg said, stroking his
beard thoughtfully.

"Me, too," Steve seconded. "We're your brothers, Lin.
We're the ones who played with you when you were little
and teased you when you got older and worried about you
when you were sick or out on your first dates. We're the
ones who love you."

"I love you, too," Lindsay answered urgently. "And you
are my brothers, the best brothers anyone could ever hope
to have. I could never feel the same way about these other
people, because the memories I have with you guys couldn't

be replaced by anything. I'm just curious, Steve. And I can't see any harm in seeing them, talking to them, finding out what they're like."

Scott had stood in the background during the discussion, watching intently but saying nothing. Now he cleared his throat. "I know this is none of my business, but I think your brothers are right, Lindsay. You've got a nice family here," he muttered with a self-conscious blush. "Why d'you want to go see all those strangers?"

Earl had his right hand on his wife's shoulder, the photograph dangling from his other hand. He gave Scott a smile of pleasure at the compliment, then turned back to his daughter. His expression turned sober, but his tone was gentle when he said, "You do whatever you need to do, Lindsay. This is something you're going to have to decide for yourself."

"If you don't meet them, you may always wish you had," Evelyn said, though with just a trace of reluctance. "I don't want you to have any regrets later."

"And what if these other people try to take her over?" Steve argued. "What if they want to replace us, try to convince her they're her 'real' family?"

"No one could do that," Lindsay refuted immediately. "And I can't imagine that they'd try. They have their own families now, twenty-five years of their own identities. Tony said that they're all married and two of them have children, so they have their own lives. They only want to meet me, Steve."

Steve didn't seem particularly reassured. "Who is this Tony guy, anyway? What's in it for him?"

"He's married to one of my—one of the sisters," Lindsay answered carefully. "He married her after she hired him to locate the rest of us. And there's nothing in it for him, except pleasing his wife and doing his job."

Greg looked at Nick. "You met the guy?"

Nick nodded.

"What did you think of him?"

Lindsay swallowed a sigh, expecting Nick to rip Tony to shreds, which would make it necessary for her to defend the P.I. She was startled when Nick answered reluctantly, "He was okay, I guess. I didn't like what he was suggesting, but he wasn't pushy or overbearing about it."

Lindsay gave Nick a quizzical look that he returned with a challenging glance, as though he thought he'd just proven that he could be reasonable, despite her accusations. "I still think it would be a mistake for you to meet them," he added. "I don't see the point in it. Curiosity about the past can get you into more trouble than you can imagine, if you aren't careful."

Lindsay knew he was cautioning her about more than this proposed meeting with the Walker siblings. There was a personal message in his words, applying to his own past. She held his gaze with her own for a moment, letting him see that his thinly veiled warnings weren't going to frighten her off. And then she turned back to her family. "I'd like to meet them. I hope you can understand and give me your support."

"Does that mean you're going despite whatever we have to say about it?" Steve demanded, sounding frustrated that his little sister wouldn't listen to him this time.

"Lindsay's an adult, Steve," Earl inserted firmly. "She can make up her own mind."

"Thank you, Daddy. I'm glad you understand."

"Just promise me you'll be careful," Earl cautioned her. "These people really are strangers to you. I'd feel a lot better if you'd take one of your brothers with you when you meet them."

"I'll go," Steve volunteered immediately.

"With a baby due in only a few weeks?" Greg asked. "I'd better go instead."

"That won't be necessary," Nick cut in flatly. "I'm going with her."

Lindsay resisted an impulse to throw up her hands in exasperation. "*No one* has to go with me. I'm perfectly capable of handling this by myself."

Nick crossed his arms, looking about as approachable and persuadable as a marble statue. "I'm going with you."

"Whether I want you to or not?" Lindsay asked in disbelief.

His thin smile was his answer. "Good thing you want me to, isn't it?" he murmured.

"What I *want* you to do is jump in a lake!" Lindsay snapped.

Steve chuckled. "This is beginning to sound serious."

"Stay out of it, Steve."

Evelyn interceded before Lindsay and Steve could get into one of the heated arguments they'd engaged in so frequently during the years. "Lindsay, I think you and Nick should decide this in private, don't you?"

"Yes, we certainly will," Lindsay agreed.

Nick nodded his concurrence. Lindsay wondered if it was as apparent to everyone else that he considered the decision already made.

Chapter Nine

"There is absolutely no need for you to go with me to Dallas," Lindsay told Nick firmly when they'd returned to her apartment. She'd thought about this all the way home. To be honest, she would have loved to have Nick go with her. She enjoyed being with him—most of the time—and would have welcomed his company, particularly since she was a bit nervous about meeting these strangers who happened to be related to her.

Still, she had no intention of taking Nick along if he was going to be as surly and defensive with Michelle, Jared and Layla as he'd been with Tony. Nor did she want him going because he thought she needed someone to take care of her, didn't trust her enough to look out for herself. She intended to make that perfectly clear.

He looked as though he'd been fully prepared for this. He didn't raise his voice or change his expression when he said, "I want to go, Lindsay."

"What about your work? You can't just desert your patients."

"I can arrange a few days off work. The partners can cover for me. You might as well accept that there's no way I'd allow you to go to Dallas alone to meet these strangers."

"You'd *allow* me?" she repeated incredulously, her fists doubling at her hips.

He held up one hand in apology. "Okay, I said that wrong," he admitted. "Obviously, I'm in no position to refuse to allow you to do anything."

"I'm glad you realize that," Lindsay shot back. "You may be sleeping with me, but you do not own me, Nick Grant."

It was clear that he didn't care for her phrasing, but he let it go. "Lindsay, please. I really need to do this."

The expression in his eyes, the entreaty in his voice, were difficult to resist. Furious with herself that she had so little willpower against this man, she allowed her arms to drop weakly to her sides. "Oh, Nick," she said with a deep sigh. "You can be so damned infuriating."

"I know," he murmured, and his tone was rueful. "God knows I've been told so enough times."

"I want you to tell me exactly why you want to go with me to Dallas," she challenged. "And be very careful what you say," she added.

He grimaced, but made an effort. "I want to meet these people," he admitted. "Find out what they're like, make sure they're on the level. And I want to be with you. I'd enjoy the chance to spend that time together. And, finally, I want the chance to keep an eye on you, whether you need it or not. You're important to me, Lindsay. I'm concerned about your safety."

"You're important to me, too, but you can't always watch over me, Nick. I'm not a delicate piece of glass to be wrapped in cotton and constantly guarded."

"I know. I just need a little more time to get used to having someone mean this much to me," Nick said, watching for her reaction.

She really hoped he wasn't just saying those things to weaken her resistance to him. She'd strangle him if she thought he was only trying to manipulate her—because he was doing so quite successfully.

"Oh, hell," she muttered. And then took a deep breath. "All right, you can go with me. But I swear, Nick, if you embarrass me or ruin this for me, I'll never speak to you again as long as I live. Is that perfectly clear?"

"Painfully," he assured her.

"Good."

"When were you thinking of going?"

"I've got a few days off at Thanksgiving. I thought I'd leave the Friday morning after the holiday. That would give me a couple of weeks to get ready and three days in Dallas, if I choose to stay that long. Can you take that long weekend off?"

"I'll arrange it."

"Fine. I'll call Tony and let him know when we'll be there."

Nick nodded. "Fine."

And that seemed to be that. Lindsay cleared her throat and glanced around the room, a little unsure of herself now that the confrontation seemed to be over. She tried to tell herself she'd won, though she wouldn't have wanted her "victory" examined too closely. "Are you hungry? I could make us something for dinner."

"No. I think I'd better go. I've got some things to do at home."

Hiding her disappointment, she managed a smile. "Okay. I have some papers to grade tonight, anyway."

"Will you go out for lunch with me tomorrow?"

"Yes. I'd like that."

"Good." He reached out and pulled her into his arms.

She lifted her face for the expected kiss. When he only held her and looked at her with a faint, quizzical smile, she asked, "What is it?"

"I'm trying to figure out exactly what it is you do to me," Nick admitted. "You make my head spin, Lindsay Hillman."

She smiled. "Funny. I was just thinking something along the same lines about you."

"Quite a pair, aren't we?"

"We have potential," she murmured, thinking of the night before.

His eyes echoed the memories. "Yeah. I guess we do."

Lindsay slid her arms around his neck. "So, are you going to kiss me or what?" she teased, giving him a coy look from beneath her lashes.

He smiled. "Why, Ms. Hillman. Are you wantonly flirting with me?"

"I believe I am."

"Good." He covered her mouth with his, his arms tightening around her waist to pull her more firmly against him.

The kiss lasted a very long time, an expression of desire, of need, of so many confused emotions that Lindsay couldn't have easily identified. Neither of them were smiling when Nick finally lifted his head.

"Are you sure you have to go?" Lindsay asked huskily, pressing closer to him and feeling his body's immediate, powerful response.

He groaned and his hands tightened for a moment at her waist. And then he released her and stepped back. "I think I'd better. I'll pick you up at noon tomorrow, okay?"

"Make it twelve-thirty. It takes that long for me to get home from church." She considered asking him to attend the services with her, then changed her mind. Her family was already speculating about Lindsay's relationship with Nick. There was no need to set off gossip among her long-time family friends at church, many of whom had been trying to match her up with someone since she'd graduated from high school.

"Twelve-thirty," Nick repeated. "See you then."

She watched him leave, then exhaled gustily and sank into a chair, covering her face with her hands and emitting a low moan. Her mind was spinning, partially as a delayed reaction to that powerful kiss, but also at the changes going on in her life. Everything had been so easy a few months ago, she thought wistfully. She'd had her job, her family, her friends. Her safe, comfortable, sometimes monotonous, but usually pleasant routines.

Now there was Nick—and a brother and two sisters she didn't know. All of them seemed to expect something from her, but she had no idea what any of them really wanted. According to Tony D'Alessandro, his wife and her siblings only wanted to meet her, to find out what she was like and how she'd fared after their separation. As for Nick—well, he obviously wanted her physically, seemed to enjoy her company, had even hinted a time or two about a relationship that went beyond a casual affair. But she couldn't have even begun to guess at his true feelings for her, other than possessiveness, overprotectiveness and desire. He camouflaged his deeper emotions so well. So damned obsessively.

An uncomfortable suspicion tapped at the back of her mind, refusing to allow her to totally reject it. What if Nick had decided it was time for him to marry and start a family, the next logical step for a successful young physician on his way to the top? What if he'd chosen Lindsay because he was fond of her family and considered her a suitable bride for a man in his position?

Yes, he was attracted to her—after making love with him more than once, she was convinced of that. But that was far from enough for her. She needed his trust, his total commitment and his love. She needed him to love her as fully, as passionately, as helplessly as she had come to love him. But she wasn't sure Nick Grant would ever allow himself to be that vulnerable to anyone. And she could never settle for anything less.

Stalemate, again.

She sighed and lifted her head. She refused to sit around moping for the rest of the evening. She had papers to grade, laundry to do, letters to write. She had a life.

If only her life weren't becoming quite so complicated. Something told her that her previously comfortable, safe and predictable existence would never be quite the same again, now that it had been invaded by Dr. Nick Grant and three mysterious, long-lost siblings.

Thanksgiving at the Hillman home was a noisy, festive affair. The house was filled with the sounds of televised football games, adults talking and laughing, a child singing to her dolly and a baby babbling at his toes. The smells of turkey and dressing, sweet potatoes and fresh-baked rolls, pumpkin and pecan pies drifted from the kitchen. Lindsay loved every minute of it.

She glanced contentedly around the filled-to-capacity den. Earl and Greg engaged in a heated discussion of who should be named Most Valuable Player of the football game currently in progress, while Paula prompted Tricia on the words to an old nursery rhyme and kept one eye on Zane, who was just learning to pull himself up onto furniture in search of interesting playthings. Steve and Kim sat side by side on the couch, holding hands and possibly dreaming about future holidays with their own soon-to-be-born child.

Evelyn had shooed everyone out of her kitchen while she made last-minute preparations for the meal she'd be serving in a few minutes. Despite all efforts to assist her, Evelyn took great pride in her holiday meals and rarely allowed anyone to interfere with her long-set way of doing things.

In one corner of the den, Nick sat talking quietly to Scott, who seemed a bit depressed by the holiday. It wasn't an uncommon reaction among the foster kids, most of whom, like Scott, had little experience with traditional family events. Lindsay hadn't been surprised when Nick had taken one look at Scott and immediately engaged the boy in a conversation about dirt-bike racing. Nick, of course, would understand exactly how Scott felt today. Lindsay vaguely remembered a couple of earlier Thanksgivings, when it had been Nick on the outside of the family circle, resisting all efforts to draw him in.

Later, after dinner had been consumed and the remains cleared away, the house would be even more crowded with visitors. Traditionally on Thanksgiving afternoon, former foster sons of the Hillman family would drop in for a visit, bringing their wives and children if they had them, to pay respect to the couple who'd sometimes been the only real parents the young men had known. Lindsay expected the first caller to be Aaron Ford, a thirty-year-old banker who'd spent three years with the Hillmans after his own family had thrown him out.

At the age of sixteen, Aaron had openly declared that he was gay—and had been viciously ostracized by his family because of his announcement. Other foster homes had refused him, but the Hillmans had taken him in without demur, giving him the love, guidance and encouragement he'd needed as much as the other boys then in residence, heatedly rejecting criticism that they were exposing their own sons to unfavorable influence. Aaron still adored the couple who'd given him a home without judging or condemning him. He visited often, as did so many of the others who'd found a home with the Hillmans when no one else had wanted them.

Her heart swelling with love and pride for her parents, Lindsay wondered for at least the hundredth time if she was making a mistake by leaving for Dallas the next morning. She had the most wonderful family in the world here. Why was she going off to meet these people she knew nothing about?

Thank goodness Nick had convinced her to take him along. She felt much more comfortable knowing he'd be there, a familiar, concerned face among strangers.

She'd seen quite a bit of Nick during the past two weeks, though their relationship hadn't progressed as far as she would have liked. He was a considerate, thoughtful, attentive escort and a passionate, exciting, generous lover—but he was still as much of a mystery to Lindsay as he'd ever been. She knew what he was like outwardly, what a genuinely kind man and dedicated physician he was, but she could no more than guess at what truly motivated him, what memories lurked behind his smooth words and practiced smiles.

Evelyn appeared in the doorway. She didn't have to raise her voice to get everyone's attention; the room immediately grew quiet. Lindsay smiled as her mother efficiently organized everyone into a hand-linked circle for the blessing—which, Evelyn decided, would be led by Greg this time. Greg didn't argue—he wouldn't have bothered even had he wanted to, since everyone knew that Evelyn would have only looked at him without blinking and calmly waited for him to begin the prayer.

Nick's hand held warmly in her right hand and her mother's in her left, Lindsay bowed her head and silently expressed her gratitude for the family she'd been given, that they were all together now and that Earl's recent, frightening illness had not taken him from them. And then she prayed that she wasn't heading into disaster—with Nick, or with the family who waited in Dallas to meet her on the following day.

During the afternoon with the garrulous, demonstrative Hillman family, Nick found himself standing on the sidelines, feeling at times as though he was watching the festivities through a thick pane of glass. It wasn't a new sensation for him—he'd often felt that way during the two years he'd lived with them during high school. The fault wasn't theirs—they did everything they could to draw him into the merrymaking.

It was Nick who held back, Nick who found himself at an occasional loss at what to say, what to do to fit in. He spent quite a bit of the afternoon with young Scott, who seemed to have some of the same feelings about the Hillman family that Nick did—affection, envy and outright bemusement, to name a few.

Lindsay, of course, had no such problems. She stayed right in the middle of the activities all afternoon, chatting with her mother and sisters-in-law, playing with her niece and nephew, teasing with her brothers and the "honorary brothers" who visited during the afternoon.

If there was ever a moment when Lindsay felt uncomfortable or at a loss for words with the others, Nick never noticed—and he watched her most of the afternoon, fascinated by the complex, whimsical, loving and articulate woman who had become such an important part of his life in such a short time. And yet, something changed when she turned to him—something that bothered him a great deal.

With the others, Lindsay was open, laughing, unrestrained. Only with Nick did she seem to choose her words with care, check her natural tendencies to touch and hug. Only with him did she seem at all self-conscious or uncomfortable.

He didn't like it. Yet he knew her hesitation was a direct reaction to his own rather obsessive reserve. He couldn't blame Lindsay for being less open with him than with the others when he had never fully opened up to her—and had no intention of doing so anytime in the near future. His fear of his past was proving to be justified in more ways than one. Not only did he worry about how Lindsay would react, whether she would pull away from him if she knew all the ugly details, but now he felt it looming between them despite his best efforts to keep it locked away.

He felt his fists tightening deep in the pockets of his slacks, and he consciously relaxed them before anyone noticed. He wouldn't lose Lindsay, he told himself fiercely. Nothing in his life had ever been more worth fighting for— not even his degree and the place in society he'd single-mindedly shaped for himself. Whatever it took—whatever he had to give—he wouldn't lose her.

Lindsay could tell Nick had something on his mind when he took her home later that evening. He accepted her offer of coffee, then paced the living room with the cup cradled unnoticed in his hands until Lindsay couldn't stand it any longer. "Nick, is something wrong?"

He stopped pacing and turned to her. "I was thinking about tomorrow."

"What about tomorrow?" Had he now changed his mind about going with her? She just might throw something at him if he had, after making such a fuss about it initially.

"It's not too late to change your mind, Lindsay. You could always call D'Alessandro and tell him something's come up."

She blinked. "Now, why would I want to do that?"

"You know why," he answered roughly. "I still think this is one hell of a lousy idea. I've had a bad feeling about it from the beginning, and the closer it gets, the less I like it."

She sighed and crossed her arms. "You're claiming to be psychic now?"

"No, I'm not claiming to be psychic," Nick snapped, setting the coffee cup on a coaster with exaggerated care, as if he'd really prefer to slam it down regardless of the consequences. "All I'm saying is that I usually have good instincts about things like this, and this trip doesn't feel right to me. You know how I feel about digging up the past."

"Believe me, Nick, I know how you feel about that. You've certainly told me enough times."

"There's no need to get sarcastic, Lindsay. I'm only trying to keep you out of trouble."

"And I don't believe there's anything for you to worry about. If you've changed your mind about going with me, say so. I'll go alone."

"I haven't changed my mind, and you're not going alone. I just wish you'd reconsider the whole thing."

"The decision has already been made," she insisted. "I'm going—with or without you."

His jaw tightened. "Fine. Just don't blame me if the whole thing blows up in your face."

"Don't worry. I won't." She glared at him.

"Damn, you're stubborn."

Despite her annoyance, the corners of her mouth twitched at his plaintive grumble. "Yes. So are you."

"Could be a problem."

"Does that mean you're sorry we ever got involved?" she demanded.

He shook his head. "No. I guess I've always been a sucker for a challenge."

"Gee. Thanks a lot."

He smiled then, for the first time since they'd returned from her parents' house. "You're welcome."

"I wish you'd sit down," she complained, relieved that the argument appeared to be over—for now, at least. "I'm exhausted from all the commotion today. How can we relax if you keep pacing the room like a caged tiger?"

"A caged tiger, hmm?" He didn't appear perturbed by the comparison, though he compliantly took a seat beside her on the couch. "You see me as a wild animal?"

"Certainly not a fully tamed one," she replied with a slight smile, thinking of all those mysterious, dark places hidden inside him. Nick was every bit as unmanageable and unpredictable as a half-tamed tiger—she just didn't seem to have the sense to keep her distance from him.

"I think you could be very dangerous, Nick Grant," she murmured, thinking of the danger her heart had been in from the moment she'd lost it to him.

His own smile faded abruptly. "No," he said flatly. "Not to you, Lindsay. Never to you."

He pulled her to him and kissed her, giving her no more opportunity to reflect on the wisdom of being with him. When he kissed her this way, there was nowhere else she wanted to be.

When Lindsay's doorbell buzzed Friday morning, she thought Nick had arrived almost an hour earlier than expected. Leaving her half-packed suitcase open on the bed, she headed for the front door, wondering if Nick had decided to make one last attempt to change her mind about the trip to Dallas. She really hoped she wouldn't have to spend the next hour waging that futile argument with him. Why couldn't he just accept that she'd made up her mind and she wasn't going to change it, no matter how nervous she'd been from the moment she'd awakened that morning?

But it was Evelyn, not Nick, who stood on the other side of Lindsay's door, a small photograph album held in her hands. "I know you're in a rush, and I probably should have called first," Evelyn said, glancing beyond Lindsay as though to check if her daughter was alone. "I decided on impulse to bring you this, and I didn't stop to think about calling to make sure you had time for me."

"Of course I have time for you, Mother," Lindsay scolded affectionately, pulling her into the room. "Always. What have you brought for me?"

Evelyn's smile looked just a bit uncertain. "I spent a few hours last night putting together some photographs of you growing up—from the time you joined our family until you graduated from college. There are several shots of you at dance classes and piano recitals, and pictures taken with your brothers and your father and me. I thought your sisters and brother might like to see for themselves that you had a happy childhood."

Touched by her mother's unselfish gesture, Lindsay took the album and clutched it to her chest. "What a nice idea! It never occurred to me that they might like to see photographs. Thanks, Mother."

"You're welcome. These photos are all duplicates, so you may keep the album after you return. I thought you might like to have it."

"Of course I want it." Still cradling the album in one arm, Lindsay threw the other around her mother's neck for a quick, hard hug. "Thank you."

Evelyn took a deep breath. "You look lovely. I've always liked that dress—it's almost exactly the same color as your eyes. Are you all packed? Is there anything I can do to help?"

"You can give me some advice about what to take," Lindsay suggested. "I was having a hard time deciding."

"I'd be glad to." A few moments later, Evelyn stood over Lindsay's suitcase, shaking her head in exasperation. She was already pulling things out and laying them aside when she began to speak. "Honestly, Lindsay, you still haven't learned to pack without wrinkling all your clothes. How many times have I told you to use tissue paper between the layers?"

Lindsay hid a smile. "I don't have any," she confessed, hanging her head. "I meant to get some, but I forgot."

Evelyn clucked her disapproval, but set to work with admirable efficiency. "We'll just have to do our best without it, then. We'll put the heavy things in first, and then..."

Lindsay stood back good-naturedly and allowed Evelyn to take over the packing, knowing this was something her mother needed to do. She waited until the time seemed right to ask, "Does it bother you, Mom? That I'm going to Dallas, I mean."

Evelyn's hands stilled only a moment before reaching for another blouse to be neatly folded and tucked into the suitcase. "Maybe a little," she admitted. "I suppose your father and I feel a bit... threatened."

"You shouldn't, you know. These people could never take the place of my real family."

Evelyn smiled faintly. "I know. Still, they *are* your blood relatives and that has to mean something to you."

"It makes me curious, that's all."

"It's more than that, Lindsay," Evelyn corrected. "You feel drawn to meet them—a need to know them. I understand. It's the way I'd feel under the same circumstances."

Lindsay tucked a strand of hair behind her ear and nodded slowly. "I suppose you're right. Ever since Tony told me about them—well, I've wanted to meet them. But that doesn't mean," she added hastily, "that I've ever been unhappy with the family I've grown up with. You know I never made any effort to track down my biological relatives, that I was never one of those adopted kids obsessed with knowing all the details of their conception or birth."

"Yes, I know. We never made any secret of your adoption, and you always accepted it very matter-of-factly. You rarely asked questions or made reference to it. I always chose to believe that was because you were happy and content with us."

"Of course that was why," Lindsay assured her, her eyes pricking with tears. "I love you, Mother. You're my real mother, just as Dad's my real father. The two of you and Greg and Steve and Paula and Kim and the kids—you're all the family I've ever wanted or will ever need. Please believe that."

"I do, darling." Evelyn turned away from the suitcase for a moment to give Lindsay a fierce hug. "I love you, too."

Lindsay swiped at her damp eyes with the back of one hand as she drew away. "I know."

Evelyn lifted a lacy half-slip and folded it with care. "You know," she mused quietly, "it's odd, but for some reason, I always half expected this to happen someday. I didn't know for certain that you had any brothers or sisters—we didn't ask many questions about your birth family, other than to determine that you were in good health and that both your parents had died. But I've always had a feeling that someday you'd be confronted by your past. I even mentioned it to Earl once, when you were little. He told me I was just being fanciful."

"You never told me you had premonitions, Mother," Lindsay murmured, fascinated.

Evelyn looked embarrassed and shook her head. "I don't, not usually. Only about this."

"So you think I'm doing the right thing?" Lindsay couldn't resist asking, suddenly needing her mother's reassurance.

Evelyn closed the suitcase. "Yes. If you don't go, you'll always wonder if you should have. Still, I have to confess I'm very glad Nick's going with you. I know he doesn't approve of the whole thing, but at least he'll be there for you if things don't work out exactly as you'd like them to."

"I know. I think Nick's one of the main reasons I have to make this trip," Lindsay admitted.

Evelyn tilted her head in question. "Why is that?"

Trying to choose the right words, Lindsay gestured vaguely with her hands as she attempted to answer. "I keep thinking that maybe Nick needs this almost as much as I do. Maybe, in helping me face *my* past, Nick will learn to come to terms with his own. I've spent so many hours thinking about this, worrying about the problems we've had—and I've decided that Nick and I can never be truly happy together until he learns to accept whatever it is in his past that he's been hiding from for so many years. He can't make his unhappy childhood go away by pretending it never happened, but that's exactly what he's been trying to do. And I think it's eating at him."

"I think you're right," Evelyn said thoughtfully. "It's that dark side of him I mentioned to you before. Like a wound that won't heal because he won't allow it to be treated. He needs to talk about his past, needs to share it with someone who cares, someone who won't judge or pity him. Someone who'll understand the pain he went through and how far he's come since. I think you could be the one, Lindsay. After watching the two of you together during the past few weeks, I'm beginning to believe Nick cares a great deal for you—probably more than he's ever allowed himself to care about anyone else."

"I hope you're right," Lindsay murmured. "But I'll never be sure of that until he learns to open up to me—to really share his feelings with me. It has to be more than words, more than superficial emotions. I have to know," she added shakily, "that Nick loves and needs me as desperately as I'm starting to love and need him."

"Oh, baby, I know." Evelyn stroked Lindsay's hair in much the same way she had when Lindsay had been a child, turning to her mother for comfort or reassurance. "You haven't picked an easy man to love, darling. I suppose I always knew you wouldn't. But I truly believe he's a good man. And you don't give up easily. I'd say if anyone has a chance of getting through to Nick Grant, it's you."

"I hope you're right," Lindsay repeated, blinking back the nervous tears she refused to shed. She swallowed hard when the doorbell buzzed again. "Speaking of Nick..."

"Well, don't just stand there—go let him in. I'll look around and make sure you're not leaving anything important behind."

Lindsay nodded and turned toward the doorway. She paused just long enough to glance over her shoulder. "Mother? Thanks for coming by. I needed you this morning."

Evelyn nodded her understanding. "I thought you might."

The doorbell buzzed again, sounding more impatient this time, and Lindsay turned to hurry through the living room, carrying the warmth of her mother's love with her. She pulled open the door with a determined smile of welcome. "Good morning, Nick."

He looked wonderful, as always, in a navy jacket, open-collared blue shirt and crisp tan slacks. Studying his expression closely, Lindsay decided he didn't look argumentative, just resigned. Which had to mean he'd reached the conclusion that there was nothing left to say that would change Lindsay's mind. He didn't like it, but he'd accepted it.

She felt her shoulders relax. "I'm almost ready. Mother's in the bedroom, making a last-minute check for me."

Nick nodded. "No hurry. Our plane doesn't leave for over an hour yet."

"I know, but I hate to rush into the airport at the last minute. I'm nervous enough about flying without worrying about missing the plane."

"You're afraid of flying? You didn't mention it before."

"It's not that bad—I'm just more comfortable on the ground than in the air," she assured him. "Can I get you anything before we go?"

"No, thanks." He brushed her lips with his own as he passed by her, into the room. "You look nice."

Her spine-length ripple of response seemed out of proportion to the casual caress—but then, she'd almost gotten used to overreacting to Nick. She moistened her lips and smiled. "Thanks. So do you."

"Good morning, Nick." Evelyn emerged from the bedroom with Lindsay's bag in her hands.

Nick reached out immediately to take the suitcase from her. "Good morning. Seeing us off?"

"Yes. I was just telling Lindsay how glad I am you're going with her on this trip. I'm sure she'd be just fine, but it makes me feel better knowing you'll be along to keep an eye on her."

Lindsay resisted an impulse to roll her eyes at her mother's old-fashioned pleasure that her daughter would have a man along to "take care of her." Thoroughly modern in some ways, Evelyn was hopelessly outdated in others—many of them having to do with Lindsay.

"Believe me, Evelyn," Nick murmured, with a glance at Lindsay. "Nothing's going to happen to Lindsay while I'm around to prevent it."

Evelyn smiled and patted Nick's arm. "That's nice to hear. I wouldn't want anyone hurting my Lindsay."

Lindsay winced at the less-than-subtle admonition. Nick probably interpreted it just as easily as she did, but he didn't even blink as he returned Evelyn's smile. "Neither would I, Evelyn. Trust me."

"I'm trying, Nick," Evelyn returned gently. "I really am."

And then she turned to give Lindsay one last hug. "Be careful, and call me as soon as you get back, okay?"

"I will. 'Bye, Mother."

A few moments later, Lindsay found herself alone with Nick. Still embarrassed by her mother's hints to him, Lindsay cleared her throat and avoided his eyes. "Shall we go?"

"Yeah. I guess so." Nick didn't exactly sound thrilled, but he swung her bag into his other hand and reached for the door. Lindsay picked up her coat and purse, made one last, quick visual check of her apartment, and followed Nick into the parking lot, wondering once again how much her life would be changed as a result of this trip to Dallas.

Chapter Ten

Tony met them at the airport. Lindsay spotted him in the crowd the moment she walked out of the jetway into the waiting area. She smiled and waved to him.

He returned the smile and took her outstretched hand in his own. "Lindsay. I'm so glad you came. Everyone's looking forward to meeting you."

Lindsay's smile wavered a bit, but she held it. "I'm a little nervous," she confessed.

His dark eyes expressed his understanding. "I know. So are the others," he assured her. "Let's just play it by ear, shall we?"

She nodded her agreement, then released his hand and glanced at Nick, who stood expressionlessly behind her. "You remember Nick, of course."

"Of course." Tony's tone was just a bit wry as he extended his hand. "Welcome to Dallas, Dr. Grant."

"Nick will do," he said, taking Tony's hand in a brief shake.

"Right." Tony turned back to Lindsay. "The baggage claim area is this way," he said with a gesture to his left.

Lindsay murmured a response, giving Nick one last glance of warning before they started walking. He returned it with a blandly questioning look back at her, though she knew he was well aware that she'd just silently ordered him to behave himself. Whether he'd choose to comply with that order remained to be seen.

The size and elegance of the home to which Tony drove them caught Lindsay by surprise. The huge Tudor was surrounded by massive security gates, behind which lay rolling, beautifully landscaped lawns that surely had to be professionally maintained. Had this been her home when he'd married her? If so, she'd been raised with more money than Lindsay would have imagined. She swallowed hard. "So—um—this is your home?"

Tony nodded. "It was Michelle's family home," he answered, confirming Lindsay's suspicion. "My two brothers and I were raised in a three-bedroom brick-and-frame house in an average middle-class neighborhood. I'm still trying to get used to living in a place where half the rooms are never even used."

"It looks like a wonderful place to raise a large family," Lindsay murmured, picturing ball games and bike rides on the sweeping grounds.

"That's what Michelle and I think," Tony agreed contentedly. "We'd like to have a baby soon—the first of several, we hope."

He parked his Jeep in the circular driveway alongside some others of modest vintage—a battered pickup and a family-type minivan—and reached for his door handle. "I'll leave the Jeep out so I can take you to your hotel later. I've arranged for a rental for your use during the weekend—I thought it would be more convenient for you than depending on us or cabs for transportation. It should be waiting for you at the hotel."

"That was very thoughtful of you, Tony. Thank you."

"You're welcome, Lindsay. Ready to go meet your family now?"

Nick spoke from the back seat, the first time he'd done so since leaving the airport. "Lindsay has a family, D'Alessandro. The Hillmans. Try to keep that in mind, will you?"

"Nick, please." Lindsay turned in the seat to look at him. "Don't make me wish you'd stayed in Little Rock."

He looked annoyed for a moment, then shook his head. "Sorry. I'll try to behave."

"I'd appreciate that." She gave him a smile, suspecting he'd reacted to Tony's choice of words because of his deep loyalty to the Hillmans. Or was she only making excuses for him again?

It seemed to Lindsay that there must have been a dozen people waiting to greet her in the enormous wood-panelled den to which Tony led them. On closer look, she saw that there were nine, counting three small children who were quietly watching an animated program on a television in one corner of the room.

Still, it wasn't the number of people there that startled Lindsay most—it was the strong resemblance to herself she saw in several of them. Two of the three women in the room had hair the exact toast brown color of Lindsay's, and eyes the same dark blue. One looked older than the other, her hair just touched with gray, her face a bit lined around the eyes.

The one who came forward first to greet her could have stepped out of Lindsay's mirror. She couldn't help staring, even as she automatically took the hand the other woman offered.

"Lindsay, I'm so glad you could come," the woman, who had to be Tony's wife, Michelle, said warmly. "I'm Michelle D'Alessandro," she added, confirming the guess.

"It's—um—nice to meet you." Lindsay spoke a bit more shyly than usual, still rather startled at meeting someone who looked so very much like herself.

Michelle smiled her understanding of Lindsay's uncertainty. "I felt the same way when I met Layla a few months ago. I suppose people who have been raised with their biological families take the resemblances for granted, but it's a bit startling when you encounter it for the first time as an adult, isn't it?"

"Yes, it is," Lindsay admitted. "I didn't quite expect it." She glanced at Nick to judge his reaction to Michelle, only to find him watching her in return. "Michelle, this is Dr. Nick Grant." She left it at that, not certain how she'd have described Nick's relationship to her if she'd tried.

Michelle shook Nick's hand and graciously welcomed him to her home, then turned to the others. "Layla—" She held out a hand, and her sister stepped forward to take it. "Don't you want to say something to Lindsay?"

Layla was obviously struggling against tears. "I don't want to embarrass you," she murmured to Lindsay, managing a shaky smile. "I know you don't remember me, but I remember you so clearly. Our mother went back to work at two jobs soon after you were born, and Jared and I took turns caring for you so she could rest during the few hours when she wasn't working. A neighbor kept you during school hours, but we had you in the afternoons and evenings. You were such a good baby, Lindsay. Your first smile was for me, your first laugh for Jared. I missed you so much when they took you away."

Touched by Layla's unmistakable sincerity, Lindsay held out a hand to her. "My mother tells me that I was healthy and happy when I was adopted, that I had obviously been treated very well during the early months of my life. Thank you for taking such good care of me, Layla."

Layla's eyes filled, but her smile grew more radiant. Lindsay had apparently chosen the right words to please her. "You're welcome." She turned her head. "I'd like you to meet my husband, Kevin Samples."

Towheaded, freckled, a few pounds overweight, Kevin Samples pumped Lindsay's hand with a friendly grin. "Nice to meet you, Lindsay. You, too, Dr. Grant," he added, offering Nick an equally enthusiastic handshake.

"Just call me Nick."

"Thanks. Those are our kids over at the TV. Dawn's eight, Keith's five and Brittany's close to three. I'd call 'em over to shake hands, but they aren't this quiet very often."

Lindsay smiled. "They're beautiful children."

"Thanks."

A teenage boy who'd been waiting patiently among the crowd, cleared his throat noisily. Studying his dancing blue eyes and infectious grin, Lindsay liked him immediately, deciding he looked like a young, masculine version of her siblings—and, presumably, herself.

Michelle gave the young man an indulgent smile. "All right, Shane, we're getting to your family. Lindsay, Nick, this is Jared Walker, and his wife, Cassie. I'll let Jared decide whether he wants to claim that scruffy teenager dancing around behind him."

For some reason, Lindsay was more nervous at meeting her brother than she had been with her sisters. Maybe because thirty-five-year-old Jared, though undeniably handsome in a rough-hewn way, was a rather intimidating-looking man. He was several inches shorter than Nick, no more than five-nine, perhaps, but looked strong and muscular, not an ounce of fat on his hard, lean body. His brown hair was functionally cut, his skin—except for a thin, recent-looking scar at his left temple—tanned by hours in the sun, his hand large and calloused when it gripped hers. A man who'd spent many hours at hard labor, Lindsay decided, relaxing a bit when she noticed the faint smile mirrored in his blue eyes. "Hello, Jared."

"Lindsay." His gaze swept her only momentarily before returning to her face, but something told her he'd missed very little in his quick examination. "It's good to see you again. I wasn't sure you'd choose to come—and I wouldn't have blamed you if you hadn't, since we're all strangers to you—but I'm glad you decided to pay us a visit."

He turned then to Nick. As the two men shook hands, Lindsay was struck by the similarities between them. It wasn't a physical resemblance, and their professions were certainly different—she remembered Tony's comment that Jared had recently purchased a small ranch close to Dallas. But still, there were other things one could detect just by looking at these two men—toughness, control, pride—several qualities that made Lindsay suspect Jared and Nick probably had a great deal in common. Maybe because they'd both been raised in foster homes, both having to learn to take care of themselves at young ages. Maybe because neither of them had found life easy, but had found his own ways of dealing with the difficulties.

About the same age as Lindsay and Michelle, Cassie Walker was small and copper-haired, her cheerful grin and merry eyes hinting at an outgoing, energetic, tenacious personality. At first glance, she seemed to be quiet, reserved, Jared's direct opposite. Lindsay suspected that the whirlwind courtship Tony had described had been due to Jared's fascination with the very qualities that made Cassie so different, and yet so suitable for him.

"Jared and I have only been married for six weeks," Cassie explained. "I work for Tony, though I'm taking a leave of absence now to get settled onto our new ranch. I think it's great that my new family keeps getting bigger."

Shane cleared his throat more forcefully. "Isn't *anyone* going to introduce me to my aunt?" he demanded, smiling at Lindsay. "What am I, chopped liver?"

"Watch your step, Shane, or I'll take you out behind the woodshed and give you a whalin'," Cassie threatened mockingly.

Shane grinned at his stepmother and stepped closer to her, so that they stood eye to eye. "You and what army?" he challenged.

"This one," Jared murmured.

Shane gulped noisily and held up his hands in surrender. "That'll work."

Lindsay laughed, already enchanted by the young man. She was comfortable with young teenagers, since she'd chosen to teach that group. Kids this age tended to still be young enough to be curious and enthusiastic, yet old enough to provide stimulating conversation whenever an adult went to the effort of listening to them. "Hello, Shane."

"Hi." He gave her a once-over as quick and comprehensive as his father's had been. "You sure don't look like an English teacher, even though Tony said that's what you are."

"He was right—I am. And thanks. I think."

"It was a compliment," he assured her. "My English teacher weighs about two hundred pounds, has muscles that could crush solid steel, and a mustache. Her name's Mrs. Newby."

Lindsay laughed. "I'm sure she's a very fine teacher."

"She has some excellent students to work with," Shane bragged, looking delightfully mischievous. "Me, for example."

"She probably considers herself extremely fortunate to have been given the opportunity to work with you," Lindsay returned gravely.

Shane grinned. "I like this one, Dad. Can I keep her, huh?"

"You've already adopted a horse and two dogs, Shane. No more pets for now," Jared answered mildly.

"I'm too much trouble, anyway," Lindsay assured Shane with a smile. "Always wanting to be walked and fed."

"Speaking of being fed..." Tony hinted with a look at his wife.

"Dinner should be ready," Michelle agreed. "I hope everyone's hungry. Betty—our housekeeper—has been bustling around the kitchen since early this morning getting ready for this. She loves having company for dinner."

Feeling a hand settle at her waist, Lindsay looked up to find Nick still watching her closely. She covered his hand with hers and smiled to show him she was enjoying the visit and didn't regret her decision to meet these people. It meant a great deal to her to share this significant event in her life with Nick, even if he was there under protest.

There was nothing formal or quiet about dinner that evening. Comfortable and familiar with the pandemonium of a large family gathering, Lindsay found herself relaxed and contented during the meal, talking easily with the others gathered around the large table in Michelle's elegant dining room.

She learned quite a bit about her siblings during the course of the meal. Layla worked selling real estate in nearby Fort Worth, and Kevin was an accountant. Jared had been in the navy for several years before leaving the service just over two years ago to be a full-time father to Shane. Michelle was heavily involved with charity work and particularly fond of her volunteer job as a "baby rocker" in the intensive-care nursery of a large Dallas hospital.

Layla and Jared shared stories with the others about the early years of their family, the years before their parents died and the children were split up. Lindsay laughed often at the funny incidents her older brother and sister remembered—though her smile faded when Jared mentioned the harder times. Their father's drinking, his death, their mother's desperate attempts to feed her large family afterward by working too hard and too long, resulting in her own death from neglect of pneumonia.

As he so often seemed to do, Shane diverted the group from the slight melancholy that had fallen over them. "Tell Lindsay the neat part—you know, the way everyone was born on different days and you each have a line in a poem," he urged.

Lindsay lifted an eyebrow in question. "What are you talking about, Shane?"

"You know, that old poem about Monday's child and Tuesday's child and so on. There were seven Walker kids and all of 'em were born on a different day—even the twins, because one was born before midnight and one after. Cool, huh?"

"Jared and I particularly remembered that because it amused our mother so much," Layla explained. "She was always quoting the poem, particularly when one of us did something that seemed to apply to our day."

"Remember when Bobby asked Mama if it was true that Michelle was full of 'grapes'?" Jared asked Layla with a chuckle. "He'd misunderstood the line of the poem for Tuesday's child."

"And you said you didn't want to be Saturday's child, because you didn't want to have to work hard for your living," Layla reminded him.

Jared shrugged. "Guess I didn't really have any choice about that. I'm still working—but at least it's at something I like doing now." He gave Layla a smile. "You were always embarrassed when we teased you about being Monday's child, 'fair of face.' Of course, you were—and still are."

Layla blushed—much the way she probably had when teased as a child, Lindsay thought in amusement. "What day was I?" she couldn't resist asking.

"Sunday," Layla and Jared replied, almost in unison.

" 'The child who's born on the Sabbath day is fair and wise and good and gay,' " Layla added, smiling at Lindsay.

"Guess you're glad you weren't born on *that* day, huh, Dad?" Shane murmured mischievously.

"I've told you it's an old poem, Shane," Jared answered admonishingly. "With the old meanings for the words used in it. Now put a lid on it."

"Yes, Dad."

Lindsay giggled, sharing a warmly amused glance with Michelle.

"They're really nice people, aren't they?" Lindsay asked Nick later that evening, when they were finally alone again in the hotel room Tony had arranged for them. "All of them."

Nick agreed, cautious as always. "The Walkers and Sampleses seemed like average types."

"What about Michelle and Tony?"

"A wealthy philanthropist and a private investigator living in a walled-in mansion with a housekeeper and gardener? Not exactly average, Lindsay."

"I suppose you're right. But, still, they're nice. I like them."

Nick nodded. "I could tell that you did."

"What about you?"

"They're okay."

"And . . . ?"

He frowned at her. "Okay, I liked them. Are you satisfied?"

She grinned. "Yes. Do you see how wrong you were now to be worried about me? They only wanted to get to know me—they don't want anything else from me that I'm not willing to offer. I'm in no danger from them at all."

"Are you trying to say 'I told you so'?"

"I'm saying it," she replied flippantly. "Told you so."

"That's an obnoxious habit, Lindsay. Not one you want to start."

"I'll keep it in mind," she answered, pleased that he was smiling a little. "I'm glad I came, Nick. And I'm glad you came with me."

He nodded again and started to unbutton his shirt. "I think I'll take a shower."

"I'm really looking forward to the cookout at Jared's ranch tomorrow. That should be lots of fun. Isn't Shane terrific? So bright and witty and personable. I think he's my absolute favorite of the bunch."

Nick shrugged out of the shirt and tossed it over the back of one of two identical striped wing chairs which sat in a corner of the plush hotel room with which they'd been provided. "Shane's definitely interesting," he agreed. "Seems older than his age, in some ways. I suppose it comes from having Jared for a father. Jared doesn't treat him like a kid, probably never has."

"No. But Shane's only lived full-time with Jared for the past two years. Cassie told me a little about Shane's background, and it's heartbreaking. His mother's an alcoholic, his stepfather, a very unlikable man who didn't treat Shane well. Jared was away a lot in the navy and Shane was badly neglected at home. Cassie said Jared tried for years to get custody of the boy, but didn't succeed until Shane took matters into his own hands and ran away from home at the age of twelve. He lived on the streets of Memphis, Tennessee, for weeks by himself until Jared found him. That's when Jared left the navy and gained full custody of Shane.''

Nick looked startled. ''Alone on the streets at twelve? It's a wonder the kid survived!''

''Cassie said he was very lucky, that he survived the experience relatively unscathed. Still, I think that's why he seems so mature for his age. He learned to take care of himself early.''

''Yeah, well, a lot of us had to,'' Nick muttered, kicking off his shoes and reaching for the buckle of his belt. ''Few people are lucky enough to have the so-called normal, TV sitcom family life you had, Lindsay. You should be grateful the Hillmans took you in, that you weren't stuck with a family of drunks or a series of unsatisfactory foster homes.''

''Of course I'm grateful for that!'' Lindsay was annoyed by his rather preachy tone. ''I've said so many times, Nick. And I'm not so sheltered or naive that I'm not aware of how difficult life can be for children. I've been teaching in public schools for three years, remember?''

Nick's slacks fell on top of the shirt over the back of the chair, leaving him clad only in white briefs. Lindsay tried very hard not to be distracted from the conversation by the sight of him, but it wasn't easy. The man was so damned delectable.

''Just don't get so infatuated with these people that you forget who your *real* family is,'' he warned, turning toward the bathroom. ''No matter how amusing and pleasant this group is, they're not the ones who were always there for you when you were little, or who took care of you when you were sick or hurt or scared.''

"Why do you seem to think you have an obligation to keep reminding me of my family?'' she demanded in exasperation. "I'm hardly likely to forget them, Nick, and I'm certain none of them asked you to serve as their representative.''

"Not in so many words," he agreed, pausing for a moment in the open door to the bathroom. "But I know they're all worried about losing you to these people claiming to be your real family. I just want to make sure that doesn't happen.''

He closed the bathroom door between them before she had a chance to sputter an answer.

Lindsay planted her fists on her hips and stared at the bathroom door for a long time, trying very hard to understand Nick Grant. Was he really so concerned that Lindsay could ever be seduced away from the family who'd given her all the love and care she could ever have asked for as a child? Or was he more worried that she could be seduced away from *him?* Was Nick feeling threatened by these people who'd so easily won her friendship and admiration?

Didn't he know how ridiculous it was to even suggest that anyone could replace her family—or him—in her heart?

She shook her head, reminding herself that Nick still had a lot to learn about being involved in a serious, loving, committed relationship. There was still so much for her to teach him.

This weekend seemed like a very good opportunity for her to start some of those lessons. Thoughtfully, she reached for the top button of her blouse.

Only moments later, Nick looked up in surprise when Lindsay swept the shower curtain aside and stepped nude into the tub with him. "I've decided I need a shower, too," she informed him, trying to look as though she wasn't aware that her cheeks were flaming at her boldness. "And, just to save time..."

He reached for her. "I'll wash your back."

She twined her arms around his neck, bringing herself into full contact with his warm, wet body. "I was hoping you'd offer."

Chapter Eleven

There were times when Nick wondered if he were destined to spend his whole life standing on the sidelines, watching others connecting and communicating and sharing emotions that, for him, were so restrained and controlled he wasn't always even sure he had them. The first sixteen years of his life had been so unpleasant, so cold and isolated that it had taken him two full years with the Hillmans to learn how to interact on a social basis. He'd spent the years since training himself—to be a doctor, to be a well-respected, successful member of society, to be the type of person who might have a chance at building a family of his own with someone. Someone who knew what family meant.

Lindsay.

He watched her with by-now-familiar fascination during the next afternoon at the Walker ranch. He'd never seen anyone fit so easily into a crowd, even among a group she'd met only the day before. Already the children were calling her Aunt Lin, tagging worshipfully at her heels. The adults seemed captivated with her—even the reserved, less demonstrative Jared, whose rare smiles appeared for Lindsay almost as often as for the wife and son he obviously adored. Lindsay and bubbly, almost hyperactive Cassie Walker seemed to have formed an immediate, genuine friendship; the others appeared to be well on the way to pledging lifelong affection for her.

It was a phenomenon Nick had observed many times during the two years he'd spent with her Little Rock family—"Princess Lindsay" was in the process of assembling an all new group of loyal subjects.

Slouched in a wrought-iron chair at one of several matching round tables on a large brick patio behind the ranch house, Nick sipped a canned soft drink, toyed with the chips and half-eaten burger on his paper plate, and watched Lindsay find her place among her second family. It was a beautiful day for an outdoor cookout—clear, unseasonably warm, the autumn air just cool enough to hint at the rapidly approaching winter. Sitting in the sun, Nick pushed the sleeves of his dark sweater higher on his forearms and hooked his left thumb in the pocket of his jeans as he tried to understand how it could all seem so easy for her.

Didn't she worry that these people might disappoint her, that they might not be all she wanted them to be once she got to know them better? That they might hurt her, if she allowed them to get too close to her, if she allowed herself to start caring for them? Was she really naive enough to think that, just because these people were related to her, they posed no emotional threat to her?

Lindsay and Shane were standing a few feet away, laughing at some silliness they were carrying on while the others mingled around them. It struck Nick again how much Lindsay seemed to fit into the group, how many physical similarities there were between her and her sisters and brother—and her nephew. Shane, with his slightly shaggy brown hair and laughing blue eyes, could easily pass as Lindsay's younger brother. Was that why she felt so comfortable with this group so quickly—because she saw so much of herself in them?

Contemporary country music, just loud enough to be heard above the laughter and the chatter of the crowd, played from a portable stereo set up at one corner of the patio. Lindsay had discovered that Shane was a serious country music fan and the two had been discussing the recent releases of some of the bigger country stars—and some of the more obscure ones for which they'd uncovered a mutual preference. His own musical tastes running along slightly different lines, Nick stayed out of the conversation, choosing instead to observe and listen. He was watching Shane when the boy suddenly grinned and gestured toward the stereo.

"Hey, Lindsay. Bet you don't know the dance everyone was doing to this song last year," Shane challenged.

Lindsay tossed her head, hooked her thumbs in the waistband of her close-fitting jeans, and gave her nephew a smug grin. "Bet you're wrong."

Shane looked delighted. "You know the 'Achy Breaky Heart' dance? No fooling?"

A moment later they were side by side, kicking and turning and gyrating their hips in almost perfect unison while the adults watched with indulgent smiles and the children with blatant admiration. As far as Nick could tell, the song was nothing but countrified disco, complete with a driving beat and lightweight, rather inane lyrics, but Shane and Lindsay seemed to love it, throwing themselves into the dance and enthusiastically joining in with the chorus. The song ended and a rock-and-roll-type country swing number began.

Shane whirled Lindsay into a laughing, spinning two-step without missing a beat.

"Looks like you've got some serious competition for your lady," an amused voice commented just before a slender, dark young man slid into the chair beside Nick at the otherwise vacant table. "I think Shane's heavily infatuated with his new aunt."

"The feeling seems to be mutual." Nick drew his attention from Lindsay to glance at Joe D'Alessandro, Tony's younger brother. Nick had been told that Joe was a medical student from Houston, staying with his parents in Dallas for the long Thanksgiving weekend and obviously a welcome visitor for his brother's in-laws.

"You know, I've been hoping for months that Michelle's younger sister would turn out to be as beautiful and sweet as Michelle. Just my luck, she is—but she's already taken."

"She is most definitely taken," Nick answered flatly, just in case Joe was subtly testing the strength of Nick's commitment to Lindsay.

Joe lifted a hand in response to the unmistakable warning in Nick's words. "It's okay. I noticed that right off."

"Good."

Joe chuckled. "You sound a lot like Tony does whenever anyone starts checking out Michelle. Must be something about these Walker sisters that brings out the primitive side of a guy."

"Lindsay's a Hillman, not a Walker."

"And Michelle was raised as a Trent, but she was born a Walker," Joe answered with a shrug. "They might not have spent their childhood together, but they're still family. Look at them."

Nick looked. The second impromptu dance had ended. Lindsay was leaning against Jared's arm as she caught her breath, while Shane stood close by with one arm draped around his young stepmother's shoulders. Layla and Michelle stood arm in arm, teasing Lindsay and Shane about their breathlessness while Tony and Kevin leaned against the patio railing and grinned in almost palpable contentment.

Family.

"Damn," he muttered, not even aware he'd spoken aloud.

"It bothers you that she's fitting in so well with them?"

"No," Nick answered immediately. "Of course not." But it did, in a way that he couldn't have explained had he tried. Deep inside himself, he was feeling...well, *threatened* seemed to be the only word to quite describe it. And grimly aware that, once again, Lindsay seemed perfectly, comfortably at ease with everyone except him.

It seemed advisable to change the subject. "How's med school going?"

Joe didn't even blink at the abrupt conversational detour. "It's a bitch."

"Yeah, well, wait until you start your internship. Med school's going to seem like a fond memory."

"So I hear. But, to be honest, I'm looking forward to finding out for myself. I finish school next semester and then I'm starting my internship at Houston General."

"What's your specialty?"

"Sports medicine. Yours?"

"Pediatrics."

"That was my second choice. You with a hospital?"

"Private clinic. Five partners. I'm the new guy there, but it's working out well. I expect I'll be there awhile."

Joe nodded. "That's what I want to do. Get set up someplace while I'm still young enough to build a solid future there, settle down, start a family. My brother, the maverick-ex-cop-turned-P.I., used to tease me about being so unadventurous in planning for the future, but now that he's married and living in a big, fancy house with a domestic staff and everything, he can't really criticize me for wanting the same things for myself."

"Your plan sounds sensible enough to me."

Joe grinned. "Yeah. I thought it might."

Surprisingly empathetic with the younger man, Nick returned the smile and then drained his soft drink.

Tony joined them a moment later, swinging his long, denim-covered leg over a chair and slouching comfortably into it. "Hey, Giuseppe. Hoping to pick up a few pointers by talking to a *real* doctor?"

Joe politely suggested that Tony kiss some portion of his anatomy that he named in Italian. And then he glanced at Nick. "You got any brothers, Nick, or were you spared that affliction?"

Nick's smile vanished. "No brothers." Something made him add, "Actually, I fit quite well with most of this crowd—I was a foster kid, too."

"Hope you had better luck with foster homes than I did," Jared growled, taking one of the three remaining chairs as he joined the conversation. "Out of the five or six I lived in, only the last one worked out."

Nick shrugged, wondering now why he'd even mentioned his experience with foster care. He rarely brought it up, but maybe he thought these people would understand better than most. "I was fortunate, I guess. I ended up with Lindsay's family. That's how I met her. She was just a little girl during the two years I lived with the Hillmans. I left when I was eighteen and hadn't seen any of them since until a couple of months ago when I moved back to Little Rock and paid a visit to my old foster family."

"Guess you noticed right off that Lindsay had grown up?" Joe quipped.

"Yeah," Nick answered dryly. "I noticed that immediately."

"Layla was happy enough with her foster family," Jared remarked. "She stayed with them for eight years, still keeps in touch with them. I guess there are some decent ones out there, though God knows I didn't have much luck finding them. From what we've found out, my twin brothers didn't, either. That's why they disappeared at sixteen and haven't been heard from since."

"You're still looking for them?" Nick directed the question to Tony.

He nodded. "For as long as it takes."

"You certainly found the rest of us quickly. Michelle said she only started looking for us in April," Lindsay said, settling on the arm of Nick's chair as the women gathered around the table to be included in the discussion. Layla and Kevin took the last two chairs, while Cassie made herself comfortable in Jared's lap. Michelle smilingly refused Joe's offer of his chair and slid onto Tony's knee, one arm looped around his neck as he unselfconsciously pulled her closer. Shane had organized a game of hide-and-seek for his young cousins, leaving the adults to talk quietly for the first time that afternoon.

Nick was distracted for a moment from the conversation and was studying the couples surrounding him. They looked so content, so much in love. So secure in that love. Would he and Lindsay ever reach that point, ever get past whatever emotional obstacle still loomed between them, invisible, but always so damned intrusive?

"Because of her foresight in registering with the reunion service, Layla was very easy to find," Tony was explaining when Nick turned his attention back to the conversation. "And Jared had made no effort to conceal his whereabouts, so we were able to trace him through his military and employment records. You were a little harder, Lindsay, since your adoption records were closed. I was able to pull strings, though. Interviewed a few of the legal and social workers who'd been involved in your case, tracked down a couple who knew bits and pieces about your adoptive family— enough to lead us in the right direction. One of my employees finally tracked you down almost a month ago. Of course, we wanted concrete confirmation before we contacted you, which was why we waited a couple of weeks after locating you."

"I understand that," Lindsay agreed. "But, I have to admit, it made me nervous when your employee kept watching me from that dark pickup. I think you should reconsider that method of keeping track of someone, Tony. I was starting to get seriously paranoid."

Nick frowned at the same moment Tony's left eyebrow shot up in question. "I'm not sure what you're talking about, Lindsay. Chuck didn't follow you around or otherwise keep you under surveillance. He simply confirmed your identity through your records in Arkansas. And he doesn't drive a dark pickup, anyway. He's got a plain brown sedan, a Chrysler. That's what he drove to Little Rock."

"You never told me about a dark pickup," Nick accused Lindsay. "What's this all about?"

She looked uncomfortable, maybe a little embarrassed. "I guess I *was* just being paranoid."

"Lindsay?" Jared, too, was frowning as he leaned in her direction. "*Has* someone been following you around?"

She lifted her hands to indicate her own confusion. "I guess not. Several times during the last couple of weeks, I've noticed a dark pickup in the parking lot of my apartment complex, and it always felt as though the guy sitting in it was watching me. When you mentioned an employee tracking me down in Little Rock, Tony, I thought of the pickup and decided that must be the explanation. Now...well, I guess he's just someone who's been waiting around for one of my neighbors. Or, if he really *is* watching someone, it's obviously not me." She smiled rather sheepishly. "I always wondered if the college student across the compound was supplementing his education with a few back-alley business transactions. The guy in the pickup could be a narc."

"I can't believe you never even mentioned this," Nick scolded, genuinely annoyed with her for not doing so. What if the guy was some pervert, one of those crazy stalkers who meant to harm Lindsay? Had she no sense of self-preservation at all?

"And risk having you call the cops on some poor guy who's probably just been waiting for his girlfriend?" Lindsay smiled and shook her head. "You're too overprotective and suspicious, Nick. No way I'd mention something like that without good reason to be concerned."

"Dammit, Lindsay—"

"Jared would probably charge over to the truck and demand to know what the guy was doing there," Cassie commented cheerfully, interrupting Nick's outburst. "My husband isn't exactly the subtle type."

Michelle giggled. "Tony would've just assigned someone to watch the watcher. There'd have been guys in trench coats behind every lamppost in the compound, all sneaking around spying on each other."

"Whereas Kevin," Layla suggested, "would have computed the statistical probabilities of the guy being a serious threat and compared it mathematically to the risk of embarrassment at taking unwarranted action."

"Thanks a lot," Kevin grumbled.

"Men," Lindsay pronounced with a deep sigh and a shake of her head.

Michelle, Layla and Cassie agreed heartily with the age-old sentiment.

"Hey, Cassie. Didn't you make a double batch of brownies this morning?" Shane asked, loping toward the patio with his three younger cousins hot on his heels. "Uh— Keith's hungry," he added.

Cassie looked skeptical. "*Keith's* hungry?"

Shane grinned, unabashed. "Okay, so *I'm* hungry. Mind if I get them out?"

"Help yourself. Anyone else want brownies?"

"I do, I do!" little Brittany insisted, jumping up and down in excitement. She was echoed with only slightly less enthusiasm by her eight-year-old sister and five-year-old brother.

"Sounds good, Cassie. Got enough for the grown-ups, too?" Joe inquired with interest.

She grinned flippantly at him. "Yeah. Once I've got you kids served, we adults will have ours."

Joe winced. "Low blow," he muttered. "You're not that much older than I am."

"Maybe not in years," she agreed. "But in wisdom . . ."

Jared snorted.

Cassie punched his arm.

The others laughed.

Nick pulled thoughtfully at his lower lip, his eyes focused on Lindsay's happy face, his thoughts turning toward their return to Little Rock the following day. As soon as they got back, he decided, he and Lindsay were going to have a long talk. And the dark pickup she'd mentioned was going to be one of the first things they discussed.

The family dined at noon on Sunday at the Sampleses' house in suburban Fort Worth. Lindsay and Nick would leave from there for the airport for their return to Little

Rock. This meal was a bit more subdued than the others had been—probably, Lindsay thought, because they were all aware that the weekend had come to an end and that it would be up to her to decide exactly how close she wanted to remain to her biological family now that the initial meeting was over.

As she sat with the adults in the dining room—Shane had graciously consented to eat in the kitchen with the smaller children—Lindsay glanced around the table, trying to decide exactly how she did feel about them. She looked first at Cassie, who'd already become a friend, someone with whom Lindsay had many things in common. Jared and Tony were already starting to feel like brothers to her—Jared in particular, she admitted silently, studying her older brother's face through her lashes. It wasn't hard to envision herself turning to him if she ever needed him, if she had a problem that, for some reason she couldn't imagine at the moment, didn't seem appropriate to discuss with her parents or Steve or Greg.

Michelle and Layla. She looked from one to the other, her heart warming. Her sisters. As happy as she'd been with her adopted family, as much as she'd adored her brothers, Lindsay had always longed for a sister. Now she had two of them. And already she loved them, though she still had so much to learn about them. She couldn't imagine never seeing them again once she left this house today.

The Hillman family would always hold first place in her affections, but Michelle, Layla, Jared and the others now had a place there, too. They were her family. And she could see now that Tony had been right on that first visit to her— there was always room in her heart for more family. It was something she'd actually learned years earlier, from the parents who always had room for another child who needed them, another foster son to love and worry over.

Lindsay had honorary brothers scattered all over the country—and now it seemed she had three biological brothers in addition to her beloved adopted ones. She was very fortunate. And she was already hoping as much as the others that the twins would be found soon, and she looked forward eagerly to meeting them. Would they, too, have brown hair and blue eyes? Would they be outgoing and spontaneous like Shane and herself, a bit shy like Layla, or rather guarded and cautious like Jared and Michelle?

"You'll call me as soon as you can find them?" she asked Tony as she and Nick prepared to take their leave for the airport.

He assured her he would. "If we find them," he added reluctantly. "I'm not going to give up, but it's not looking very promising now. As hard as we've looked, we've come up with absolutely nothing after the twins ran away nearly fourteen years ago. I can't even guarantee they're still alive."

Lindsay nodded. "I know. But I'd like to be kept informed."

"You will be," he promised.

Lindsay turned to Michelle. "I'm really very glad you hired Tony to start looking for us," she said honestly. "I'm glad I had this chance to meet you all."

"Oh, Lindsay, so am I," Michelle answered, her smile trembling. "I was so nervous about starting the search, so concerned about how it would all turn out, but now I have the brother and sisters I always wished for when I was a lonely child, as well as Tony's big, wonderful family. I've never been happier."

"I want to stay in touch with you all," Lindsay said, including everyone in the announcement. "You're family, and I don't want us to lose contact again."

Layla wiped at her eyes with the back of one unsteady hand. "I'll never stop regretting that we were separated so young," she admitted. "We should have been together, should have grown up together. It was wrong—horribly wrong—to split us up, and I spent a lot of years grieving over that loss. I'm just glad we're back together now. I don't ever want us to lose touch again, either."

"This time there'd be no one to blame but ourselves if it happened," Jared said, putting an arm around Layla's shoulders. "I felt guilty for a lot of years because I couldn't stop what they did to us, let the guilt almost eat me alive as I was growing up. Now I realize that we couldn't help what happened to us when we were kids. But we can damn sure make an effort to stay together now."

He put his free arm around Lindsay's waist. She smiled up at him and returned the hug. A moment later, Michelle joined them, the others standing back to let the siblings share this moment of bonding. Lindsay's eyes were damp when she finally stepped away. She knew how hard it must have been for Jared to share his emotions that way, to open up so much when he tended to be the type to keep his feelings to himself.

She couldn't keep looking at Nick, standing so still and inscrutable behind her, watching. Like Jared, Nick had developed his obsessive reserve as a defense against the unpleasant things that had happened to him, learned to control his emotions because there were so many things in his life that had been out of his control. Was it possible that Nick, like Jared, would someday learn to relax that control? Was she foolish to allow herself to believe that he would?

Lindsay kissed Layla's children, promising she'd see them again soon, then turned to Shane. He was perhaps the hardest to say goodbye to. She'd fallen hard for this particular nephew. "Practice up on those dance steps," she told him. "I'll be expecting you to dazzle me on my next visit."

"Dazzling the ladies is my number-one talent," Shane assured her gravely, eliciting groans from his father and stepmother. "Don't be a stranger, Lindsay."

"I won't," she promised, and kissed his cheek, pleased when he gave her an enthusiastic, rib-threatening hug in return.

Nick shook hands with everyone, thanked them politely for their hospitality, agreed they'd have to do this again sometime soon, and then slipped an arm around Lindsay's waist, hustling her to the door with the excuse that they had to be getting to the airport. Her farewells said, Lindsay didn't try to linger.

She took one last, emotional look back over her shoulder as she and Nick drove away from Layla's home in the rented car they would turn in at the airport. Even as she felt the pull of wanting to be back with her family in Little Rock, she was aware of another tug of regret that she was leaving this family behind.

Something told her she'd spend the rest of her life balancing her feelings for her two families, always aware that Walker blood ran through her, affecting her almost as deeply as her Hillman upbringing.

Chapter Twelve

Though she hadn't consciously thought of the dark pickup since she'd mentioned it in Dallas, Lindsay found herself automatically looking around for it as she climbed out of Nick's car in the parking lot of her apartment complex upon their arrival from the airport. Nick watched her. "Do you see the truck?" he demanded.

Embarrassed at being caught in her paranoia, Lindsay shook her head. "No."

"I still can't believe you never mentioned that. Even if it turned out to be nothing, you should always let me know if there's something—or someone—bothering you," Nick scolded. "What if the guy *had* turned out to be someone to worry about?"

It seemed easier to concede than to argue. "All right, Nick. Next time I think someone's watching me, I'll let you know."

He scowled, apparently not at all mollified. "You're not taking this seriously, are you?"

She sighed soundlessly. "Trust me, Nick. I take you very seriously."

He muttered something unintelligible and lifted her bags out of the trunk of his car.

Though she'd been gone for just three days, Lindsay entered her apartment with the odd feeling that she'd been away for much longer. How could her life have changed so much in only three days? she mused, snapping on lights and automatically glancing around to make sure nothing had changed in her absence. She had left Little Rock certain that she'd never belong to any family other than the one with which she'd grown up. Now she felt a definite, powerful, permanent connection with the two sisters and brother she'd met in Dallas, and with their families.

She still loved the Hillmans, still felt a part of them, would always give them her first loyalty. And yet, her other family now meant a great deal to her, as well. She couldn't imagine losing them again, now that they'd found each other.

Three days. Three very important days.

She called her mother to let her know she was back, and also because she just needed to hear her mother's voice again. Evelyn seemed genuinely pleased that Lindsay had enjoyed the visit in Dallas and said she wanted to hear all about it. Lindsay promised to drop by the next afternoon to tell her everything. "Have the coffee on," she said with a smile. "I'll be there at four."

Nick's arms encircled her waist from behind when she hung up the phone. "Feels good to be home, doesn't it?" he murmured, resting his cheek on her hair.

"You aren't exactly home," she reminded him, thinking of the large, elegantly decorated house in which he seemed to spend very little time.

"It feels like I am," he replied, pulling her closer. "It's too lonely at my place. I like it better here."

She was both surprised and touched by his confession. He rarely gave her glimpses of his vulnerabilities, and she was always disarmed when he did. She turned her head to look over her shoulder at him. "Do you get lonely, Nick?"

"When I'm not with you, I do. You've become an important part of my life, Lindsay."

"You're important to me, too. I only wish . . ."

"What?" he urged when she bit her lip and fell silent.

"I only wish I could understand you better," Lindsay confessed carefully. "Sometimes I feel so close to you . . . but at other times, I'm not sure I know you at all. I don't know what you're thinking, or what you're feeling, or what you want."

"Right now, I'm thinking that I'm glad we're finally alone together again," he murmured, his lips moving against the soft skin at her temple. "I'm feeling good because you're in my arms. And if you don't know what I want—" he moved his hips against her bottom, letting her feel his need for her "—then you're not paying very close attention."

She sighed and shook her head. "That's not what I—"

Her words were muffled by his mouth when he turned her suddenly in his arms and kissed her with a fiery hunger that quickly ignited her own desire. And suddenly nothing else mattered except that he was with her and he wanted her and she wanted him. She wrapped her arms around his neck and went on tiptoes to press herself full-length against him, hugging him as tightly, as closely as she could, holding him as though she'd never have to let him go. And his arms

locked around her with the same intensity, the same possessiveness, the same near desperation.

For a long time they stood there, entwined, their mouths
fused, hearts pounding in unison. And then their hands were
moving, seeking, kneading, tugging at buttons and zippers
and hems, demanding even as they pleaded. They didn't
bother to go to the bedroom, but undressed each other
where they stood, falling naked to the living room carpet,
heedless of the tangled garments beneath them as they
arched, writhed, undulated.

Lindsay held Nick's head between her hands when he
kissed her breasts, then tangled her fingers in his hair when
his head lowered. Her breath caught in her throat, then
seemed to hold there. Her heart pounded in her chest, then
seemed to stop altogether. *"Nick!"*

He surged upward, lying half on top of her as he cupped
her flushed face in his unsteady hands, staring at her as
though he were trying to memorize every detail of her face,
almost as though this would be his last time to look at her.
"Lindsay," he muttered, his voice raw. "You're so beautiful. God, how I need you."

"Oh, Nick." She touched his face, trying urgently to read
him. "Do you really need me?"

Did this strong, capable, obsessively self-sufficient man
really need anyone?

"More than my next breath," he answered huskily,
sounding so sincere, so earnest that her eyes filled with tears.

"Nick..." But she couldn't find words to respond to him,
so she had to express her feelings with actions. She caught
his face between her hands and lifted her mouth to his,
wrapping her legs around his, urging him to her.

Nick didn't need a second invitation. Supporting himself
on his forearms, he surged into her, and Lindsay arched to
meet him, his name a broken whisper on her lips. She clung

to him, her fingers digging into his back, feeling his hot, pliant skin grow slick and damp beneath her touch, feeling the muscles bunch and ripple as he moved within her, driving her higher and higher until finally she bowed beneath him with a cry of joyful pleasure. The ripples went on for a very long time, leaving her drained and sated when they finally faded, only dimly aware that Nick had shuddered with his own release while she'd been lost in her own.

The floor was hard beneath her, the carpet a bit scratchy, but she didn't care, wouldn't have traded her place in Nick's arms for the finest bed, the softest mattress. She snuggled into his damp, salty shoulder and closed her eyes to savor the moment for as long as it lasted. Wishing it could last forever.

Knowing that all too soon it would have to end.

Nick waited until after he and Lindsay had shared a lengthy, lazy shower before gathering his nerve to talk to her seriously. "There's something I want to discuss with you."

Looking distracted, she finished French-braiding her damp hair and tied the end with a black ribbon to match the black jeans she wore with a red-and-black patterned sweater. "Okay. How about over dinner? I think I have something in the freezer I could thaw in the microwave. I'm getting a bit hungry, aren't you?"

"No." Aware of how bluntly he'd spoken—making her look at him in startled question—he softened his voice. "Not yet. I'd really like to talk first, if you don't mind."

"Sure. Of course. What is it, Nick?"

He cleared his throat and glanced at the couch. "Maybe you'd better sit down."

She bit her lip. "This sounds serious."

"Yeah. It is."

Beginning to frown, she perched warily on the edge of the couch. "All right. What is it? What's wrong?"

"Nothing's wrong," he assured her quickly, realizing that he'd worried her with his grave tone and expression. He tried to smile. "At least, I hope not. I just want to ask you a question."

She relaxed. "Oh. All right, Nick. What did you want to ask me?"

For just a moment, it occurred to him that he should be on his knees or something—and then he dismissed the idea as quickly as it crossed his mind. He'd look like a fool. He wanted her to marry him, not laugh at him. He cleared his throat again, wondering why it suddenly seemed so hot and tight. "Lindsay, I—er—what I'd—uh— Oh, hell."

Disgusted, he shoved his hands in his pockets and glared at her. "I want you to marry me. Will you?"

She blinked. Then blinked again. Her cheeks went noticeably pale.

Something told him he hadn't exactly swept her away with romance.

Trying to recover his usual aplomb, he spoke again before she had a chance to answer him, deciding that since he was lousy at pretty, flowery speeches, he'd be better off using the talents he *did* have. Logic, reason, common sense. He'd make her realize that there was no rational reason for them not to be married, despite her perfectly natural doubts.

"You know we're good together, Lindsay. There's been something between us from the beginning, something neither of us was able to resist. We've got a lot in common, we're dynamite in bed, we share many of the same goals and values. You wanted me with you when you went to Dallas—one of the most important events in your life—and you understand and accept the demands of my job. And I'd never interfere with your job or your responsibilities, or brush it off as less important or less demanding than my own. I know how much it means to you.

"I get along fine with your family—both your families, actually—and I've always known I wanted a family of my own someday. Being around your parents and your brothers, and watching the happily married couples in Dallas, has made me realize how much I want what they have. I want it with you, Lindsay. I want you to be my wife, the mother of my children. I want to spend the rest of my life with you. Will you marry me?"

She was silent for so long that he became concerned. His fists tightened in the pockets of his dark slacks. "Lindsay?"

"I . . . can't believe you're asking me this. Not now," she admitted, her voice shaken, her face still pale. "We still have so many things to work out. So much left to learn about each other."

"That will come with time," he assured her. "We have so much going for us, Lindsay. Such a solid foundation for a marriage. We'll deal with the rest later, once we have the security and commitment of marriage working for us."

She looked down at her tightly clenched hands, hiding her expression from him.

Frustrated by his sudden inability to read her, he took a step closer. "Lindsay. You will marry me, won't you?"

"I . . . I can't, Nick."

He froze, unable to believe she'd actually turned him down, unable to accept her answer as final. Stunned by the depth of the pain that had slashed through him with her refusal. "Why can't you, dammit?"

"I don't want to be married because it's the sensible, logical thing to do," she answered with just a hint of bitterness. "I don't want to marry you because we're good in bed and you get along well with my families. Or because you think I'd make a suitable, compatible doctor's wife.''

''What *do* you want?'' he challenged.

''I want to be loved,'' she threw back at him, her chin lifting proudly.

He stiffened, a muscle twitching in his jaw. ''Oh.''

Of course she'd want the pretty words, he realized, chagrined that he'd made such a mess of his proposal. He knew Lindsay well enough to understand that she was sentimental and sensitive, a bit naive and idealistic. Why had he forgotten that when he'd been making his practical, prosaic speech about the advantages to their union?

''Of course I love you, Lindsay,'' he said rather awkwardly, uncomfortable with the words he'd spoken to no one before. No one. ''I thought that was obvious.''

She looked up at him then, and her face was so sad that his heart twisted. If he hadn't known better, he'd have sworn her expression held a deep pity for him. Why in the world would Lindsay pity him?

''It's not enough, Nick,'' she said, her dark eyes gleaming with what might have been suppressed tears. ''I'm sorry, but it's just not enough.''

''Dammit, what do you *want* from me?'' Was she so eager to see him crawl?

''I want it all,'' she whispered. ''Your emotions, your fears, your flaws—your past.''

He winced and spat a curse from between clenched teeth, frustrated and irritated that she was still harping on that. That she insisted on digging into his past, battering against the control he'd spent so many years building. ''Believe me, Lindsay,'' he told her roughly, ''you don't really want to know. You think you do, but you don't. Trust me.''

She rose slowly to her feet, shaking her head and looking so calm and distant that he wanted to reach out and shake her, anything to make her respond to him again. "The problem," she said firmly, "is that you don't trust me. You want to pat me on the head and tell me not to worry about things that don't concern me, even though those things are still locked inside you, still controlling so much of what you do, what you feel, what you allow other people to know of you. I don't know if you're hiding your past from me, or if you're the one hiding from the past, but it can't work. I can't marry you if you won't truly share yourself with me."

He shook his head. "You don't know what you're asking."

"Yes, I do. I'm asking you to let down those damned barriers of yours, give up that rigid control you hold over your emotions. I'm asking you to give as much to me as you're asking from me."

Fully angry now—and terrified that he was losing her, despite everything he'd done to make her his—Nick snatched a small porcelain figure off a nearby table and hurled it at a wall, hearing it smash even as he shouted at her. "You want me to lose control, Lindsay? You want me to tell you that the last time I lost control I damned near killed a man? You want to know that I was once moments away from taking a life with my bare hands? You really think you could live with me if you knew exactly what I've seen, what I've done, what I'm capable of doing?"

As suddenly as his temper flared, it evaporated, leaving him appalled at what he'd done, what he'd said, the way Lindsay was looking at him. His stricken gaze went from the broken shards of porcelain scattered on the carpet to her stunned, colorless face. "Oh, hell."

Lindsay started toward him, her hands reaching out to him. "Nick—"

He held up his own hands to ward her off, half-afraid that if she touched him now he'd shatter as completely as the little figurine. "No."

"Nick, I'm sorry. Please, talk to me."

He shook his head, avoiding her tearful, all-too-expressive eyes. "I'm tired," he muttered, taking a step backward—toward the door, toward the safety of solitude. "We're both tired. We need some time alone."

"Nick, please—"

"Not tonight, Lindsay," he said wearily, taking another step away. "I'm just not up to it tonight. Give me time," he added roughly. "I really just need some time."

She didn't try to stop him when he spun on one heel to leave, though he thought he heard her whisper his name just as the door closed behind him. He stood for a long time on the walk outside her apartment, alone in the shadows, wondering if he'd spend the rest of his life paying for a youth that hadn't been of his making, for mistakes made out of anger and frustration and pain. Wondering if he was destined to spend the rest of his life alone.

He didn't go straight home, though he'd intended to when he drove away from her apartment. Instead, he found himself on the freeway, headed east of Little Rock, away from the exclusive, well-groomed neighborhood in which he'd made his home, past the thriving metropolitan area of the city, into an area of old, empty storefronts, peeling, faded frame homes and scraggly, barren yards. The sun had set and shadows spread, but even the darkness couldn't hide the destruction, the ugliness. He could almost smell the hopelessness, the despair, almost touch the heavy gloom of the poverty-devastated neighborhood.

As he drove, he fought the memories of violence and pain, of a mother who assuaged her misery with mind-dulling chemicals, of the father who'd died in a bloody, senseless fight, and the series of men who used and abused the widow and son he'd left behind. Echoes of screams and obscene shouts, of glass breaking and fists connecting with flesh, of drunken threats and vicious ridicule ran endlessly through his mind.

"Why do you let them do this to us?" he heard his own angry young voice asking from so many years in the past. *"Why do we have to take this from them?"*

And his mother, her youth and looks gone, her spirit dead, had looked at him from the depths of her bottle and asked with near pity, *"Who's going to put food on our table, huh? You?"*

"Yes," he'd answered earnestly, pleadingly. *"I will. Somehow, I will."*

But she'd only laughed at him, and the laugh had held no humor, no affection.

No hope.

His hands gripped the steering wheel until his knuckles whitened and his palms ached. It had been so long since he'd allowed himself to remember, so long since he'd opened those old, mental doors. He'd worked so hard to escape, so hard to leave it all behind.

Tried so hard to pretend it had never happened.

Only to have it all crash back down on him with the sound of a porcelain figurine shattering against Lindsay's wall.

He slammed on his brakes to avoid hitting a cringing, ragged, half-starved dog, which immediately streaked away, into the gloom. And then he asked himself what he was doing here, why he'd come back to a place he'd left sixteen years ago with a vow that he'd never return.

His foot still flattening the brake pedal, he dragged his hands through his hair and then scrubbed wearily at his face, wishing he knew what to do next.

He'd tried so hard to shield Lindsay from the ugliness of his past, to protect her from the part of himself that lurked in the shadows like that half-wild dog, angry, hurting, prepared to snap at any hand that reached out to it. Now, despite his efforts, it appeared inevitable that she would demand to hear it all. He'd lose her if he refused to discuss this with her...but could she ever look at him the same way once she'd heard it all? Would he ultimately lose her either way?

Had he only been fooling himself that anything had really changed for him, despite his respectable career and lucrative practice? Was he fated to always live alone, to always hover on the fringes of other families, never to belong to one of his own?

Lindsay had given him a taste of heaven—but now he found himself trapped in an old, too-familiar hell. Hurting as he hadn't hurt in more years than he could remember. Wanting her, needing her—praying she cared enough to stay with him, even after she learned everything about him. Wondering if even loving, caring, tender-hearted Lindsay could be that trusting and understanding.

A harsh, sudden honking from behind made him aware that his car was sitting motionless in the middle of a road. He pulled his foot off the brake and stamped the accelerator, heading back the way he'd come, speeding away from the physical remains of his past, though he knew the worst reminders of his youth couldn't be so easily left behind.

He desperately wanted to return to Lindsay. Yet, he found himself afraid to do so, afraid of what he'd see in her eyes after his violent outburst earlier. He didn't think he'd be able to bear it if he saw fear there.

No, he needed time alone. Time to think, to regroup, to plan. Tomorrow, when he was rested and calm and composed, he'd go back to Lindsay and make her understand how little the past mattered, how much he was willing to offer for the future.

Whatever it took, he wouldn't lose her. God help him, he couldn't lose her.

He wasn't at all sure he'd survive intact if he did.

Lindsay pressed a cold cloth to her burning, swollen eyes, trying to find relief from the discomfort of a bout of hard, uncontrollable weeping. It wasn't like her to cry that way, had never been her habit to give in to despair, but she hadn't been able to stop crying after Nick left. The expression in his eyes when he'd walked away had broken her heart.

She couldn't bear knowing how deeply he was hurting, and realizing that there was nothing he would allow her to do to help him.

What had happened to him when he was a boy? What horror had he lived through that had left him so battered and angry and afraid? What had driven him to the act of violence he'd alluded to, an ugly, painful memory that was eating him alive?

What would it take to ever make him trust her enough to tell her everything? How could she ever hope to understand him, to help him, if he refused to show her his pain?

He'd asked her to marry him. And for one brief, stunned moment, she'd wanted nothing more than to joyously accept, to throw herself into his arms and make believe that all their troubles were over, all the obstacles behind them. But her fear had been stronger than her pleasure. Even then, she'd known that she and Nick could never make a relationship work—much less a marriage—unless they tore down the emotional walls between them. How could they be husband and wife when they couldn't even be confidants? How could they share a lifetime if they couldn't share their feelings, their fears, their pain?

She paced her apartment, aching, tired, torn. She thought of calling him, but couldn't bear the thought of trying to make stilted conversation over the telephone. She thought of going to him, but couldn't face the possibility that he might turn her away. She wondered if he would leave her life as suddenly, as devastatingly as he'd entered it.

She loved him. She needed him. She wanted him. And yet she didn't really know him. Couldn't know him until she understood what drove him, what hovered so threateningly between them.

Until she knew what had put that heartbreaking look in his beautiful, tormented eyes.

But would he ever give her the chance to find out?

Chapter Thirteen

Though Lindsay had worried that her chaotic emotions might interfere with her teaching on Monday, she found that her work helped her keep her mind off her problems. She enjoyed teaching, genuinely liked most of the teenagers who filled her classes, and was usually able to remain objective about—and committed to—those who caused her problems. Teaching wasn't an easy job, particularly with modern, streetwise, sometimes aggressive teenagers, but Lindsay truly believed she could make a difference in these young lives if she worked at it hard enough. And she worked even harder that day than usual.

She was almost sorry to have her last class end. She hadn't heard from Nick since he'd left her apartment the night before, and she wasn't sure what to expect from the evening. Would he show up on her doorstep? Would he call? Would he ever come to her again?

"Miss Hillman?"

Immediately masking her frown, Lindsay looked up from her paper-littered desk to find two popular teenage girls on the other side, watching her in obvious concern. "What is it, Heather? Jennifer?"

It was Heather who spoke, pushing her long, permed, teased and sprayed hair out of her pretty, made-up face. "Are you okay? You're not sick or anything, are you?"

"I'm fine, thank you. Why do you ask?"

"Usually you stand by the door and see us off when the class ends," dark-haired, dark-eyed Jennifer explained shyly. "Today you look worried about something."

Annoyed that she'd let her personal problems creep into her work, after all—even if she had managed to hold them off until the end of the day—Lindsay forced a bright smile. "Really, I'm fine. But I appreciate your concern."

She stood and walked them to the classroom door, making light conversation, asking about their extracurricular activities, apparently successful in distracting them from their concern for her. She held on to her smile until the last student had departed.

She spent a few more minutes chatting with fellow teachers, then another fifteen minutes with paperwork at her desk. She took her time straightening her desk after that, until she finally remembered that she'd promised to be at her mother's house at four. It was almost that now. Sighing impatiently at her thoughtlessness, she took her purse out of her desk and headed for the parking lot.

Since she'd delayed so long, most of the other faculty were already gone, and the parking lot was nearly deserted. She noticed that Steve's car still sat in the principal's space, and thought for a moment about going in to see him, since they'd only had time for a few hasty exchanges during the busy day. But then she decided to wait. Steve had always been too perceptive where she was concerned. He'd be bound to notice that something was bothering her, and he'd surely guess that Nick was the "something" in question. She really didn't want to discuss the situation with Steve yet.

She needed very badly to talk to her mother.

She'd go straight to her mother, she thought wistfully, just as she had when she was a child. And she knew her mother would be just as supportive, just as loving, just as helpful as she'd always been in the past.

She had almost reached her car when someone spoke from behind her. "Miss Hillman? Lindsay Hillman?"

She turned to find a handsome, well-groomed middle-aged man standing behind her, impeccably dressed, giving her a friendly smile. "Yes?"

Keeping his left hand in the pocket of his beautifully tailored dark suit slacks, he held out his right hand. "I'm Bob Carter. Tony D'Alessandro's an old friend of mine, and he asked me to look you up this afternoon and check on you."

"Check on me?" Lindsay repeated in confusion, though she shook the man's hand.

"Yes. After your eventful weekend in Dallas, he wanted to make sure you were okay. I can see by looking at you that there was no need for him to be concerned."

"No, of course not." Lindsay backed toward her car, suddenly uncomfortable with the man's slick, genial manner and rather thin excuse for disturbing her. "Tell Tony that I'm fine and I'll be in touch with them soon. Now, if you'll excuse me, I have to—"

Carter motioned with his right hand toward a large, dark blue sedan that sat very close to them. "I'd like for you to take a little ride with me, Miss Hillman. There are some things I want to discuss with you."

No way was she getting into a car with this stranger, no matter how respectable his appearance. "Why don't we go back inside the school," she suggested instead, thinking that she'd lead him straight to her brother's office. "Whatever you have to tell me can be discussed in the administration office."

His bland smile never wavered. "I don't think so. Get in my car, Lindsay."

She looked wildly around the parking lot, hoping to see someone—anyone—to whom she could turn for help. Unfortunately, Carter had chosen his timing well. Except for a couple of cars, the parking lot was deserted. She frantically calculated her odds of escaping him if she started running toward the front door. She was younger than this man and probably in better shape. Surely she could—

The gun that suddenly appeared in his left hand put an end to that idea. She wouldn't get two feet.

"What do you want from me?" she asked, the question little more than a stunned, disbelieving whisper. Things like this simply didn't happen to her! How could it be happening here, in broad daylight, in her school parking lot? Where *was* everyone?

"In the car," the man repeated with a quick glance around and a small, meaningful motion of the gun. "Now."

There was nothing else to do. She had a better chance of escaping a moving car, should the opportunity arise, than surviving a gunshot from this close range. Trembling, frightened, vigilantly watching for the first opportunity to get away, she got into the passenger seat of the dark sedan, wondering if he'd noticed that she'd discreetly set her key ring on the hood of her car as she'd passed it. Praying he had not. Following Carter's instructions, she fastened her seat belt as he climbed behind the wheel, hearing him snap the power locks on the doors just before he started the engine.

Hoping someone would see her—*Steve, where are you?*—she looked desperately over her shoulder as Carter drove swiftly out of the parking lot. Her hopes rose when she spotted a male teacher watching the car from the open outer door to one classroom. She wondered if she could lift a hand to wave for help.

"Turn around and keep your hands in your lap," her kidnapper ordered, his eyes on the rearview mirror. And then he looked at Lindsay with a smile that froze her blood. "We wouldn't want anything to happen to you, now, would we?"

Nick had been having a hell of a day. Everything that could go wrong, had. Medical emergencies, equipment malfunctions, overanxious mothers interfering with the efficient treatment of their sniffly children. Though he'd performed his job with his usual competence, he hadn't been able to put Lindsay out of his mind for a moment, and his inner tension made him rather curt with everyone except the children. Only with them could he smile and tease and find temporary relief from his personal problems.

He'd hoped to get away an hour early, planning to go straight to Lindsay—though God only knew what he'd say to her when he got there—but even that fell through when an unusually heavy number of minor emergencies kept all the staff running throughout the afternoon.

When he was called to the phone late in the day, Nick steeled himself for yet another annoyance, pessimistically prepared for the worst, considering the way his day had gone so far. He certainly hadn't expected to hear Steve Hillman's voice on the other end of the line. "Steve? What can I do for you?"

"I've been trying to call you at home," Steve replied, sounding worried. "You didn't by any chance pick Lindsay up at school earlier this afternoon, did you?"

Nick's fingers tightened on the receiver. "I haven't left the clinic since I got here this morning. What's going on?"

"I wish I knew. I'm still at the school. Lindsay's car's sitting outside, and I found her key ring on the hood. I can't find Lindsay anywhere. The janitorial staff and I have torn this place apart looking for her."

"Her key ring was on the hood?" Nick repeated, his stomach clenching.

"Yeah."

"Did she have any meetings this afternoon, any professional events to attend?"

"Not as far as I'm aware. In fact, she'd promised to stop by Mom's house on her way home to tell her about the trip to Dallas."

"You called Lindsay's apartment?"

"Repeatedly. I thought maybe she'd had car trouble and had called for a ride home, but she doesn't answer. I started her car and there's nothing wrong with it."

"You've talked to your mother?"

"Yeah. She hasn't heard from her. She was expecting her at four. Nick—I'm starting to get scared, here. This doesn't make sense. It's not like her."

"Have you contacted the police?"

"No. I was hoping you'd know something."

"Call them," Nick ordered curtly. "I'm on my way."

"Oh, hell. You think there's reason to be scared, don't you?"

"Call the cops, Steve. And keep calling all Lindsay's friends—everyone you can think of who might know something. I'll be there in a few minutes."

It took him fifteen minutes to get away from the clinic. It felt like hours. No matter how many times he tried to reassure himself that Lindsay was all right, that this would turn out to be nothing more than an oversight or a misunderstanding on someone's part, deep inside he knew something was terribly, dangerously wrong. He couldn't stop thinking about that damned pickup truck she'd mentioned, wondering sickly if it was in some way involved in her disappearance.

Disappearance. Oh, God. *Lindsay.*

Both the Hillman brothers were waiting in Steve's office when Nick arrived, their faces creased with worried frowns. "Have you heard anything?" Nick demanded the moment he walked in.

"No. The last anyone saw her, Lindsay was in her classroom, doing paperwork at her desk," Steve answered. "I've started calling every member of the staff, but I haven't been able to reach everyone yet."

"Keep trying."

Steve picked up the phone and flipped a card in his Rolodex file. "I intend to."

Nick turned to Greg. "The police have been notified?"

"They asked a few questions over the phone, made some notes, but they said that's about all they can do until she's been missing twenty-four hours," Greg answered tightly.

Twenty-four hours. Nick made a sound of disgust. "Damned if I'm going to sit here and do nothing for twenty-four hours."

"None of us are," Greg assured him. "We're just trying to decide what to do next."

Momentarily overcome with frustration, Nick slammed a fist down on Steve's desk. "Dammit, where *is* she?"

Greg placed a hand on his shoulder. "We'll find her, Nick. This has got to be a mistake. I'm sure she'll turn up at any minute and chew us out for overreacting again."

"I wish I could believe that," Nick said grimly.

"We have to believe it," a new voice said from the door-way behind them. Earl Hillman entered the office, Scott tagging at his heels. The older man's eyes held steady on Nick's face. "We have to believe it," he repeated firmly. "Lindsay's okay, Nick. We'll find her."

Nick swallowed his fear. "Yeah. I'm sure you're right." *Please, God, let him be right.*

"Your mother stayed home in case Lindsay calls there," Earl said, turning to Greg. "Have you called Patty Terry? Your mother said that she and Lindsay sometimes meet here and go to movies together."

"Steve called her earlier," Greg confirmed. "Patty hasn't heard from Lindsay since the day before she left for Dallas."

"Maybe she's walking around the track behind the gym," Scott suggested. "You know, like those exercise walkers do sometimes. Want me to go look?"

"Why don't you do that, Scott. That's a good idea," Earl told him kindly.

Scott all but ran from the office, obviously glad to have something constructive to do.

"Why would she have left her keys on the hood of the car?" Greg fretted, as though to himself, pacing restlessly around the room. "It's not like Lindsay to be absent-minded."

"She wouldn't have left them there deliberately," Nick muttered, his mind racing in its quest for answers, for possibilities. "Unless—"

Greg turned. "Unless?"

"Unless she wanted to leave a message."

Paling, Greg shoved his hands in his pockets. "What sort of message?"

Nick answered reluctantly. "That something was wrong. That she didn't leave here voluntarily." *The dark pickup. Could Lindsay have been driven away in a dark pickup?*

"No," Earl said flatly, as though he couldn't even bear to consider that possibility. "No, she just laid them there and forgot them. She's probably at a meeting or a dinner right now, maybe with some of her teacher friends. She'll feel very foolish when she realized where she left her keys," he added.

Nick hoped he was right.

It was after seven o'clock by the time they all conceded there was no reason for them to remain at the school. Steve had contacted all the teachers he could, only a few remaining to be tried again later. Scott had thoroughly searched the grounds of the school, finding nothing. The janitorial staff had helped in one last search of every room, closet and cranny of the buildings, turning up no clues.

Nick had begun to feel like an automaton, mechanically going through the motions with the rest of them, while inside he was a helpless mass of confusion, panic, hope and despair.

Lindsay had been missing for nearly four hours. Not so long, really, but somehow he knew something was wrong. Terribly wrong.

He'd told her he loved her. He hadn't told her how much, he realized grimly. Hadn't even realized it himself until he found himself facing a very real possibility of losing her forever. These weren't feelings he could keep under comfortable control, as he'd tried from the beginning to do. These were feelings that could destroy him if given rein.

"We should go back to our house," Earl said finally. "There's nothing else we can do here."

"Her car—what if she comes back for it?" Steve asked. "She won't even be able to get into it without the keys."

"We'll leave a note telling her to have whoever she's with bring her to our house," Earl said. "Steve, you got some tape or something we can stick the note to the car window with?"

"Yeah. And I'll call her neighbor at her apartment complex and ask her to please call if Lindsay shows up there," Steve added, reaching again for the telephone.

"Better bring your list of teachers' phone numbers with you," Nick reminded Steve. "We'll want to contact the rest of them, find out if any of them know anything."

Steve was already dialing. "Yeah. I'll do that."

Evelyn met them at the door. "Have you heard anything?" she asked, wringing her hands.

Earl shook his head. "You?"

"Nothing." Her breath caught. "Oh, Earl, where is she?"

"I don't know," Earl said, looking helplessly frustrated. "I just don't know."

Carrying his files of telephone numbers, Steve headed determinedly toward the kitchen. "I'll spread this stuff out on the kitchen table. I'm going to keep calling teachers until I find someone who knows something."

"I'll go with you," Greg offered. Scott tagged along after the brothers, leaving Nick alone with Lindsay's parents.

"Nick, you look as though you could use a drink," Earl commented, trying to speak with his usual gruff confidence. "What can I get you?"

Nick shook his head. "Nothing, thanks."

Evelyn reached out to lay an unsteady hand on Nick's arm. "Come sit down, dear."

Nick had taken two steps toward the den when the doorbell rang. He whirled toward the sound, hope rising. If it was Lindsay, he thought fleetingly, safe and sound and surprised that anyone had been worried because she'd disappeared without a trace for hours, he had a few pointed words for her. And then he intended to tell her just how much he loved her, and that he never wanted to risk losing her again, no matter what it took on his part.

But it wasn't Lindsay standing on the porch when Earl jerked open the door. It was, instead, a uniformed police officer.

Nick felt his heart stop, even as Evelyn took his arm again, this time for her own support.

His hat in his hands, the young officer greeted Earl and stepped into the entryway. "I just heard about Lindsay," he said, a look of worry creasing his handsome ebony face. "I had to stop by. Have you heard anything?"

Evelyn sagged against Nick's side in obvious relief. Nick quickly wrapped an arm around her waist. "Oh, Thomas, I was afraid you were here with bad news," she murmured.

The officer reached both hands out to Evelyn in apology. "I'm sorry, I didn't mean to frighten you," he told her sincerely. "I stopped by to see if there was anything I could do to help."

Evelyn stepped away from Nick to take the young man's hands in hers. "Thank you, Thomas. Oh, this is Dr. Nick Grant, Lindsay's boyfriend. Nick, Officer Thomas Kennedy, another one of our former foster sons."

A little disconcerted at hearing himself introduced as Lindsay's "boyfriend"—the term sounded much too innocent and uncomplicated for the serious, potentially devastating feelings he had for her—Nick shook the officer's hand. He'd said only a few words of greeting when Greg, Steve and Scott joined them in a rush from the kitchen, having heard the doorbell and obviously hoping for good news. Looking relieved that Thomas wasn't there on solemn, official business, yet disappointed that there was still no word from Lindsay, they greeted him, then returned to their calling in the kitchen.

Evelyn, Earl and Thomas sat in the den, quietly discussing the events of the afternoon. Unable to sit still, wishing he could think of something—anything—to do, Nick paced from one end of the room to the other, restless, edgy, only half listening to the others' conversation. It was clear from the beginning that Kennedy agreed the family had good reason to be worried. "This just doesn't sound like Lindsay," he commented.

Evelyn shook her head. "She said she'd come by this afternoon. I can't imagine why she'd have said that if she'd made other plans."

"Does anyone know if something happened to upset her?" Thomas asked, glancing at Nick as he spoke. "Any—uh—quarrels, or anything like that?"

Guiltily remembering the way he and Lindsay had parted Sunday night, Nick shoved his hands in his pockets and took a defensive, feet-apart stance. "Even if she were mad or upset, Lindsay wouldn't knowingly worry her family like this," he said, evading the question.

"You're probably right," Thomas agreed. "It was just a thought."

"Shouldn't the police be out looking for her?" Earl demanded, glaring at the young officer as though he was personally to blame for the regulations.

Thomas didn't take offense. "There's not really anything they can do at this point, Earl," he explained. "But, if it makes you feel any better, everyone's been given the information about Lindsay's disappearance and they'll be keeping their eyes open. I made sure of that."

"I appreciate it," Earl murmured, "but the only thing that will make me feel better is to have Lindsay back with us."

She'd been missing for over five hours.

Steve and Greg appeared in the doorway, wearing identical somber expressions. "We may have something," Steve said. "I've reached one of the teachers who gave us some information."

The others froze. Taking an involuntary step forward, Nick spoke first. "What information?"

Steve drew a deep, shaken breath. "Doug Jeffers—one of the history teachers—happened to be standing in the door to his classroom when Lindsay left this afternoon. He saw her get into a large, dark blue sedan with a well-dressed, middle-aged man. At first he thought it must be you, Dad. Then he noticed the Texas plates on the car. He knew she'd just gotten back from Texas, so he didn't think much about it until I called."

Texas. Nick scowled. "Did the guy say Lindsay got into the car voluntarily?"

Dammit, were her sisters and brother still wanting something from her, even after the weekend she'd just spent with them? Why wouldn't they leave her alone?

Steve nodded. "Apparently. Doug thought she looked a little stiff, and wondered why she was leaving her own car in the parking lot, but he didn't see anything to make him unduly concerned. He said she looked over her shoulder at him as they drove away, but then turned around and didn't look back."

Earl turned to Nick. He, too, was frowning. "You know how to reach D'Alessandro?"

"I've got his card in my wallet."

Steve motioned toward the kitchen. "Call him."

Nick started toward the doorway, then hesitated. This was the only lead they had, he thought pensively. For some reason, he was reluctant to pursue it by telephone. He looked at Greg. "Even if D'Alessandro doesn't know anything about this, he seems to be a damned good P.I.," he said, his mind busy with possibilities. "We could use him here."

Greg caught on immediately. "We could be there in less than two hours in my plane."

"Let's go."

"You're going to fly to Dallas? Now?" Evelyn looked from Nick to her son in obvious confusion. "But what if Lindsay shows up and it turns out it was all a mistake?"

"Then we've wasted a trip," Greg answered with a shrug, though the look he gave Nick didn't hold a great deal of hope that Lindsay would suddenly turn up on her own. Like Nick, he had apparently come to the conclusion that Lindsay hadn't left the school parking lot voluntarily. It simply made no sense that she would have willingly gone with a stranger and disappeared for this many hours with no word to her habitually overprotective family. "Call Paula for me, will you, Mom?"

Pulling on his jacket, Nick paused to hand Tony's card to Earl. "Call one of these numbers if you hear anything. D'Alessandro will know what to do."

"You seem to have a lot of confidence in this guy," Earl said rather gruffly.

Nick hesitated only a moment. "He's the best hope we've got until the police can get involved," he explained with a darting look at Officer Kennedy. "We'll be in touch, Earl."

"Be careful," Evelyn urged them, wringing her hands.

Greg and Nick both assured her they would be. And then, with a quick, low word of instruction for Steve, they rushed to Nick's car.

"Do you think we're acting impulsively? Flying to Dallas like this, I mean?" Greg asked on the way to the airport.

"At least we're doing something," Nick answered with a shrug. "I don't think I could have kept pacing that room much longer without taking something apart."

"I know the feeling. I was about ready to get in my car and just start driving, looking for her."

"Even that would have been better than the waiting."

Greg looked out the window for a long, silent minute before turning back to Nick. "You really care about Lindsay, don't you? It's really serious between the two of you."

"Yeah," Nick said hoarsely. "Damned serious."

"We'll find her, Nick."

"We have to," Nick agreed. He refused to even think about the alternatives.

Chapter Fourteen

Having been summoned by the security intercom at the gate, Tony D'Alessandro was waiting at the open front door of his home when Nick and Greg drove up in the car they'd hastily rented at the Dallas airport. It was eleven o'clock, and though he'd been taken aback by hearing Nick identify himself at that hour, he'd opened the gates without question. Now he wanted to know why Nick had returned to Dallas at this late hour, only a day after he'd left with Lindsay. "What's going on?"

"Have you heard from Lindsay?" Nick asked bluntly, wasting no time with preliminaries.

"Not since the two of you left here yesterday. Why?"

"Have you authorized anyone to contact her in Little Rock? Someone described as well dressed and middle-aged, driving a large, dark blue sedan with Texas tags? Does that sound like one of your people?"

Tony shook his head, beginning to frown. "No. What's happened, Nick?"

"Lindsay's missing," Nick answered bleakly. "No one has seen her since she got into the car I just described as she was leaving the school where she teaches. That was at four this afternoon. She was supposed to have visited with her mother on her way home, but she never showed up. Her car is still sitting in the school parking lot. We found her key ring, with all her keys on it, lying on the hood of her car."

"Lindsay's missing?" Michelle stood in the doorway, clutching a satin bathrobe to her throat, her blue eyes—so like Lindsay's, Nick thought with a pang—wide with distress. Nick heard Greg catch his breath at the sight of Michelle, and knew that Greg, too, was shaken by Michelle's uncanny resemblance to Lindsay.

"Come inside," Tony ordered, holding the door for them. "I want to hear everything from the beginning."

Running a hand through his hair, Nick entered the house, aware of a deep sense of disappointment. "I was hoping you'd know something about this," he admitted.

"I wish I did," Tony answered gravely. He looked at Greg. "I'm Tony D'Alessandro. This is my wife, Michelle, Lindsay's sister."

Greg handled his own introduction. "Greg Hillman. Lindsay's brother."

Michelle hardly seemed to hear the introductions. She had turned to her husband, her face deathly white, eyes haunted. "Tony? Do you think she's been . . . kidnapped?"

Tony hesitated. "It's a possibility, Michelle."

"Oh, God." Nick hadn't thought she could go any whiter, but she did. "Oh, Tony. . ."

Tony slipped a bracing arm around her shoulders. "I know, sweetheart." He looked at Nick and Greg. "Michelle was kidnapped when she was eight," he explained tersely. "She was held for five days before she was rescued."

Five days. Shaken, Nick touched Michelle's hand. "I'm sorry."

Michelle drew a deep breath, obviously shaking off the old memories as she concentrated on the present situation. "We don't know that anything's happened to Lindsay," she said, reassuring them as well as herself. "Tony will find her," she added with encouraging confidence.

As though by habit, Tony picked up a pencil and pad the moment they entered the den, making notes of everything Nick and Greg told him. "There's definitely reason to be concerned," he agreed unnecessarily, now looking as worried as the others. "We have nothing to do with this, Nick. I hope you believe that."

Nick nodded, instinctively certain Tony was telling the truth, even without Michelle's convincing distress as proof. "Yeah. So, what do we do now?"

"I'll make some calls. I've got a few connections in Little Rock. I'll call them as soon as I've dispatched a couple of my own guys. The police won't be able to do anything for a while yet, but we don't have their regulations to hold us back. I'll need the name of the teacher who saw Lindsay leave. Chuck will have a lot of questions for him."

"Tell him to call my brother Steve at my parents' house," Greg suggested. "Steve can get him in contact with the teacher."

Tony made a note. "I'll get started. Michelle, use the other line and set up a charter flight to Little Rock for Nick and Greg and me. Oh, and call Jared. He'll want to know what's going on."

"We don't need a charter plane," Nick informed them. "Greg's a pilot. We came in his plane—an eight-seater."

Tony nodded. "Good. We'll want to get in the air as soon as we can. I'll take a cellular phone with us."

For the first time in his stubbornly independent life, Nick found himself looking to someone else to take charge, almost humbly asking for help. He caught Tony's arm in a white-knuckled grip. His voice was almost unrecognizable, even to him. "Find Lindsay, Tony. Whatever it takes, whatever you have to do—find her."

Tony searched Nick's face with sympathetic eyes. "We'll find her, Nick. This is what I do, remember?"

Nick sighed and released him. "I just hope you're as good as I think you are."

"I am. Better." Tony managed a tight, reassuring smile and then went into action.

It was dark and stuffy in the closet. The approximately three-by-six foot space barely gave Lindsay room to move around, though she tried pacing from one end to the other as a means of holding off the panic that threatened to overtake her. A metal bar ran the length of the empty closet, and she bumped her head on it more than once when she turned to retrace her few, jerky steps. She stopped every few minutes to try the door, as though the lock that held it closed might have magically vanished since the last time she'd checked. At least it gave her something to do besides cry.

She was scared—and she was terribly confused. What was she doing here? What did he want from her?

The man who'd abducted her from the school parking lot, the one calling himself Bob Carter, had refused to answer any of her desperate questions, ordering her, instead, to shut up and cooperate with everything he told her to do. He'd driven her to an alleyway not far from her school, where he'd parked the car, wrapped a blindfold of some sort

around her eyes, tied her hands behind her and ordered her
to lie down in the back seat.

Sometime later—it could have been minutes or hours for
all she knew, disoriented by fear and bewilderment—he'd
put the gun in her back and brought her into the place. He'd
untied her hands and shoved her roughly into this closet.
She'd heard the locks snap even as she'd reached up to
snatch off the blindfold—not that it had done any good,
since the closet was dark and she'd been even further hampered by her night blindness.

What did he want from her? Why was he holding her
here? Over and over, the questions repeated in her mind, but
no logical answer presented itself. The man hadn't looked
like a criminal, more like a respectable businessman, but his
eyes had held a cold determination that told her he'd re-
solved to go through with whatever he'd planned for her.
His hands had shaken just a bit, telling her he was anxious,
probably unaccustomed to this sort of activity, but he'd
looked desperate enough, determined enough to terrify her.

She'd been kidnapped. But why? What could he possibly
hope to gain? At first, she'd wondered frantically if he were
a rapist, taking her someplace private where he could tor-
ture, maybe even kill her. Perhaps he was, but he'd given no
indication so far that he was interested in her physically.

Not, she thought with a sick clench of her stomach, that
he couldn't still prove to be just that. All-too-clear memories of famous, gruesome crimes lurked at the back of her
mind as she wondered if Carter—or whoever he was—was
only biding his time before attacking her. Toying with her,
perhaps. Playing on her fears.

She shuddered, touching a wall before turning to pace the
five steps to the other end of the closet. What else could he
possibly want? Money? Surely not. Her family was hardly
wealthy. Even combining all their resources, her parents and

brothers would have a hard time coming up with enough ransom to make the risks of kidnapping worthwhile. Could Carter have mistaken her for someone else, perhaps? But, no. He'd called her by name.

She thought of her family's fear for her. They'd know something was wrong by now. They'd know she was in trouble. They'd be sick with worry. Her eyes filled with tears and she stumbled, bumping her head again on the metal bar.

But mostly, she thought of Nick. Even when her mind whirled with questions and unpleasant possibilities, even as she longed for the comfort of her family, even as she tried to think of some way to escape this locked room, Nick was never out of her thoughts. She wanted him so desperately, prayed that he'd find her, tried to imagine how he must be feeling now. Did he know how much she loved him? Would she ever have the chance to tell him?

Would she ever have the opportunity to help him shake off his past and give them a chance at a future together?

Would she never see Nick—or any of her family—again?

She tried the door one more time, found it still locked, and rested her head wearily against its rough, dusty surface, finally giving in to the despair that had threatened for hours. "Nick," she whispered brokenly. "Oh, Nick, where are you?"

Nick was still in Dallas, impatient to get away. Tony had been on the telephone for half an hour, calling in every contact he had to assist with the search for Lindsay. Jared had arrived a few minutes earlier, having left his ranch immediately after Michelle called. Though he said Cassie would have liked to assist in the search, she'd elected to stay home with Shane, who'd been upset by the news that his newly discovered aunt was missing.

"Okay," Tony said, hanging up the phone and standing. "Chuck's on his way to Little Rock, and an associate there is already making calls. Michelle, you stay by the phones here in case Lindsay or someone from her family calls. The rest of us can head for the airport now. Greg, is your plane ready for takeoff, or should we call and take care of it from here?"

Greg shook his head. "I left instructions for it to be topped off and ready to fly."

Tony nodded. "Good. Jared, I assume you're going with us?"

"Damn straight."

The corner of Tony's mouth twitched at the familiar response. "Right. Let's go, then." He kissed his wife, promised he'd be in contact the moment he had any news, then turned for the door.

Followed by Nick, Jared and Greg, he'd taken only a few steps when the phone rang. All of them stopped and turned toward the sound. Michelle snatched up the receiver just as it began to ring a second time. "Hello?"

Tensely, Nick watched her face for a sign. His throat tightened in foreboding when her eyes went wide with what appeared to be shock, the little color that had returned to her cheeks fading again.

"Carter?" Michelle whispered, her hand tightening visibly around the telephone receiver. "Where are you? Why are you calling?"

Nick didn't know the name, of course, but from the way Tony and Jared reacted, he assumed they did—and weren't happy that he'd called. He looked from one to the other, studying their almost identical looks of distaste.

And then Michelle regained his full attention when she demanded, "Where is she, Carter? What have you done with my sister?"

Jared spat a curse from between clenched teeth. Tony dashed out of the room, and Nick assumed he was headed for an extension phone. Nick and Greg looked at each other in frowning question, then back at Michelle.

"You really have gone crazy if you think you'll get away with this, Carter!" she was saying furiously. "How dare you touch my family? My father *trusted* you, dammit!"

And then she stiffened, her anger transformed to fear. "No," she whispered. "No, Carter, please. Don't hurt her. She hasn't done anything to you."

Nick's fists had clenched at his sides, every muscle in his body tensing for battle. If someone had taken Lindsay—if he hurt her—Nick wouldn't rest until he had the bastard's throat in his hands.

"Yes, I'm listening," Michelle said tautly. "All right. Yes, I'll be waiting. Carter, please—"

And then her voice faded and she lowered the receiver slowly away from her ear. "He hung up."

"Who hung up? Michelle, who has Lindsay?" Nick demanded, stepping toward her.

"His name is Carter Powell," Tony said from the doorway, his face dark with anger. He crossed to his wife, sliding an arm around her shoulders as he continued to fill Nick and Greg in. "He's a bail-jumping, crooked lawyer with a grudge against me. Not long after I met Michelle, I found evidence that Powell had been stealing from her—and from several other clients, incidentally—for several years. When I gave the information to Michelle, she called the police. Powell was arrested. His rich wife dumped him—as did his sexy young mistress—and his law firm canned him. He faces disbarment and a prison sentence. He blames me."

"So he took Lindsay?" Looking stunned, Greg shook his head. "That doesn't make sense."

"He wants money," Michelle explained shakily. "He says we owe him enough to set up comfortably in another country. He's holding my sister for ransom. He pointed out that he could have just as easily taken one of Layla's children— or Shane," she added, glancing tearfully at Jared. "He called himself a 'reasonable man' for not taking one of the children, and he promised to release Lindsay unharmed if we cooperate with the money."

"I'll kill him," Nick said dispassionately, beyond anger now. He'd gone oddly numb, his thoughts centered only on getting his hands on this Powell guy—after he'd found Lindsay, of course.

"I'll help you," Jared muttered, his hard, cowboy face set in white-lipped fury. "That son of a—"

"Now, wait a minute, you two," Tony warned, holding up a hand. "We'll find Lindsay. Powell's an amateur at this. He doesn't know what he's up against."

"You've got *that* right," Jared said coolly.

"Where are you supposed to make the drop?" Greg asked, pushing aside his own concern for his sister to help work out a plan.

"He said he'd call us back. I think he wants us to stew awhile."

"The police?" Greg suggested.

Michelle quickly shook her head. "He said…he said he'd kill her if we brought the police in."

"Will he?" Jared asked Tony.

Tony shrugged, hesitating only a moment. "I don't know," he admitted. "He's desperate. He's already lost everything else. That makes him dangerous."

His banked temper suddenly igniting again, Nick slammed one fist into the other palm in an explosion of pain and fury. "Dammit, I knew nothing good would come of this reunion!" he snarled, futilely looking for something to blame for Lindsay's peril. "I told her nothing good could come of digging up the past."

Michelle gasped, her hand going to her throat.

Greg reached out to touch Nick's arm, soothingly, but Nick shook him off, refusing to be so easily mollified.

Jared snarled something Nick didn't even try to catch.

But, again, it was Tony who made himself heard most effectively. "You think any of us would have contacted Lindsay if we'd known this would happen?" he asked, his tone icy. "For all we know, Carter found her before we did and only waited until after we'd met her before grabbing her. He's known about Michelle's family from the time they were separated."

"Oh, Nick, don't you know how sorry we are that this has happened?" Michelle asked, her blue eyes filled with unshed tears. "Don't you know that I'd trade places with Lindsay if I could to spare her this?"

Only then did Nick remember that Michelle had once been a kidnapping victim herself. And he'd been an insensitive jerk. "I'm sorry," he muttered awkwardly. "I just—dammit, I love her. And I *hate* feeling helpless!"

Michelle was the first to reach out to him, despite her obvious distress at his words. "We understand, Nick. You're frightened for her—we all are. But Tony will find her. Trust him."

It was hard to argue with her absolute faith in her husband's expertise—or with his own instinctive belief that D'Alessandro knew what he was doing. Nick drew a deep, calming breath and nodded. "All right. What do we do now?"

"I make some more calls," Tony answered, still a bit stiff after Nick's outburst, which had been so painful for Michelle. "We wait for Powell to call back. Then we go get Lindsay."

He made it sound so simple. Though he knew it wouldn't be that easy, Nick allowed himself to be reassured. He needed all the confidence he could find to get through the next few hours.

Lindsay sat on the floor, her knees drawn up, arms tight around them, forehead down. She didn't know how long she'd been here, but it seemed like days. She tried to tell herself it could only have been a matter of hours, guessing that it was around midnight. If only she could see her watch.

She was tired, thirsty, dispirited. She was beginning to believe she'd never leave the closet, that Carter had locked her in here to die. That she'd never be found until it was much too late.

She ached all over. Having tired of pacing and trying the doorknob, she'd finally tried to batter her way through— hammering with her fists, feet, shoulders, throwing herself at the solidly built door again and again until she'd finally been too tired and bruised to continue. She hadn't conceded defeat, she told herself wearily. She was only resting until she'd recovered enough strength to start again.

When the door suddenly opened, she gasped and jerked her head upward, praying for rescue. Momentarily blinded by the light streaming in from the other room, she couldn't at first see who stood in the closet doorway. And then he spoke. "I've brought you some food and water. Get up."

It was Bob Carter—or whatever his name was. Disappointed, Lindsay sat still, fighting her fear, blinking furiously in an attempt to clear her vision, knowing she had to be ready for the first opportunity to get away.

"I said get up! Now!" He wasn't as calm as he'd been earlier. Either something had happened since, or his own anxiety was building. Either way, Lindsay didn't like it.

She pushed herself slowly upright, wincing when her abused muscles protested. And then she stumbled, reaching out to steady herself against the wall.

With a sound of impatience, Carter grabbed her arm and pulled her toward him. "What's wrong with you?"

"I have night blindness," she snapped in return. "It will take a few minutes for my eyes to adjust to the light."

His grip loosened somewhat on her arm. "There's a chair to your left," he said gruffly. "Sit down."

Still squinting, Lindsay turned her head and located the chair he'd pointed out. A battered folding metal chair was the only item of furniture in the small, dingy room. A bare light bulb hung above it. The floor was a dull, filthy-looking, once-green linoleum, the walls had been painted white maybe thirty years earlier and not touched since. There was no window.

"I'll stand."

"I said *sit*." He pushed her roughly toward the chair.

Hearing the edge of temper in his voice, Lindsay perched on the very edge of the cold metal seat. "All right. I'm sitting. Now what?" She held her chin high as she spoke, refusing to show him how frightened she was.

Surprisingly enough, he chuckled at her defiant tone. "Damn, but you look just like her," he startled her by saying with a shake of his graying head. "Sound like her, too, when she gets in a temper."

The only person Lindsay so closely resembled, as far as she knew, was... "Michelle?"

Carter's smile vanished, his face hardening. A chill slithered down Lindsay's spine. "Yeah. Michelle," he snarled. "Thanks to your bitch of a sister and her gigolo of a husband, I'm reduced to this. A few months ago, I had it all. A partnership in an old, established law firm. A wife and a home in one of the most exclusive Dallas neighborhoods. A beautiful mistress in Houston. D'Alessandro took that away from me. Now he'll pay.''

Stunned—strangely enough, Lindsay had never even considered that her abduction might be connected with her family in Dallas—she stared at him. "You've kidnapped me to get back at *Tony?*"

"I'm holding you for ransom," he corrected her, his dark eyes gleaming. Lindsay didn't at all like the expression in their depths, nor the faintest hint of madness in his voice. "They owe me," he emphasized. "They drove me to this. I warned D'Alessandro that he didn't know who he was messing with, but he just wouldn't listen. Had to impress Michelle, so he could get his hands on all that money.''

"Tony loves Michelle," Lindsay couldn't help protesting. "He isn't interested in her money.''

Carter's harsh obscenity made her flinch. "If you really believe that, you're as stupid and naive as your sister. I took care of her for twenty-four years. I handled her adoption, took her out of foster care and gave her to one of the wealthiest families in Texas. I saw that she had money for college. I made sure she had the means to keep up the Trent estate, along with its staff, after Harrison and Alicia died. Anything she needed, all she had to do was call me. Yet she threw me over without a second thought when that lying, smooth-talking Italian crawled into her bed.''

"I'm sure Michelle appreciated everything you did for her," Lindsay suggested uncertainly.

Carter sneered. "She had me arrested. She begrudged me even a small portion of all that money she inherited, even though she was damned lucky to have it in the first place. It wasn't as if she'd even been born to it. She was just some common, stray kid Alicia and Harrison took a fancy to. A grubby orphan from a miserable, alcohol-riddled, penniless couple with more kids than brains. She didn't deserve it all."

Lindsay shuddered, realizing just how far over the edge this man had gone. He talked like a fanatic, convinced of his own superiority, his own righteousness.

Unless she did something quickly, she was beginning to believe she would never leave this house alive.

"Why did you take me?" she asked, wondering if there was any reasoning with a desperate madman. "Michelle and Tony hardly know me. I only met them a few days ago. What makes you think they'd give you anything in exchange for my safety?"

Carter nodded, almost in approval, as though she'd made an excellent point. "I thought of snatching one of the kids— that bunch from Fort Worth. It wouldn't have been hard. They play out in their front yard all the time. A little candy... a kitten, maybe... But it would have been a bit more risky. Too close to home, and the cops tend to act faster when little kids are involved."

Oh, God. Lindsay pictured the smiling, innocent faces of Layla's children. Dawn, Keith, tiny Brittany. And this man would have taken any one of them without a second thought, had it not been more inconvenient for him. He'd obviously rejected the idea only for practicality, not from any sense of conscience.

Wouldn't a man who was capable of stealing a child be as likely to commit murder if it became necessary in his opinion?

"Still," she said hoarsely, trying one last time to appeal to whatever rational part of him remained, "I'm practically a stranger to the D'Alessandros. They have no particular loyalty to me."

He looked at her again, derisively. "I think you already know better than that. Michelle's been looking for you for

months. Now that she's met you, she'd do anything for you.
I could have gotten you at any time over the past three
weeks," he added smugly. "I've had someone watching you
for that long. I simply thought it better to let Michelle spend
some time with you, get attached to you, before I made my
demands. And it worked. You should have heard her beg me
not to hurt you."

The dark pickup. So she hadn't been paranoid.

Nick's going to be furious when he finds out, she thought
inconsequentially. *He won't be able to resist pointing out
that I should have told him about the truck the first time I
saw it.*

But would she ever have the opportunity to hear Nick's
lecture? Oh, how she hoped she would!

"You've called Michelle?" she asked numbly.

"Yes. And it's about time for me to call again, to arrange the exchange of money. You can eat something while
I'm out of the room. Oh, by the way, there's no need to try
the door. It will be locked, and I'll be just on the other side."

"No, wait. Please, I—"

But Carter only gave her a vaguely threatening look and
let himself out of the small room, firmly closing and locking the door behind him.

Lindsay sagged in the chair, trying to assimilate everything he'd told her, wondering why he'd been so expansive.
Had he simply been unable to resist an opportunity to brag
about his resourcefulness? Had it been a while since he'd
had anyone to talk to? Or—she swallowed—was he so confident that she wouldn't be around later to tell anyone what
he'd said?

He'd left the food lying on a newspaper spread on the
floor. A sandwich wrapped in waxed paper, an apple, a
canned cola. The thought of food made her stomach turn,
but she was thirsty enough to down half the cola without

caring that it was warm. She spent a few futile minutes looking for a means of escape, but the windowless room offered no alternatives other than the door. She tiptoed closer to the door, pressing her ear against it as she carefully tried the knob.

As she'd expected, it was locked. She closed her eyes and tried to listen through the wood for sounds from the next room. She could hear her captor speaking. Was there someone with him? she wondered in despair, afraid she'd never escape if he had assistance. Was it the man from the dark pickup?

But then she realized that Carter was talking on a telephone. It seemed hard to believe that this dump with no furniture would have a phone. He must have spent many hours planning this abduction, down to the last detail.

She strained to hear his words, realizing that he must be talking to Michelle or Tony. She caught snatches of threats, of commands to leave the police out of this, of smug derision aimed at Tony. She heard him name two streets she recognized, located in the least desirable, most dangerous portion of the city. A drop-off point? she wondered, biting her lip as she tried to plan, fought to stay calm.

She had to get away. She had too much pride, too much to live for to go along with this man without resistance. She'd been prepared to fight for Nick's love, to risk everything for their happiness. Now she was fully determined to fight, if necessary, for her life. The only advantage she could think of in her favor was that Carter could be underestimating her—that he thought her too frightened and vulnerable to confront him.

He was wrong.

It was now or never, she decided, taking a deep breath and squaring her shoulders, listening for approaching footsteps. The moment Carter opened the door, she would make her move. He was older, perhaps slower than she; she had a chance—a small chance—of getting away from him if she took him by surprise, didn't give him an opportunity to pull out his weapon.

If there was someone else with him . . . well, that was just a risk she'd have to take.

Chapter Fifteen

It almost worked.

The moment Carter opened the door, Lindsay shoved past him, intent on running as fast as she could, without looking back. Had she not been wearing a full denim skirt, she might have made it. Caught by surprise, Carter made a frantic snatch at her, his fingers just snagging the hem of the garment. He tugged hard, almost jerking her off her feet. Lindsay fought him, playing a desperate game of tug-of-war with the heavy fabric, putting all her strength into the effort, her breath catching in ragged sobs.

"Dammit, be *still!*" Carter exploded, just before the back of his hand crashed against the side of her face.

Multicolored stars exploded before her eyes. Lindsay reeled, the salty, coppery taste of blood filling her mouth, her stomach wrenching in response to the pain and the violence. She staggered, fighting to stay on her feet, and falling when he caught her arm and threw her bodily back into the windowless room. She landed on the floor on all fours, her knees taking the brunt of the heavy impact, one ankle twisting sickeningly beneath her. She cried out in pain.

"One more stunt like that and you *won't* live to regret it, is that clear?" He was furious and made no effort to hide it.

Lindsay didn't even try to answer. She was trying too hard not to be sick. She wouldn't give him that satisfaction.

The door slammed and she was alone again, curled in a dazed, bleeding, aching ball on the filthy floor. Her ankle throbbed and burned, and a savage pounding in her head made her moan. The taste of blood was making her gag. She wiped the back of one shaking hand across her mouth, and it came away bright red. She reached unsteadily for the soda can, rinsing her mouth out with the warm liquid, wincing when the acidic carbonation burned the cut her teeth had sliced into the soft flesh when Carter's knuckles had made contact with her cheek.

For just a moment, she found herself losing all hope of getting out of this alive. She thought of the family she loved so deeply, the new family who could have meant so much to her, given time. She thought of Nick and all they could have had if they'd been able to work out their problems—and only then did she start to cry.

She never would have believed she could have fallen asleep there on the hard linoleum floor, surrounded by dirt and dried blood and old newspaper. Perhaps she'd simply given in to exhaustion and pain, escaping into the blessed oblivion of unconsciousness rather than facing the bleak, lonely present.

She dreamed of Nick, dreamed that he was holding her, kissing her, loving her, promising he'd never leave her again, never let anyone hurt her again. She wanted so desperately to believe him, wanted so much for him to help her, to shelter her. But then a large hand shook her rudely awake, and he was gone again, leaving her no one to depend on but herself.

"Back in the closet," Carter ordered curtly, pulling roughly on her arm to force her to her feet. "It's time for me to go."

Time for the ransom exchange, Lindsay realized groggily, pushing her tangled hair away from her sore, bruised face. So why was Carter putting her back in the closet?

"You're not going to let me go, are you?" she asked quietly, the words hard to form through her dry, swollen lips.

He didn't meet her eyes. "As soon as D'Alessandro drops off the money and I'm convinced he hasn't called in the cops, you'll be released," he told her.

He's lying, she thought with certainty. He had no intention of giving her back to her family.

Carter pushed her into the closet. She caught her balance and turned to face him. "How do you know he'll show up?" she dared to ask.

"He'll show up," he answered confidently. And then he reached into the pocket of his jacket and pulled out the gun he'd brandished in the school parking lot. "D'Alessandro's going to pay for what he did to me."

"What are you—"

He slammed the closet door before she could finish her question, throwing her back into the suffocating darkness.

What was that madman planning to do to Tony? She hugged her arms to her chest and shivered, remembering the cold, savage look in Carter's eyes. Tony was in danger— terrible danger—and there seemed to be nothing Lindsay could do about it.

Hearing the distant slam of an outer door, she knew she was alone in the house. Carter obviously knew she wouldn't be able to scream for help, or he would have gagged her.

Where was she? Just how isolated was this place? What were the chances that someone would find her if he never returned?

She took a deep breath to avert panic. She had to get out. One way or another, she had to get out.

She threw herself against the door again, groaning when her bruised shoulder slammed into the unyielding wood. "Dammit!" she shouted, comforted by the sound of her own angry voice.

Taking the doorknob in both hands, she shook it as hard as she could, cursing, kicking the door, fighting to escape.

Nothing.

"Think, dammit. *Think!*" she ordered herself, frustrated by the total blackness surrounding her.

Her thumb brushed a hole in the doorknob. She froze, then painstakingly ran her fingers across the cold, hard surface, trying to visualize the lock. The hole was small, and round, not large enough for a key. An interior privacy lock, she realized. One meant to secure a bathroom or bedroom door operated by a push button on the other side. Carter obviously hadn't been greatly worried that she'd find a way out.

She remembered the time little Tricia had locked herself into the bathroom at Lindsay's parents' house. Greg had freed her by poking an ice pick into the hole on the outside of the doorknob, pressing some inner mechanism to release the lock.

If only Lindsay had something long and sharp to push into this hole. But Carter had taken her purse and made sure the deep pockets of her denim skirt were empty, leaving her with nothing but her clothing and her flat leather shoes. She didn't even have a barrette or hairpin, having left her hair loose around her shoulders that morning. It seemed like so very long ago since she'd dressed for school.

"*Think*, Lindsay!"

She stilled, her breath catching in her throat. Slowly she touched a hand to the soft, braided leather belt threaded through the loops of her denim skirt. Her belt.

Her breath escaped in a jubilant gasp. Her obnoxious, smugly confident, undoubtedly mad captor had over-looked something, after all. His insane thirst for revenge had finally made him sloppy.

Frantically, her fingers made clumsy by haste, she unfas-tened the belt and jerked it out of the loops. A moment later she was poking blindly at the doorknob with the long metal tongue of the belt buckle. She laughed out loud when she heard the mechanism give, felt the knob turn in her hand. The sound of her own laugh unnerved her; it sounded al-most as unhinged as Carter's.

Carter had closed the door and turned off the light in the windowless room connected to the closet. Lindsay groped her way across the room, cursing her limitations, flinching every time her twisted right ankle bore her weight. Hurry-ing as much as possible, she didn't realize the metal chair was in her path until she stumbled over it.

It collapsed beneath her, causing her to fall heavily on top of it, her breath leaving her in a painful whoosh when her ribs connected with the hard metal. Something sharp caught her forearm; she suspected that the old chair had a few jag-ged edges. Already she could feel the sticky warmth of fresh blood on her skin, though she didn't yet feel the pain of the cut.

The second door opened even more easily than the first had. Lindsay was half tempted to kiss her belt buckle, but didn't have time to spare for giddiness.

"*D'Alessandro's going to pay for what he did to me.*"

No. She didn't have time to waste.

She limped rapidly into a small, dirty kitchen, looking around wildly for the telephone Carter had used, planning to call 911 and have the police meet her at the intersection she'd heard him name. There was no phone. She looked blankly at the empty telephone jack on the dirt-smeared wall. Could it be in another room? But she'd been so sure she'd heard Carter talking in this room.

She closed her eyes with a groan when she realized what he must have used. A portable, cellular phone. She should have known from the beginning that it was unlikely that this vacant, dilapidated bungalow would be furnished with phone service.

She turned toward the outer door, hoping it hadn't been secured with dead-bolt locks, which would require a key. If so, she'd be forced to break through a window somehow. But the flimsy, aging doors were ridiculously inadequate, the locks no more effective than the two she'd already handled.

Lindsay threw open the kitchen door and rushed outside, intent only on reaching Tony in time to warn him that the man waiting for him was armed and vengeful. Shivering in the damp, cold, foggy night air, she wished desperately for a telephone with which to call the police—call Nick—but she was afraid there wasn't time to find one. It might be too late already, she thought grimly.

Frustratingly hampered by her limited vision, which was made even worse by the heavy fog that hung eerily white in the air around her, she squinted into the shadows, trying to find some clue as to her location. The neighborhood seemed hauntingly deserted, a row of empty, boarded-up houses and bare, rutted yards. No wonder Carter hadn't been worried about anyone hearing her scream. Chances were the only people around, if any, were vagrants looking for shelter from the cold, early December temperatures. Even if one of them heard her, the chances were slim she'd find assistance from that quarter. Might even find herself in more trouble than she was already in.

Her hands held in front of her to prevent her from running into anything, she stumbled desperately down the broken, uneven sidewalk, trying not to think about how alone, how vulnerable she was on these deserted streets. She thought she knew where she was now, thought she recognized a few of the hazy landmarks ahead, and it wasn't a neighborhood that was safe for a lone woman at night—or even in broad daylight, for that matter. Some of the rundown houses she passed looked occupied, and she considered stopping to ask for help, but fear drove her on. Fear of what could happen to her if she stopped, fear that once she stopped running she'd collapse, fear for Tony.

The only comfort she found was that, if she was indeed where she thought she was, the intersection Carter had named was only some eight to ten blocks away.

She could make it that far—maybe.

She had no choice.

She began to run, her gait broken by the throbbing ankle, her breathing ragged, her head, arm and shoulders aching. She fought dizziness, telling herself it was only panic making her light-headed, assuring herself that she'd come this far and wouldn't be stopped now. The ripped right sleeve to her once-white blouse looked almost black when she glanced down at it. Her right arm felt heavy, strangely numb. She couldn't think about that, couldn't allow herself to dwell on how much blood it would take to discolor the sleeve to that extent.

A staggering, odorous figure shuffled out of the shadows of one of the vacant houses. "Where ya goin'?" it mumbled, reaching awkwardly out to her. "Hey, honey, where ya goin'?"

She gasped and swerved out of the man's way, somehow finding the strength to increase her speed, though fire coursed up her leg with each jarring step she took. She could have wept with relief when she realized that the vagrant hadn't tried to follow her. It had to be three o'clock or later; thank heaven old downtown Little Rock was nearly deserted at that hour on a weekday morning.

She stumbled over a broken piece of concrete and moaned when her teeth connected sharply with her already-damaged lower lip, bringing the taste of blood back to her mouth. *Tony,* she thought dimly, struggling onward. *Remember Tony.*

Yet it was another name that hovered in her shaky consciousness, giving her strength when she would have fallen, keeping her going when she would have given up.

Nick. Oh, Nick, I need you. Where are you?

She would probably never remember the details of that run. By the time she reached the alley, she was in more pain than she'd ever known—her head, her ankle, her arm, her lungs. She'd begun to think longingly of just falling to the pavement and letting the darkness have her. But she'd made herself run three more steps, and then four, and somehow she kept going.

There was an alley between two vacant, shabby commercial buildings at the intersection she'd heard Carter name. By now, she'd almost convinced herself that she hadn't heard him clearly, after all, that she probably had no chance of intercepting Carter before he could harm Tony. She should have stopped somewhere and called the police, she thought, her face wet with tears and exhaustion. She'd been wrong to try to stop this herself.

Still, she found herself slipping as silently as possible into the alleyway, struggling to see in the darkness, grateful for the dim lighting provided by a nearby halogen security lamp. It didn't give her much vision, but enough that she could see darker shadows against the grayness. At the end of the alley—was that a big Dumpster? Wasn't that a logical place for the drop Carter would have ordered?

She took a step forward. Stopped when she heard Tony's voice. "Powell?" he said, sounding startled.

Who was Powell? The man who'd called himself Carter? Lindsay opened her mouth to shout a warning to Tony about the gun. The cry was drowned out by the sound of a shot.

Her scream was instinctive, ripped from her throat in anguish, despite the danger to herself. Was Tony dead? Had he died trying to rescue her?

Oh, Michelle, I'm so sorry.

And suddenly there were other shadows, at least three men surrounding the one that must be Carter—or Powell, or whoever he was. And there were voices—shouts—sounding like Greg and Jared and... "Nick?" she whispered as the multilayered darkness began to spin around her. She put all her strength into one last cry. *"Nick!"*

And then she fell.

The moment the gun went off, Nick lunged forward, taking Powell with a flying tackle straight from his college football training. He heard the gun clatter against the pavement even as Powell landed heavily beneath him, sensed that someone—probably Jared—had rushed forward to grab it. He heard Greg yell Tony's name, heard Tony answer, heard Jared shout a question at someone—Powell?

And then he heard the scream, heard his name. *Lindsay.*

She was okay. She was here. Powell had brought her for the exchange. Or had he intended to take her with him as a shield against the retribution he must have been expecting?

Powell was struggling, swinging wildly, spitting obsceni-
ties in a voice edged with insanity. "I'll kill her," he warned
wildly, one fist connecting ineffectively with Nick's jaw.
"I'll kill her."

This final threat to Lindsay—no matter how pathetically
impotent—was all Nick needed to release the fury that had
been building inside him for so many long, anguished hours.
His fury escaping in a low, feral growl, he slammed Powell
to the pavement and wrapped his hands around the man's
throat, fully intending, at that moment, to kill him.

Powell clawed at Nick's wrists, bucking helplessly beneath him. The halogen lights illuminated both the fear and
the madness in the older man's widened eyes. Nick tightened his fingers.

Other hands grabbed him, tugging at his arms, his shoulders. "Let him go, Nick," Tony urged. "C'mon, man,
we've got him. Let him go."

"He's beaten, Nick," Jared seconded. "Let us have him."

Both men sounded as though they fully understood
Nick's actions, even as they tried their best to stop him.

Staring into Powell's eyes, knowing he had only to tighten
his fingers a bit more to exact full revenge for Lindsay's abduction, Nick froze. And realized that, no matter how much
he hated this man, he couldn't kill him. Tony and Jared had
nothing to do with it; even had they not been there, Nick
wouldn't have finished what he'd started.

He was a doctor. He saved lives. He didn't take them.

He loosened his hands, hearing Powell gasp frantically for
air, hearing Tony and Jared give identical exhalations of
relief.

"Nick! Nick, get over here! Lindsay's hurt! Oh, hell, it
looks bad."

Greg's shout had Nick on his feet, Powell forgotten.
Leaving the man to Tony and Jared, he rushed toward the

end of the alley, where Greg knelt beside a small, huddled form.

"Lindsay!" Oh, God, was he going to lose her, after all?

He pushed Greg out of the way, letting the full light from behind them fall on Lindsay's pale face. "Let me see her."

Greg obligingly moved out of the way, though he stayed close. "I've got the flashlight," he reminded Nick.

"Good. Put it on her face."

She was alive, though deeply unconscious. There was no color in her face, other than the bruises on her cheek that stood out so dramatically against her paleness. Nick recognized the marks of a powerful, openhanded blow—and was almost tempted to turn back to finish the job on Powell. For the first time in his professional life, he found himself having to fight for control, having to focus himself into the objectivity required for the performance of his job.

Her broken breathing and her shallow pulse made Nick's stomach clench. He ran his hands carefully, tenderly over her, searching for injuries. Her right ankle was horribly swollen, burning hot to the touch. But it was the long, jagged, still-bleeding rip on her arm that concerned him most. She'd lost so much blood.

He wrapped his hands around the cut, applying pressure to the torn blood vessels. "Get to the car," he ordered Greg. "Call an ambulance."

It wasn't necessary for him to urge Greg to hurry.

"Hang on, baby," he whispered, his eyes locked on Lindsay's pale, still face. "I love you, Lindsay. Can you hear me? *I love you.*"

But she only moaned in response, a low, broken, forlorn sound that pierced Nick's aching heart.

* * *

Her mouth was so dry. Her lips felt parched and cracked. She moistened them with her tongue, then flinched when a twinge of pain resulted. How had she cut her lip?

Forcing her eyelids open, Lindsay blinked against the soft light that assaulted her. Then blinked again when she saw Nick sitting on the side of her bed, holding her left hand and looking down at her with tears in his beautiful blue-gray eyes.

Tears? She closed her eyes again, certain she must be imagining things. Nick didn't cry. He'd never allow his control to slip that far.

"Lindsay?" Even his voice sounded different—raw, husky, less crisp and certain than usual.

She opened her eyes again. "Nick?"

His tender smile broke her heart. He touched her face with unsteady fingers. "How do you feel, sweetheart?"

She was in a hospital room, dressed in a thin cloth gown and covered with a crisp white sheet. And she ached all over. She vaguely remembered being poked and prodded, fussed over and annoyed with questions and not-so-gentle ministrations. "Was it a truck or a bus?"

Nick looked confused. "What?"

"Whatever it was that ran over me. A truck or a bus?"

His smile deepened a bit. "Oh. Yeah, I guess you would feel that way."

The memories crashed back down on her, causing her fingers to tighten spasmodically in Nick's. "Carter," she said urgently. "He had a gun. He wanted to kill Tony."

"Tony's fine," Nick assured her, soothingly.

"But I heard a shot."

Nick shook his head. "Tony ducked."

She sagged into the thin pillow in relief. "Thank God. I was so afraid...."

And then she frowned. "Were you there?"

"Yeah. I was there."

"Oh. How...?"

"I'll tell you my side later. First, what about you? Do you remember what happened to you?"

She made a face that pulled uncomfortably at her bruises. "Vividly."

"Want to tell me about it now?"

"Could I have a drink of water first? My mouth is so dry."

"Of course." He released her hand to reach for the plastic pitcher on the stand beside the bed. Lindsay reached automatically with her right hand for the plastic cup he held out to her, then flinched and cried out softly as a fiery pain shot all the way up her arm.

Nick moved swiftly, easing her arm back down to her side, the plastic cup cradled in his left hand. "Let me help you, babe. That arm's going to be sore for a while."

"The metal chair," Lindsay murmured, looking down at the long row of dark stitches marking her red, swollen arm. "There must have been a sharp edge on it somewhere."

The cut looked deep. She didn't even want to think of the scar it would leave. At the moment, that didn't seem particularly important.

Nick held the straw to her lips, letting her take several long, refreshing sips before pulling it away. "Okay?"

"Yes, much better. Thanks."

"You lost quite a bit of blood from that cut." His voice was oddly flat, unnaturally calm. "Gave us a real scare."

"I'm sorry. I did it when I was trying to escape and warn Tony. The lights were out in the room and I couldn't see anything, so I just fell right over the chair."

He returned to his place on the side of the bed, taking her left hand in both of his own. "Tell me what happened to you, Lindsay."

She did, from the time the man identifying himself as Bob Carter had approached her in the school parking lot, until she'd heard the shot in the alleyway just before she'd passed out. It didn't take long to tell the story. She left out a lot of the details. Like how frightened she'd been. How she'd almost given up hope of ever getting out alive. How horrifying the painful run to the alleyway had been.

Nick didn't seem to need the blanks filled in to understand the ordeal Lindsay had been through. His hands tightened almost painfully around hers, his expression making her squeeze his fingers and whisper, "It's okay, Nick. It's over. I'm fine, really."

He lifted her hand to his face, cradling her palm against his cheek. "God, Lindsay, I thought I'd lost you. I thought I'd never see you again."

"I had a few thoughts along that line myself," she said unsteadily. "I kept telling myself that I had to get away, had to get back to you."

"I love you, Lindsay. I don't know if I could have gone on if anything had happened to you."

A surge of joy went through her, settling in her heart. He'd said the words to her before, but she hadn't been sure he meant them then. Now there could be no doubt of the sincerity in his deep voice. "Oh, Nick. I love you, too. I need you so badly."

His laugh was shaky. "Do you? I wasn't the one who broke you out of that place where Powell had you stashed. I wasn't the one who ran eight blocks with a sprained ankle and a slashed arm. You've accused me of being overprotective, of not giving you enough credit for taking care of yourself—it appears that you were right. I'm not sure you need me half as much as I need you, sweetheart."

For Nick to admit that he needed *anyone* was a miracle in itself. Lindsay's eyes filled with tears. "Trust me, Nick. The need is mutual."

"I've been such an idiot," he muttered, frowning in self-censure. "So convinced that I could always stay in control. Of my past, of my emotions...of you. Since you were taken, I realized how shaky my control really is. I was wrong to keep things from you, Lindsay, wrong to believe that ignoring my past would make it go away, that rejecting your past would protect you from the things I went through. You were right to resist my efforts to control you the way I tried to control everything else in my life. I'm sorry."

"Why were you so afraid of the past, Nick?" Lindsay asked carefully, almost holding her breath as she voiced the sensitive question.

"I didn't want to lose you," he answered simply. "I was afraid that if you ever knew everything about my background that you'd always wonder if the violence and ugliness I'd locked up inside me would escape to harm you."

"Oh, Nick," she whispered. "You are such a caring, giving, *gentle* man. I know you'd never hurt me—or anyone else, unless you were fighting for your own life or the life of someone you love."

"It wasn't always that way, Lindsay," he admitted slowly. "Before I came to your family, I *was* violent. Angry enough, frustrated enough to be dangerous. I'd seen so much, lived through so much, had to learn so early to fight back to protect myself, that I didn't think I could ever be turned around. I was taken out of my dysfunctional family when I finally tried to kill the man my alcoholic mother was living with at the time, a man who'd hit me—and her—one time too many. I *would* have killed him if someone hadn't pulled me off. I wanted him dead, and I wanted it to be at my hands. It took me a long time to deal with what I'd almost done."

"You were young, Nick. You were defending yourself."

He shook his head. "You were just a little girl when I came to your family. You probably don't remember the hard time I gave your father, how hard he worked to straighten me out. He almost gave up a couple of times, but something kept him at it. And there came a day when he finally made me realize I had to finally take responsibility for my own future. I could either go on as I was, fighting everyone around me, flaunting the rules, end up dead or in jail—or I could make something of myself."

He cleared his throat. "I decided to make something of myself. I realized I wanted to be someone who belonged with a family like yours, someone who fit in with nice people, decent people. Someone worthy of a woman like you."

"So you locked away all the ugly memories, all the dangerous emotions," Lindsay murmured in understanding.

He nodded. "Yeah. It seemed like the only way to put it behind me. I've always believed the violence, the ugliness was still there—that I wouldn't be able to control it unless I kept it firmly locked away."

"But you locked the good emotions away with the bad. All you left yourself were safe, superficial feelings, carefully planned goals and actions."

"Yes," he admitted. "And that wasn't enough for you."

"No. I want all of you, Nick. The good and the bad, the past, present and future. I could never have been satisfied with less."

"I understand that now. While you were missing, I realized that I couldn't control the past any more than I could control the future. I found out once and for all that I'm not a victim of that past, that I'm no longer the angry, violent threat to myself or others I might once have been. I wanted to kill Powell," he confessed, watching her closely as he spoke. "I wanted to punish him for daring to touch you. But when I had the opportunity, when I held his throat in my hands—I couldn't go through with it."

"Of course you couldn't."

"I'm not saying I wouldn't kill if I had to," he added, as though compelled to be totally honest now that he'd started this. "If it came to a choice between your life or someone else's, I'd do whatever I had to do to protect you."

"I know. It may not be a pleasant thing to realize, but it is human. We're capable of doing a great deal when our own lives or the lives of those we care about are threatened. I suppose that's something *I* learned during this ordeal," she added, remembering that desperate run through the darkness.

Nick took a deep breath. "Unlike you, I can't go back to my past, Lindsay. I wouldn't want to. But I can face it now, with your help. I can tell you about it, work out my feelings about it with you. And I'm pleased for you that you've found your own past. Tony and Jared were ready to risk their lives for you, and your sisters were sick with worry about you. You're very fortunate that you've found these special people. I'll never do anything again to try to come between you and your family—either of your families."

"You won't have to," she said softly, lovingly. "You're a part of both those families now. You belong, darling."

He groaned and lowered his head to kiss her, taking care not to hurt her split lip. "I don't deserve you, Lindsay," he murmured against her cheek. "But I love you."

"I love you, too. And I hope that marriage proposal is still open, because I don't ever want to let you out of my sight again—at least, not for long."

He lifted his head to smile down at her. "The proposal stands. Does this mean you've changed your answer?"

"Yes. The answer is yes, Nick. With all my heart."

He kissed her again, and she didn't care about the twinge of protest from her lip. Nick's kiss would make it better.

"Yep, she's awake," Steve's voice announced from the doorway. "Hey, Lindsay, if you can stop the gushy stuff for a few minutes, you've got an awful lot of family waiting out here to make sure you're okay."

Lindsay tore her gaze away from Nick's loving face to smile brightly at her brother. "I want to see my family. *All* of them," she added gaily. And then she looked back at Nick when Steve stepped out to usher the others in. "No matter how large my family becomes, Nick, I want you to know you'll always be first with me," she assured him, just in case there was any lingering uncertainty.

He brushed his lips against her bruised cheek. "Thank you, Lindsay. And you'll always be the most important part of my life. I love you."

Yes, she thought with a contented smile, he really did.

There were no longer any secrets between them.

Epilogue

They were married on Valentine's Day. Nick groaned at the unabashed sentimentality of the date, but because it amused Lindsay, he didn't protest overmuch. Even two months after her kidnapping, he still found it almost impossible to deny her anything she wanted. He'd come so close to losing her.

The wedding was a large, cheerful, splashy affair attended by the Hillman family, a whole platoon of former foster sons, Nick's professional associates, Lindsay's many friends and some of her students, and ten very welcome guests from Dallas. The Hillmans had been a bit stiff around Lindsay's biological family initially, but their mutual affection for Lindsay formed a basis for friendships to begin. As Earl said, there'd always been room in his clan for a few dozen more.

"Oh, Nick, wasn't it *wonderful?*" Lindsay asked with a sigh, pulling a brush through her hair as they prepared for bed that night in the Jamaican resort room in which they'd spend their two-week honeymoon.

"It was a circus," he answered indulgently, watching her with growing impatience to try out the luxurious, oversize bed behind him. "But we're married and that's all that really counts."

Lindsay set down the brush and turned to him, her sheer negligee swirling around her as she gave him a loving smile. "You did very well today, considering all the rampant, sloppy emotionalism you had to deal with. You even handled yourself quite nicely when Mother burst into tears and threw herself into your arms."

Nick grimaced. "Yeah, well, she was—um—just a little overcome by all the excitement, I guess. It has to be stressful watching your youngest child getting married."

"We'll keep that in mind when it happens to us."

Struck by the pleasant image of having children with Lindsay, Nick smiled. "Yeah. Guess we will."

"Oh, Nick." She took a step toward him and wrapped her bare arms around his neck. "I loved everything about today. The wedding was beautiful. And it was so wonderful having all my family there—*all* my family. Hillmans, Walkers, D'Alessandros, Sampleses, all my special foster brothers. I'm very fortunate to have so many people who care about me."

He turned his head to kiss the thin white scar on her right forearm. "We're both very lucky," he agreed fervently.

She looked pensive for a moment. "Do you think Tony will ever find the twins?"

He shrugged, answering candidly, "I don't know, Lindsay. Maybe not. But at least you've been reunited with the others."

"I know. It's just that, like Tony, I've come to understand that when it comes to family, when it comes to love, there can never be too many or too much. Life is too precious, too beautiful to spend it alone.''

She'd always be a dreamer, he mused, always an optimist. And he, perhaps, would always be a bit of a cynic, with a tendency toward pessimism.

They balanced each other quite nicely, he decided contentedly.

''Big families are nice,'' he agreed, putting his hands at her waist to pull her more tightly against him. ''But right now, I'm glad the others aren't anywhere near us. That I have you all to myself for the next two weeks.''

Her blue eyes gleamed as she snuggled closer. ''You'll always have me, Nick. For a lifetime.''

''Even that won't be enough,'' he murmured, lowering his mouth to hers. ''But we'll make the most of it, anyway.''

She returned his kiss with an enthusiasm that promised that she, too, intended to make the most of their time together—this night, the next two weeks...and the rest of their lives.

* * * * *

OFFICIAL RULES • MILLION DOLLAR BIG WIN SWEEPSTAKES
NO PURCHASE OR OBLIGATION NECESSARY TO ENTER

To enter, follow the directions published. **ALTERNATE MEANS OF ENTRY:** Hand-print your name and address on a 3"×5" card and mail to either: Silhouette Big Win, 3010 Walden Ave., P.O. Box 1867, Buffalo, NY 14269-1867, or Silhouette Big Win, P.O. Box 609, Fort Erie, Ontario L2A 5X3, and we will assign your Sweepstakes numbers (Limit: one entry per envelope). For eligibility, entries must be received no later than March 31, 1994 and be sent via 1st-class mail. No liability is assumed for printing errors or lost, late or misdirected entries.

To determine winners, the sweepstakes numbers on submitted entries will be compared against a list of randomly preselected prizewinning numbers. In the event all prizes are not claimed via the return of prizewinning numbers, random drawings will be held from among all other entries received to award unclaimed prizes.

Prizewinners will be determined no later than May 30, 1994. Selection of winning numbers and random drawings are under the supervision of D.L. Blair, Inc., an independent judging organization whose decisions are final. One prize to a family or organization. No substitution will be made for any prize, except as offered. Taxes and duties on all prizes are the sole responsibility of winners. Winners will be notified by mail. Chances of winning are determined by the number of entries distributed and received.

Sweepstakes open to persons 18 years of age or older, except employees and immediate family members of Torstar Corporation, D.L. Blair, Inc., their affiliates, subsidiaries and all other agencies, entities and persons connected with the use, marketing or conduct of this Sweepstakes. All applicable laws and regulations apply. Sweepstakes offer void wherever prohibited by law. Any litigation within the province of Quebec respecting the conduct and awarding of a prize in this Sweepstakes must be submitted to the Régies des Loteries et Courses du-Quebec. In order to win a prize, residents of Canada will be required to correctly answer a time-limited arithmetical skill-testing question. Values of all prizes are in U.S. currency.

Winners of major prizes will be obligated to sign and return an affidavit of eligibility and release of liability within 30 days of notification. In the event of non-compliance within this time period, prize may be awarded to an alternate winner. Any prize or prize notification returned as undeliverable will result in the awarding of the prize to an alternate winner. By acceptance of their prize, winners consent to use of their names, photographs or other likenesses for purposes of advertising, trade and promotion on behalf of Torstar Corporation without further compensation, unless prohibited by law.

This Sweepstakes is presented by Torstar Corporation, its subsidiaries and affiliates in conjunction with book, merchandise and/or product offerings. Prizes are as follows: Grand Prize—$1,000,000 (payable at $33,333.33 a year for 30 years). First through Sixth Prizes may be presented in different creative executions, each with the following approximate values: First Prize—$35,000; Second Prize—$10,000; 2 Third Prizes—$5,000 each; 5 Fourth Prizes—$1,000 each; 10 Fifth Prizes—$250 each; 1,000 Sixth Prizes—$100 each. Prizewinners will have the opportunity of selecting any prize offered for that level. A travel-prize option if offered and selected by winner, must be completed within 12 months of selection and is subject to hotel and flight accommodations availability. Torstar Corporation may present this sweepstakes utilizing names other than Million Dollar Sweepstakes. For a current list of all prize options offered within prize levels and all names the Sweepstakes may utilize, send a self-addressed stamped envelope (WA residents need not affix return postage) to: Million Dollar Sweepstakes Prize Options/Names, P.O. Box 7410, Blair, NE 68009.

For a list of prizewinners (available after July 31, 1994) send a separate, stamped self-addressed envelope to: Million Dollar Sweepstakes Winners, P.O. Box 4728, Blair NE 68009.

SWPS693

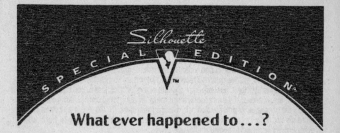

Silhouette
SPECIAL EDITION™

What ever happened to...?

Have you been wondering when a much-loved character will finally get their own story? Well, have we got a lineup for you! Silhouette Special Edition is proud to present a *Spin-off Spectacular!* Be sure to catch these exciting titles from some of your favorite authors.

TRUE BLUE HEARTS (SE #805 April) *Curtiss Ann Matlock* will have you falling in love with another Breen man. Watch out for Rory!

FALLING FOR RACHEL (SE #810 April) *Those Wild Ukrainians* are back as *Nora Roberts* continues the story of the Stanislaski siblings.

LIVE, LAUGH, LOVE (SE #808 April) *Ada Steward* brings you the lovely story of Jessica, Rebecca's twin from *Hot Wind in Eden* (SE #759).

GRADY'S WEDDING (SE #813 May) In this spin-off to her *Wedding Duet, Patricia McLinn* has bachelor Grady Roberts waiting at the altar.

THE FOREVER NIGHT (SE #816 May) *Myrna Temte*'s popular *Cowboy Country* series is back, and Sheriff Andy Johnson has his own romance!

WHEN SOMEBODY WANTS YOU (SE #822 June) *Trisha Alexander* returns to Louisiana with another tale of love set in the bayou.

KATE'S VOW (SE #823 July) Kate Newton finds her own man to love, honor and cherish in this spin-off of *Sherryl Woods*'s *Vows* series.

WORTH WAITING FOR (SE #825 July) *Bay Matthews* is back and so are some wonderful characters from *Laughter on the Wind* (SE #613).

Don't miss these wonderful titles, only for our readers—only from Silhouette Special Edition!

Fifty red-blooded, white-hot, true-blue hunks from every State in the Union!

Beginning in May, look for MEN MADE IN AMERICA! Written by some of our most popular authors, these stories feature fifty of the strongest, sexiest men, each from a different state in the union!

Two titles available every other month at your favorite retail outlet.

In July, look for:

CALL IT DESTINY by Jayne Ann Krentz (Arizona)
ANOTHER KIND OF LOVE by Mary Lynn Baxter (Arkansas)

In September, look for:

DECEPTIONS by Annette Broadrick (California)
STORMWALKER by Dallas Schulze (Colorado)

You won't be able to resist MEN MADE IN AMERICA!
